RIDE THE PINK HORSE

DOROTHY B. HUGHES (1904–1993) was a mystery author and literary critic. Born in Kansas City, she studied at Columbia University and published her mystery debut, *The So Blue Marble,* in 1940.

Hughes published fourteen more novels, three of which were made into successful films (*In a Lonely Place, The Fallen Sparrow,* and *Ride the Pink Horse*). In the early fifties, Hughes largely stopped writing fiction, preferring to focus on criticism, for which she would go on to win an Edgar Award. In 1978, the Mystery Writers of America presented Hughes with the Grand Master Award for lifetime achievement. *Ride the Pink Horse* is her ninth novel.

SARA PARETSKY is the *New York Times* bestselling author of twenty-two novels, including the renowned V. I. Warshawski series. She has received both the Grand Master Award from the Mystery Writers of America and the Cartier Diamond Dagger from the Crime Writers Association of Great Britain, among many other accolades. She lives in Chicago.

T0017307

RIDE THE PINK HORSE

DOROTHY B. HUGHES

Introduction by
SARA PARETSKY

AMERICAN MYSTERY CLASSICS

Penzler Publishers
New York

Published in 2021 by Penzler Publishers
58 Warren Street, New York, NY 10007
penzlerpublishers.com

Distributed by W. W. Norton

Cover image: Andy Ross
Cover design: Mauricio Diaz

Paperback ISBN 9781613162026
Hardcover ISBN 9781613162019

Library of Congress Control Number: 2020925074

Printed in the United States of America

9 8 7 6 5 4 3 2

RIDE THE
PINK HORSE

INTRODUCTION

He hadn't wanted to come here. He'd wanted it less and less as the bus traveled further across the wasteland; miles of nothing, just land, empty land. Land that didn't get anywhere except into more land, and always against the sky the unmoving barrier of mountains. It was like moving into a trap.

The man we know only as Sailor has arrived in Santa Fe at an inauspicious moment: it's Fiesta weekend. Sailor is a Chicago gangster, single-mindedly hunting his former patron, a U.S. Senator named Douglass: he believes Douglass has cheated him out of a substantial amount of money. So single-minded is Sailor's pursuit that he didn't learn about Fiesta before he got on the bus in Chicago. He didn't know the hotels would be fully booked, didn't know that he'd end up sleeping on the ground next to a hand-cranked Merry-Go-Round, unable to bathe or shave or change his clothes.

Sailor is out of his depth as soon as he gets off the bus. He's angry to find himself in "a dump" of a town. He compares everything he sees to its superior Chicago counterpart. Yet in this dump, his usual sense of direction deserts him as he tries to navigate streets packed with Fiesta-goers.

Dorothy Hughes is often described as an avatar of noir. Sarah Weinman calls her "the world's finest female noir writer." If noir, in Megan Abbot's words, is a world where "everyone is fallen [and] right and wrong are not clearly defined, [perhaps] not even attainable," then Hughes belongs there. Sort of.

Her people do know the difference between right and wrong, and some are able to choose right, including Dr. Hugh Densmore, hero of Hughes's final novel, *The Expendable Man* (1963). Sailor, in contrast, has a cynical lack of belief in a morally good life. He longs for a "clean girl," meaning not one free of venereal disease, but instead one free of the corruption that fills his own world.

Like her younger contemporary, Dorothy Salisbury Davis, Hughes finds evil more beguiling to explore than good, and her exploration is rich in detail, all culled from Sailor's third-person interior monologue.

Sailor is a product of Chicago's Irish-Catholic slums. He prides himself on having left the grime and cruelty of his childhood behind. As the novel unspools, events around him force him to remember his mother's efforts to provide for the family—as a washer-woman—while his drunken father beat up her and the children.

Sailor is constantly trying to assure himself that he doesn't behave like his old man. "He wasn't any bum," he keeps saying: he knows how to dress—the best-dressed man on the senator's staff—he'd been to college for a year and a half, but the dirt that encrusts him throughout the book degrades his sense of self. He has wants/needs that can be met only through the senator's money. He's sure that as soon as he's paid, all will be well.

Ride the Pink Horse is claustrophobic. The action is contained within the small downtown of 1947 Santa Fe, where Sailor feels hemmed in by the surrounding mountains. He's hemmed in, too, by a small cast of characters who keep showing up despite the large crowds. Don José, who owns the hand-cranked merry-go-round; an Indian girl named Pila in town with her Hispanic cousins; and MacIntyre, "Mac," a Chicago cop who's been part of Sailor's life since he first busted Sailor for stealing cars.

Along with Don José, Mac offers the novel's moral counterpoint to Sailor. He comes from the same slums as Sailor, with the same abused childhood. For all the years he's known Sailor, he's hoped that he can bring a latent sense of decency in him into life.

Hughes shows us signs of the moral core Mac has occasionally glimpsed in Sailor. For instance, troubled by the possibility that the Indian girl, Pila, will follow her Hispanic cousins into a life of quasi-prostitution, Sailor gives her some of his dwindling money—along with a lecture to go back to her pueblo and leave the bright lights of Santa Fe behind. And as his physical condition deteriorates, he develops a reluctant empathy for the Indians and the Hispanics whom he initially denigrates as "spics." He can't quite admit that he's as much an outsider as they are, but he is inhabiting their same shadowy world on the fringes of the money and power he yearns for.

Don José is respected by all the Santa Feans who live outside the world of white, moneyed incomers, but Sailor will call him only Pancho Villa because of a superficial physical resemblance to the outlaw. Even when Don José gives him a place to sleep, gets him medical care when he's wounded, and worries over his emotional state, Sailor cannot rise above Pancho Villa in his mind. The racism Hughes observed in the Southwest is a theme of *Pink Horse,* as it is of most of her later novels. As Hughes grappled with the nature of evil, she created villains out of the white moneyed people who displaced the Spaniards and the Indians. In *Pink Horse,* Don José is a good, moral man—despite his alcohol consumption, which reminds Sailor of his own brutal father. Don José also tries to educate Sailor on the history of race in the southwest.

Those passages are a bit flat, didactic, but they stand in contrast to the stereotyping prevalent in most mid-twentieth century crime fiction, including Chandler, where Black characters are woolly-headed, or shines, or monkeys, prone to rolling their eyes in terror when danger threatens. In fact, in *The Expendable Man,* the central character is a Black medical doctor of high moral character who unwittingly gets sucked into a world of white depravity.

Lawrence J. Oliver, Jr. discusses Hughes and race in "The Dark-Skinned Angels of Dorothy B. Hughes's Thrillers" (*MELUS,* Vol. 11, No. 3, Autumn, 1984). He says that a pitfall for white writers who wanted to counteract racist stereotyping was to fall into a different trap—to create one-dimensional stereotypes where people of color are the suffering servants of society. Oliver believes Hughes's non-white characters are too saintly, too forgiving of the damage done to them. By denying them anger, she deprives them of a full humanity.

This is somewhat true for *Ride the Pink Horse,* but Don José doesn't sugarcoat the history of bloodshed between Spaniards and Indians in the early fights over who controlled the Southwest. Don José also tries, for inexplicable reasons, to save Sailor from his hard-driving demons.

The policeman Mac also tries to save Sailor. Near the end of the novel, he offers something close to a Christian sermon on right and wrong, on the possibility of choosing the right path.

> Mac said, "I don't want anything to happen to Senator Douglass. I told you that before. Moreover, I don't want anything to happen to you." He took a long drink of beer. "Why I should care about that, I don't know, Sailor," he said in that quiet way of his. As if he were wondering about it for the first time. "All these years, every time I've tried to give you a hand, to steer you right, I might as well have hollered down a well. I don't know why I've thought you were worth saving. Why I still think so."...
>
> [Sailor walks away, thinking] "Mac was getting preachy again."

Even more than its concern with race and history in America, *Ride the Pink Horse* is a novel about good and evil, sign-posted by religious imagery, which come from the Catholic tradition in which Sailor grew up. The processions stir up his bitter memories of childhood services where the priest paid no attention to the domestic sufferings of the women and children in the parish. Sailor's nervous wandering through Santa Fe in the dark keeps calling those memories back to him. In the penultimate scene where Mac "was getting preachy again," the cop is depicted as unmistakably Christlike.

Hughes wrote poetry as well as prose, and many of the poems explore the questions both of race and religion which dominate *Ride the Pink Horse*. Her "Down South" is a powerful meditation on lynching, but the bulk of her poems come out of the New

Testament: "Miserere," "Lullaby from a Stable," "Golgotha," "Prodigal."

In "Miserere,"

> There will be no reprieve though
> Love turn cold
> And Life to sullen ash: always the lance
> Will pierce his side; always he must toss
> Beneath a sleepless sky, and never still
> The sound of women beating empty breasts,
> The silence of despair. Though he protests,
> His tortured prayer will be to no avail...

These poems are not sentimental, any more than Hughes's novels are. Hughes lays bare the essential loneliness with which we all wrestle. It's a loneliness that makes many of us choose the wrong path, in Mac's language, because that's where we find companionship and a superficial comfort.

In pure noir, where, as Megan Abbot says, everyone is fallen, characters exist without hope. Hammett's *Red Harvest* makes the reader weep from the misery that afflicts everyone in Poisonville. In *Ride the Pink Horse,* Hughes offers a more nuanced portrait of human suffering. If you step back far enough from it, the whole world looks like Poisonville. Up close, though, small acts of kindness may get the loneliest Chicago gangster through the night.

SARA PARETSKY
Chicago
November 2020

RIDE THE
PINK HORSE

PART ONE
Zozobra

One

HE CAME in on the five o'clock bus. He was well to the back and he didn't hurry. He remained seated there, his eyes alone moving while the other passengers churned front. His eyes moving and without seeming to move, through the windows on the right where he was seated, across the aisle through the left-hand windows. He saw no one he knew, no one who even looked as if he came from the city.

A hick town. He didn't like hick towns. He uncramped his legs, slid out into the aisle soon enough to seem to be one of the surge without being of it. Only someone who was aware, as he was, would know he was alone, separate. The hayseeds he'd traveled with out of Kansas City across the plains into mountain land didn't know. The yokels sagging on the concrete loading slab in back of this dump station didn't know. It was habit that shoved his right hand into his coat pocket as he stepped off the bus. Not nervousness. He had no nerves; caution yes, but no nerves.

There was no one he knew. He went around the bus to the rear where an officious bastard in a khaki-drab coverall was pulling baggage out of the compartment, dumping it on the concrete. The sheep stood like sheep waiting.

He didn't. He walked over to the heap and yanked out his old valise. The officious bastard started sputtering. The bastard was a greaser, a spic; he needed his face shoved in. Sailor pulled his claim check out of his left-hand pocket, shoved it into the bastard's coverall pocket. This wasn't the time or place to push in a guy's face. He didn't want to land in the hoosegow, hick towns were sometimes tough. Particularly on strangers. Besides he didn't want his approach telegraphed. He was to be a surprise, a little surprise package for the Sen.

His mouth twitched as he walked away. Time enough to take care of officious bastards after he'd taken care of the Sen. His mouth wasn't twitching as he moved heavy-heeled into the grimy bus station.

His valise was too heavy. It pulled down his left hand and shoulder. His right hand, habitual, was in his right pocket. There wasn't need for it.

The small station was littered with papers, smelling of people who didn't wash. But there weren't many people, only a few on the dirty benches. On one bench, two Indian women. They had broad flat faces, and their hair was cut like on Dutch dolls, banged to their polished black eyes, squared just above their ear lobes. The women billowed fat under calico, blue and pink and green, a different color for every skirt and petticoat. One squaw had over her head a purple shawl bordered in bright pink flowers. The other's shawl was orange and green like a Halloween pumpkin. The women looked cheap and sweaty but they wore a mint of jewelry, silver earrings and heavy chains of silver and turquoise, a lot of chains and massive bracelets, lots of big silver and turquoise bracelets on their broad brown wrists. They looked like something out of a circus but he didn't snicker. Something about them kept him from wanting to snicker. They were the first Indians he'd ever seen.

On another bench there was a woman all in rusty black from

her shawl to her shoes, the kind of shoes nuns wear. She was as fat as the Indians but she was a spic. There was a little runt of a spic guy with her, in overalls and a shabby dark gray jacket, a greasy hat pulled down over his ears. A mess of little girls was with them, lined upon the bench in their cheap patent-leather slippers and cheap straw hats, their starched clean print dresses. They were all spics but they might have been Indians as well. He knew all the black silent eyes watched him as he hardheeled to the desk.

He asked, "Where's a hotel?"

The fellow behind the desk was any fellow behind a desk in a bus station. He saw too many people to care about any, tired, harassed even in this hick dump. "Inca on the corner. Cabeza de Vaca around the corner."

Sailor nodded, his nod meant thanks. He was chary of words. The fellow said, "You won't get a room."

He jerked his head around. Suspicious. "Why not?"

"Fiesta," the fellow said. Then he was busy with the phone ringing and the sheep starting in through the rear doors.

Sailor slid on outside. He didn't want gab with the ticket agent anyway. He'd find a room. The Inca was a dump. One of those corner hotels with a lobby the size of a dime, a big green fern taking up most the space. Good enough till he found the Sen, after that he'd be moving to a real hotel.

No rooms. He accepted it because the old man behind the desk wasn't insulting. He was an old gentleman; he regretted it but there were no rooms.

From the corner you could see the sign *Cabeza de Vaca Hotel*. It hung over the sidewalk, a big sign, and Sailor cut across the narrow street and started towards it. This was a big hotel, an old one. There was a porch, with armchairs, most of them filled with cackling old men in faded brown panamas. As he passed they looked at him as if he were a stranger. But without interest, only porch curiosity.

The lobby was big and cool and shabby old. Dark. Not a bad place to hole up while he was doing business with the Sen.

The fellow behind the desk was immaculate in gabardine, an expensive handwoven tie. The kind of a handsome clerk you'd expect at The Stevens, not in a shabby old hotel in a hick town. There were no rooms.

The hotel was big enough to hold everyone who'd be coming to a hick town the end of summer.

He got a little tough. "What's the idea?"

The clerk gave a surprise titter. "It's Fiesta."

"What's Fiesta?"

The clerk tittered again. "Fiesta—" he began. He picked up a pink handbill from the desk. ". . . tells you about it."

He took the sheet only because it was pushed into his hand. Took it and thrust it in his left-hand pocket. The clerk wasn't laughing now. He was arranging his tie. "You won't find any rooms during Fiesta—" he began but his voice trickled away in the direction of a pretty girl with hair that curled like a baby's.

Sailor went out again to the sidewalk. The bag was heavier than before. He was hot in the late sunset afternoon; he was sticky and bus-soiled, crumpled. He didn't believe there were no rooms to be had. If he were shined up, he could get a room quick enough in the Cabeza de Vaca. He ought to punch that fancy clerk right in the nose. But how was he going to get clean without a room?

He lugged the bag back to the corner and followed the street past The Inca towards town. There'd be other hotels. Or a motor court. He turned right at the top of the street, turned to the tinkling sound of music and people. Turned with a city-dweller's instinct toward the heart of town.

A half block, past J. C. Penney's, a grocery store, a drug store and he stood on the village square. He stopped there, against the glass front of the drug store, and he set down his valise. This was what the clerk had been talking about. This was Fiesta. Overhead were strings of colored lights. In the center of the square was a small green park, trees and benches and a bandstand draped in red-and-orange bunting. A low cement wall ran around the park with entrances at each corner. Entrances hung with grotesque papier maché standards. In the street that circled the park were thatched booths, smelling of food, the acrid smell of chile; stacked with cases of pop, decorated with gimcracks, cheap canes topped with celluloid dolls wiggling feathers, and cheap sticks with flimsy yellow birds floating from them, balloons on brittle wooden sticks. This was Fiesta: a run-down carnival.

He picked up his valise again, he'd seen a hotel sign halfway up the street. This one shouldn't turn him down. It was next door to a pool hall. There were no armchairs rocking on a porch, no ferns in the lobby. The bulky clerk was in shirtsleeves. A pinball machine jerked and clattered, almost drowning out his words.

No rooms.

Sailor jutted out his chin. "What's the matter? Don't I look like I got the price of a room? Listen here—" He was reaching for his roll but he didn't.

The bulky guy said, "This is Fiesta. You didn't expect to blow in and get a room during Fiesta, did you? Even us, we got reservations months ahead for Fiesta."

"What's this Fiesta stuff?"

"You mean you came to town right now without knowing it

was Fiesta?" The big guy didn't snicker, he just looked as if he were seeing a sight. "Every year for two hundred and thirty-four years there's been a Fiesta here. Account of—"

"Skip it," he said. He would read about it off the pink handbill in his spare time. He didn't care about Fiesta, he was here on business; the sooner it was over the better. "Where am I going to sleep tonight?"

The guy shook his head. "You better go on to Albuquerque. There's nothing in town." He saw by Sailor's scowl that was no good. "If you got a reason you got to be here, I don't know. You might try the Chamber of Commerce. Maybe they got a private room listed." Doubt plucked at his heavy chin.

The Chamber of Commerce. And some wise guy wanting to know who you were and where from and what you doing in our dump. He wasn't having any. He reached for the valise and then he tipped his hat over to the other side of his head. "How about me leaving the bag here for a little? Maybe I can clean up my business and go on to Albuquerque." He gave it the pronunciation he'd heard on the bus, Albukirk. He knew his business would take longer than that but if he could get rid of the weight he was tugging, he could look around for a place to stay.

The big guy said, "Sure." Friendly enough. "I won't be responsible for it but you can leave it." He wasn't interested. "Put it behind the counter. I'm on duty till nine. You'll be back before nine?"

"Sure." He pushed the bag around behind the counter. The lock was good. The guy wasn't curious anyway. "Sure," he said and he went outside into the pale pink dusk.

He stood there for a moment getting his bearings. This side the square shops. The left side more shops, nothing fancy, nothing like Michigan Boulevard, more like Clark Street. Except for the corner, a fancy shoe store all glass. Right side of the square was the good side, ticket office, a white bank, better shops. And across was a long low, dun-colored building set back from a covered walk. Took up the whole block. It might be a hotel, no sign, but worth looking into.

That was all of the town. The four sides and in the center the park, the village green, all gaudied up and tinkling music. Not many people walking around, a few.

He turned and strode on up the street to the corner. Across, cat-a-corner, was a real hotel, a big one. Not that it looked like one; it was a dun-colored, plastered mass, 'dobe, the wise guys on the bus called it, with terraces and walls, like an old Spanish hacienda. He knew it was the hotel; he'd remembered La Fonda from the signboards coming in, La Fonda, the Harvey House. He stepped across the narrow street, passing the hotel's corner shop slowly. Rich stuff in the windows. Mex and Spanish and Indian. He knew without anyone telling him that the dark hideous wooden statue, the tarnished silver beads flung across the base, were loot, out of some old palace.

He walked more slowly. La Fonda was class; from the outside he knew that. He wasn't class. He was soiled and smelly, he looked like he'd just come off a four-day bus trip. His money was as good as anybody's. He might pretend he'd motored across the country, mention his Cad just casually.

He didn't turn in at the arch. He started to but there were two babes coming down the walk, two babes that had just been washed and ironed in white linen. They didn't have anything more on their minds than lying around getting that golden glow on their skin. He didn't want to pass them; he didn't want to watch them look down their noses at this bum. He walked on, passing the garden wall, a high wall to keep out the muck but let them hear the gashing laughter, the tinkling ice of the elect behind the wall. On past drab brick, the barren, gravel playground of a parochial school. End of the block. A cathedral across. Gray-brown stone and squat towers. A cathedral blocking the way.

He turned on his heel and walked back, past the school, the garden wall, into the hotel. He didn't give a damn whom he passed or who looked up or down their noses. This was a hotel.

It didn't look like a hotel; it was more like a Spanish hacienda inside than it was out. Cool, dark and rich, a high, timbered ceiling, soft leather couches and chairs. There were oil paintings on the walls, Indian and Spanish. French doors opened to a patio, a splash of pale light with gaudy umbrellas, bright swings carelessly placed around a tiled fountain. The fountain banked with red geraniums.

This was where the Sen would be staying. This was for rich blood, for the sleek and the clean, for the names on the society page, the boxes at the opera, the clubhouse at the track. Not for him.

He was truculent because he was ashamed to ask for a room here. The clerk was just somebody in a dark suit and thin hair. Courteous but firm. There were no rooms. This was Fiesta. Everything had been reserved months ago.

He took another look around the lobby, not a big lobby like the Palmer House, you could lose this one in one corner of the Palmer House, but it seemed spacious. It wasn't noisy but it was gay, there was movement, and from the bar the usual bar racket. He could use a cold beer but as his tongue thirsted he turned on his heel and walked out of the hotel. Walked hurriedly away.

He didn't want to bump into the Sen yet. The Sen looking at him as if he were dirt. He'd pick his own meeting place, nothing accidental. After he was cleaned up, bathed and pressed.

He went out and crossed to the ticket-office corner. There was still the big building across the square. He walked towards it past the little white bank and the shops but when he crossed to the building he saw what it was, a museum. It came like a door slammed in his face and he was angered. There had to be a place to stay in this dump. Against the walls of the old museum was a frieze of Indians, a frieze a block long. They sat there on the wide walk, women and children and suckling babies, all in calico and shawls and black, bobbed hair, the women's bulbous breasts and worn brown wrists jeweled with silver and turquoise. Spread before them on the walks were their wares, bows and arrows and painted drums, beaded doodads, clay birds and vases and ash trays. Behind them, safe from pawing souvenir collectors and curio hagglers were the good things: heavy woven rugs, strands of turquoise, massive silver belts. He'd known it all along: Fiesta was any cheap carnival. Having Indians hawking the junk didn't make it any different.

And then he realized. They weren't hawking the stuff; they were as silent as if they didn't know he was standing there. But they knew. Their black eyes, even the kids' black eyes slanted like Chinks, were watching him. Not with curiosity, not even with particular interest. They looked at him as if he were some kind of a specimen they hadn't seen before. There was no expression on their brown faces. It gave him a queer feeling, as if he, not the Indians, were something strange.

He stood there, helpless anger knotting his nerves. Monotonously cursing the Sen, the dirty, double-crossing, lying, whoring Senator Willis Douglass. It was the Sen's fault he was in this God-forsaken town and no place to rest his feet. He hadn't wanted to come here. He'd wanted it less and less as the bus traveled further across the wasteland; miles of nothing, just land, empty land. Land that didn't get anywhere except into more land, and always against the sky the unmoving barrier of mountains. It was like moving into a trap, a trap you couldn't ever get out of. Because no matter how you tried, no matter how far you traveled, you'd always be stopped by the rigid mountains. He didn't like it at all when they moved into this town, his destination. Because this was the center of the trap; it was a long way back to civilization in any direction. The only thing to do was get out quick.

As he stood there he heard again the tinkling music. He turned as if he wanted to find where it came from, as if that were important. As if he hadn't been routed by the guard of silent Indians. A small merry-go-round was in the corner of the park, motionless at this hour. Two spics were sitting there, playing a violin and a guitar. Playing for themselves; there were no customers. For all its gala disarray the park was deserted.

He stepped off the curb without direction, crossed the narrow street and entered the little park. He walked to the merry-go-round, not intending to, but because there was life there and the absence of life on the streets and in the holiday square was suddenly a little fearful. He didn't intend to speak to the spics but there he was leaning against the enclosure.

"Not much business," he said. He saw the third man as he spoke, a big brigand, a Pancho Villa, fat and shapeless and dirty, but his brown face was curiously peaceful. He was leaning against the weathered, dark red pickets of the enclosure. His overalls were worn and faded, held up by dirty knotted string; his blue shirt smelled of sweat and his yellowed teeth of garlic, his hat was battered beyond shape. But his face was peaceful, even happy.

The fat man said happily in his spic accent, "It is because they burn Zozobra."

The tinkling music kept on in the background. An old man squeaking a violin, so old his fingers were warped, so old his face was without meaning, a small man shriveled into age. The man at the guitar was thin to gauntness, greasy black hair falling over his eyes, his empty black eyes.

"What's Zozobra?" Sailor asked.

"You do not know what is Zozobra?" The brigand wasn't patronizing, he was surprised. He hitched up the dirty string. "It is Old Man Gloom." He chuckled deep in his fat belly. "We must burn Zozobra, Old Man Gloom, before the Fiesta commence. When Old Man Gloom he is dead, we have no more troubles. We laugh and dance and make merry. Then there is La Fiesta."

The man at the guitar began to sing in a flat, nasal voice. The fat man chuckled, "See? Ignacio sings to you how Zozobra must die."

Sailor lit a cigarette, scratching the match hard on his heel. "So Old Man Zose is dead and there's no business, Pancho?"

Pancho Villa hitched up his pants. His sigh was light as a leaf falling. "There is too much business. Tio Vivo grows old. Tomorrow, the next day, too much business for poor old Tio Vivo. He is happy to rest a little while."

Tio Vivo was the brigand's little merry-go-round. A hand-cranked merry-go-round, gondolas alternating with fierce white and pink and brown wooden horses. The big paw rested tenderly on the neck of one pink horse. The brown eyes were soulful with love of his battered old carousel.

"Tio Vivo grows old and I grow old too. We are happy to rest this little moment in the Plaza while everybody he goes to burn Zozobra."

He saw then the direction Pancho's eyes pointed. He saw the twos and threes hurrying away from the Plaza. Everyone goes to burn Zozobra. Everyone. If that was the thing to do, that was where the Sen would be. It might be possible after all to see him tonight, under cover of the celebration, to get it over with and out of this dump.

He said, "Thanks, Pancho. I guess I better get on my way if I want to see Old Man Zose kick the bucket."

The fat man laughed and laughed. As if Sailor had pulled a good one. He said, "Yes, you had better hurry." And he laughed some more, hitching himself comfortably against the palings. "Hurry, hurry," he laughed because he didn't have to hurry. Because he was comfortable here by his old Tio Vivo, with the violin and guitar stroking the deepening twilight. Because he had learned long ago that Zozobra could burn without his moving from his comfort.

Sailor flicked away his cigarette stub. He would follow the late stragglers and find his way to Zozobra. To Zozobra and the Sen.

It was as he turned that he saw McIntyre. And for the moment the works thumping inside of him were frozen.

The man was leaning against the pale wall of the little bank. A tall, thin man with a horsey face. A quiet man who didn't belong here. Who didn't belong against the wall of a hick bank with a red ribbon tied around his pants and on his head a flat black hat with little colored bobbles hanging from the brim. If Sailor hadn't frozen for the moment he'd have doubled up laughing. But he was frozen, the hand that had flicked the cigarette was frozen in mid-air.

Softly from behind him, softly and in sympathy he heard Pancho. "Trouble?"

The works started ticking again that fast. "No," he said short-ly. His mouth twisted into a grin that the big greaser couldn't see. "No trouble at all," he said.

He walked on out of the Plaza then, sure of himself. Trouble wasn't waiting for him. McIntyre hadn't followed him here. Mac had been here first. There wasn't another bus in until midnight; he knew the schedule. There wasn't a train into Lamy until morning. The trains didn't come to this town. Mac hadn't just driven in from Chicago. He'd been here long enough to buy a silly Spanish hat and a red sash. To know about Fiesta. He wasn't after Sailor; he was after the Sen.

The grimace held on Sailor's face as he walked up the dark-ening street the hurrying stragglers had taken. Past a library, a vacant lot, past houses. He wasn't the only one who'd caught up with the Sen. McIntyre was here. Tonight the villagers were burning up their troubles. But the Sen wasn't burning his. They'd caught up with him at last.

Two

HE'D WALKED two blocks before he got a sense of direction. There was a swarthy policeman on duty here, diverting cars. There were more people hurrying up the hill. He walked past the cop without even an under-the-eye glance. When he'd passed the big pink building he could see the lights beyond and across. Across on the other road a million pinpoints of light, headlights trying to move forward. Ahead the lights of pageantry. The stragglers were walking faster now; they weren't laughing and talking; they saved even that energy to spur them on before the show began. There was a current of excitement transmitted to him in their rapid silence, a current that lengthened his own stride. He pushed on with them until he came to the footbridge that led into the dark arena.

But he stopped there on the outskirts. He hadn't expected anything like this. He hadn't thought a hick town had this many people. The football field was packed with them, a shifting electric mass of people, like State Street on the day of a big parade. The day Roosevelt was there. He couldn't find the Sen in this haystack. He'd have been better off to have stayed with Pancho and Tio Vivo. Better to be hunting a room.

He could have turned around and beat it back to the Plaza

but he didn't. He did what the others were doing, threading forward for a better position in the crowd. And he saw Zozobra.

A giant grotesquerie there ahead on the terrace, a gray specter at least forty feet tall with a misshapen head, hollow eyes, pointed flapping ears, shapeless flapping mouth. A giant puppet with giant clawlike hands, palsied hands lifting and falling. Out of the flapping mouth a sepulcher voice was threatening, scolding. Little threats, yet mouthed by him they were as purest obscenity. *It's going to rain. It's going to rain and spoil your fun . . .*

Zozobra. Made of papier maché and dirty sheets, yet a fantastic awfulness of reality was about him. He was unclean. He was the personification of evil.

For the moment the personification held Sailor motionless. Then the spell passed and he could see the figures behind the effigy. He could recognize the under-rasp of the loudspeaker that made words for the giant to speak. About him Sailor could hear scraps of conversation. *Shus outdid himself this year . . . the best Zozobra yet . . . isn't Sloan wonderful . . . wouldn't be Zozobra without his voice . . .* The evil was manmade; it wasn't real.

Scraps of conversation but nothing about the Sen. Voices but not the Sen's voice. He threaded further forward and was halted by the quiver of excitement from the crowd. White sheeted mounds were creeping down the far stone steps to posture and scrape before the obscene specter. A lean devil dancer bounded forward in frenzied ritual. A quiver went through the mass as the sheeted figures stooped and laid fire on the dry fagots piled before the evil god. The figures scuttled. Only the dancer remained on the steps before the giant, now ranting hysterically before the onlicking flames. The words became hideous groans. The dancer leaped free of the consuming fire. The mob cheered as the crimson tongues caught the skirts of Zozobra, lapping higher and higher.

Sailor turned his eyes away. Noise was staccato, skyrockets flaring into the sky, fire crackers exploding as the flames ate away the body of evil. He'd had enough. He'd wasted enough time with this charade. He was here to find the Sen. He began edging through the crowd.

But wherever he turned he found himself looking up again at the terrace where that hideous groaning face floated above the fire and smoke and noise, above the crowd's lust for destruction of evil. In destroying evil, even puppet evil, these merrymakers were turned evil. He saw their faces, dark and light, rich and poor, great and small, old and young. Fire-shadowed, their eyes glittered with the appetite to destroy. He saw and he was suddenly frightened. He wanted to get away.

He couldn't get away. Even as Zozobra couldn't get away. He was hemmed in by the crowd. By the unmoving crowd waiting for the final consummation, holding their cheers until the ghost face alone floated in the flame and smoke. And a band somewhere in the darkness struck up a lusty dirge.

The crowd broke then, laughing, talking too loud, as if for a moment they too realized the bestiality they'd conjured in themselves. As if they would forget. Children squeaked and skipped, here and there a baby in arms cried. People were moving and their feet kicked dust to add to the fumes of smoke. Across on the far road the traffic jam squawked horns and on this side of the field the police held back the people to let pass the cars with badges. The big shots' cars.

He knew then he'd been a fool to think the Sen would be on foot, would be part of a motley crew. One of those cars would be carrying the Sen out of the dirt and confusion. He'd be back in La Fonda with a fancy drink and a fancy woman before the plodders were halfway down the hill.

Sailor pushed with the crowd out of the dark field. He hadn't noticed before how many were in fancy dress, Spanish and Mexican and Indian. All dressed up for the Fiesta. He understood now why McIntyre was wearing a Spanish hat and sash. In his dark city suit and hat, Sailor stuck out like an Indian would on the Gold Coast. He ought to get himself some fancy duds if he didn't want to be conspicuous. Even here, stumbling over the dark stubble, people were giving him the curious eye.

And suddenly he saw the Sen. He was so close he could have touched him. Only the Sen was behind the glass-and-steel protection of an official car and the cops were holding back Sailor with the other peasants to let the tin gods roll by. It was the Sen all right. You couldn't miss that weasel face, the long snout, the sleepy-looking eyes, the thin brown hair receding from the forehead. You couldn't miss him even if he was dressed up in a Spanish black velvet jacket with a red bow under his sloping chin. The car rolled by too fast for Sailor to see who else was in it. He saw only the Sen and he wasn't uneasy any more. His hunch was right. The Sen was here, not hiding out but playing it big, thinking he was safe. Like as not still wearing the mourning band on his sleeve. Sailor spat in the dust after the big black limousine.

When he reached the pavement he cut through the people hurrying down the hill. It might be he could reach the hotel as quickly as the Sen. The cars weren't making much headway. Even those of the elect, allowed to travel on this side of the field, had to creep down the street. There was a traffic tangle at the corner of the pink building. He might beat the Sen to La Fonda, be waiting for him when he came into the fancy lobby. Be waiting with his hand in his right hand pocket where it was now. Not looking for trouble, just a few words with the Sen. No action, just words, but the comfort of a hand on cold steel. When you came up against the Sen you needed what comfort you could find.

He was delayed on the corner while the cops let a line of cars pass. He looked into each one as it crept by, not seeming to look, standing there with the other sheep waiting by order of the law. The Sen wasn't in any of these cars. Sailor was restless waiting and he watched his chance to break through the line for the opposite sidewalk. The cop yelled something as he broke but Sailor didn't pay any attention. He was safe on the other side, with another endless stream of people. No spic cop was going to keep him standing on a corner all night. He had business.

The Plaza was alive now. It was wriggling with people, and the street that surrounded it, blocked from traffic, was filled with people. He could hear the tinkling music of Tio Vivo before he reached the Old Museum. He didn't enter the Plaza, he walked big along the bank side of the street not even remembering McIntyre until he had reached the bank. Mac wasn't there any longer. Mac had business here too.

It wouldn't be so bad if McIntyre too were waiting for the Sen in La Fonda lobby. Give the Sen a scare. He'd be easier to talk to scared. Not that Sailor would talk before a Chicago copper, but it wouldn't hurt to have the Sen think he might. Sailor had been striding along feeling good but at the bank he was stopped.

Stopped by an unmoving mass of people jamming to the corner, jamming the walks and the streets, packed like cattle here in the open street. Sailor shoved off into the street behind the crowd where he could crane his neck up and see what they were looking at. Zozobra was dead. His ghost couldn't have beat the crowd downtown.

He looked up just as music blared through the loudspeaker, just as the crowd sighed and sucked its breath and whistled, just as the floodlights were flung on the high terraces of the hotel. He saw it all as a kaleidoscope, the lights, the Spanish orchestra in the corner abutment, the pretty boy leader with the lavender powder on his face. He saw the throne and the dark girl in crimson velvet robes ascending it, the old duck in knee britches and plumes placing the crown of gold on her head. The crowd cheered and the Spanish princesses in white satin preened before the throne. There wasn't a chance of eeling through to the hotel. These weren't separate people; they were a solidified mass. Only darkness on the terraced roof would give them fluidity again.

Sailor stubbed on across to the one familiar spot in this alien night. Knee britches was blaring through the microphone. He spoke in Spanish and the crowd cheered. When he finished he spoke again in English, spic English, and the crowd again cheered. "Viva las Fiestas," he cried and the crowd echoed, "Viva las Fiestas." Anything went with these peasants; Old Man Gloom was dead, bring on the Fiesta.

A woman was singing in Spanish, her voice, distorted by the mike, deafened the night. Sailor leaned against the tired fence palings of the merry-go-round. The musicians were standing at the far end, peering up into the sky. Only Pancho Villa was where he was before, big and motionless, one hand on the neck of the pink wooden horse.

He had a wide smile for Sailor. "You see Zozobra burn, no? Zozobra is dead. Viva las Fiestas!" It was as if he were host and anxious that Sailor should enjoy the carnival.

"Sure." Sailor took out his pack of cigarettes. This time he passed it to Pancho. He scratched the match on the peeling, dark-red paint. "Sure he died, but where's the customers?"

Pancho laughed deep. His hand stroked the pink horse. Smoke trickled out of his nose and his big mouth. "This time it is the Queen. The show on the roof for the Queen. After it is over, Tio Vivo and I must work." The sigh came out of his belly but he brightened. "Tonight not so much work. It is late and the muchachos must go home to bed. Tomorrow, ah—" The sigh was long.

Music again blasted the speaker and the sound of dancing, heels tapping, castanets clicking. Sailor dug his elbow between the palings. "This is a spic town. Why'd the Sen pick a spic town?" He didn't know he'd spoken aloud until the brigand answered.

"Spic?" He said it "speec" like a spic. "Spic? I do not know that spic"

Spic. Hunkey. Mick. Kike. Wop. Greaser. Sailor felt for translation. "Mex," he said.

Pancho was solemn. Big and sweaty and shapeless, he was dignity. "No," he said. "This is not a Mex town. This is an American town."

"Then why does everybody talk—" He halted at the word. He supplied, "Spanish?"

Pancho was no longer offended. "It is Spanish-American. The Fiesta, it is Spanish. It tells of my people who come so long ago and conquer the Indian. So long ago." His sigh wasn't unhappy now. It was the leaf falling. "Before the Gringo soldiers, the English-speaking, come and conquer the Spanish. Now we are all one, the Spanish and the Indian and the Gringo." His yellow teeth smiled. "If I were Ignacio I would make a song about it. We are all one in the Fiesta." He shook his head. "I do not like spic. We are not Mexican, Mister. Mexican is south, below the border. I have been to Mexico," he boasted.

A gourd rattle and a chorus of harsh voices broke over the mike. Pancho's eyes leaped with love. "The Mariachi! Ah . . ." He started lumbering to the far end of the enclosure. "The Mariachi are Mexican," floated over his shoulder. "From Guadalajara of Jalisco."

Sailor circled the paddock to where he could crane up to the roof. The Mariachi were singing, strumming and beating their crude wooden guitars. "Guadalajara . . ." they sang. The shouting proud song of the homeland. They wore enormous straw sombreros and white peasant suits with red sashes, woven rugs over their shoulders. Their faces were carved of wood, brown, wrinkled, impassive. The faces of cut-throats, but they carried guitars not machetes; they made fierce music not war. This was Fiesta. The solid mass went wild but the Mariachi showed no emotion. They sang again, a wild, cruel song, baring their teeth, pounding with their knuckles on the gourd-like guitars, sweeping the catgut strings with maniacal speed.

Fiesta. The time of celebration, of release from gloom, from the specter of evil. But under celebration was evil; the feast was rooted in blood, in the Spanish conquering of the Indian. It was a memory of death and destruction. Now we are one, Pancho said. A memory of peace but before peace death and destruction. Indian, Spaniard, Gringo; the outsider, the paler face. One in Fiesta. The truce of Fiesta. Why had the Sen come to this strange foreign place? Did he think he'd be safe in a Spanish-American town? Did he think the native truce was for him too?

Sailor's mouth twisted. This dump might seem out of the world but the busses came in regular from Chicago. It wasn't that far from Chicago.

And again he saw the Sen. Not standing down in the street cricking his neck; not the Sen. He was up on the second roof, where the pretty young Queen sat; trust the Sen. All dressed up in his tight black velvet pants and velvet monkey jacket, the red bow flopping under his chin. He was too far away for Sailor to see his face; he was too far up. There wasn't a guy so far up he couldn't be pulled down. The Spanish pulled the Indians down and that's why there was the Fiesta. Then the Gringos pulled down the Spanish and that's why the Spanish were spics cranking up an old merry-go-round, smelling of dirty sweat. While the Sen sat on a roof leching at a phoney Queen.

A woman in white was dancing on the highest roof, white doves fluttering from her hands. Around her girls in white were releasing white doves, the birds winging up against the blue-black sky. The orchestra got more excited and the crowd oohed and aahed. Someone was singing Spanish into the mike. It looked as if the thing was about to break up.

Sailor didn't want to be trampled by the sheep. He crossed the Plaza to the Old Museum, boosted himself up on the ledge. He wasn't afraid of the Indians' eyes now. He wasn't the lone stranger. After the mass turned into people again, he'd find his way to La Fonda. The Sen wouldn't run away. He didn't know Sailor was here.

He pushed his hat on the back of his head, lit a cigarette and watched the Plaza fill with moving people. Smoke smudged from the chimney pots in the thatched roofs, and the acrid stench of chile became more acrid. His stomach remembered that he hadn't eaten since noon. A dry sandwich, a cup of coffee somewhere along the line. He'd eat later. What he thirsted for was a cold bottle of beer. Ice cold. Time enough for that after he met up with the Sen. He could wait.

Through the tree leaves and the colored lights and the moving people he saw across the Plaza a patch of the hotel where he'd dumped his bag. He'd forgotten it. Past nine now. He wasn't worried about the bag. He wasn't even worried about a place to sleep. He'd bunk with the Sen if the big shot couldn't find a room alone for him. He could pick up the bag later, or let the Sen pick it up.

About time to move. He dropped down from the ledge to the street, almost colliding with two giggling girls. The littlest one said "Hello." She was thin as a child and painted like a whore. He went past her, past other girls and women and children and men, not seeing them. He went past Tio Vivo, whirling now, children clinging to the wooden horses, the thin music trying to be gay.

He rolled down the street past the thatched booths to the intersection, crossed over to La Fonda. The roof show was over but the walk in front of the hotel was jammed with people. He shoved through them into the lobby. It looked like The Sherman when the Democrats were meeting in convention. Only the Democrats didn't wear fancy costumes. Finding the Sen was still a needle in the haystack, even if it had narrowed to one particular haystack. He fought his way across the lobby to the Cantina but he couldn't push inside. There were fifty or more ahead of him trying to push their way into the tightly packed cocktail bar. He'd have to wait.

He turned away and started back across the lobby. But he stopped. The switchboard, the single house phone, brought the first right idea he'd had tonight. The place to catch the Sen was in his room. He might not be there now but the desk would furnish the number. He hitched his shoulders and began a casual walk forward as if the desk clerks were conscious of him and of his purpose.

The quiet voice spoke behind him. "Hello, Sailor."

He didn't turn. He halted in his tracks. Then slowly he swiveled. "Hello, Mac," he said. McIntyre still wore the silly black hat with the bobbles, the red sash winding his white pants.

The bobbles were red and green and yellow. "Come for Fiesta?" he asked.

Sailor said, "Sure," hearty as if he meant it.

The Sen couldn't have hired McIntyre to protect him. It couldn't be that. Mac wasn't the Sen's man. He'd gone in when the reform commissioner was appointed. He'd been against the Sen for too many years to have gone over to his side. "You here for Fiesta?" Sailor asked.

"Yeah," McIntyre said.

"Kinda interesting, isn't it?" Two guys from Chicago talking it over in a foreign town. "See Zozobra burn?"

"Yeah, I saw it," McIntyre said.

Close-mouthed, McIntyre. Tight-mouthed and gimlet-eyed, his eyes going through what you said into what you were thinking. Sailor stirred. The silly hat struck him again. He laughed. "Have to pick up a costume, I guess. Only got in this afternoon." He wanted to ask and he did. "You been here long?"

"A week," McIntyre said.

Sailor kept satisfaction out of his face. "Well, be seeing you," he said. His foot was out to move away but McIntyre spoke again.

"Where you staying, Sailor?"

It was a casual question but he was afraid of it. It caught him flat and he answered the truth. "I haven't got a room yet. Kind of hard to find one during Fiesta." He wouldn't put it past Mac to have him jugged as a vag. If it suited his purpose. He laughed quick. "If I'm out of luck, I got a friend here who'll put me up."

"Yeah," McIntyre said. Not "Yeah?" but "Yeah."

He knew the cop was thinking of the Sen and he ought to have been thinking of the Sen too but the funny thing was, he hadn't been. He'd been thinking of the merry-go-round man, of fat, dirty Pancho Villa. If he was out of luck, Pancho would take care of him.

This time he broadened his smile. "Be seeing you, Mac," he said and this time he walked away. Walked away while McIntyre was saying, "Take care of yourself, Sailor." Saying it like he might need to walk carefully. McIntyre didn't know what he knew. McIntyre didn't know Sailor had the Sen where he wanted him.

He walked out of the hotel, not stopping at the desk. Because he'd had a quick one, a real one in the dome. McIntyre was trailing the Sen and the farther Sailor stayed away publicly, the safer he'd be. Mac knew a lot of things. He might know that Sailor was one of the Sen's boys. Was, meaning, had been. But again, he might not know it. Tomorrow was time enough to get the Sen's room number. The Sen wouldn't be running away. Not before he knew Sailor was looking for him.

Sailor went out again into the cool of night. After the fumes of perfume and liquor and body stench in the lobby, the night was a cool drink. He still hadn't had that cold bottle of beer. He still wanted it though the edge was off want after the stink of liquored breaths in the hotel. He didn't care to be caught in another trap like that one. If he could have beer here on the Plaza it would have a taste.

He stopped at one of the thatched booths and asked. The wizened woman could barely speak English. Her head was bound in a blue turban and there were chile stains on her white apron. "No beer," she said. Her smile was toothless. "Pop." He didn't want pop but the cold moisture clinging to the bottles made his dry throat ache. He bought a coke and he drank it standing there, everyone around him speaking in foreign tongue, Spanish-speaking. He felt suddenly lonesome, he who was always separate and never lonesome. He felt uprooted, he who had no roots but the Chicago streets; a stranger in an alien place. He finished the pop and walked on. His throat wasn't dry but he still had a beer thirst. Pancho could tell him where to cure it. His faith in Pancho was childlike. But even as he mocked the faith, it became the stronger.

He swung down into the park and over to Tio Vivo. He couldn't get near. It was ten o'clock but the kids were still lined up knee deep, pushing against the red palings. The music strummed with a thin brightness, Tio Vivo spun about, young not old, around and around. Over the heads of the kids he could see the brigand, sweat running from his broad brown face, his muscles bulging as he wound the crank that sent the horses galloping over their circled course.

Later he'd see Pancho. About a beer and a room. He lit a cigarette and strolled on, out of the Plaza, back to the ledge under the portal of the Old Museum. It was occupied now; in one corner a thin mother with a weary, hopeless face held a sleeping child across her lap. Two brown-skinned punks with loose lips took up the rest of the ledge, swinging their legs over the edge, boasting in spic of their intended prowess during La Fiesta.

Three

HE LEANED against the wall watching the movement of the Plaza, the dark leaves turning under the strand of lights, the Spanish musicians sawing their strings in the lighted bandstand, the shrill of laughter and the thin whine of tired children, the cries of the vendors. Over it all he could hear, or thought he could hear, the tinkling music and the whir of Tio Vivo.

In the streets the costumed, giggling girls walked clockwise and the slack-mouthed boys counter-clockwise. They spat insult and their eyes invited as they passed. Until the game was worn dull and they stopped together to regroup boy and girl, girl and boy.

"Hello." He hadn't realized that he too was a part of the Fiesta night until she spoke.

It was the same kid he'd almost bumped into earlier. She was just as immature as he'd thought on first glance, her breasts barely formed, her legs and arms thin, child-voiced, wise-eyed. Her small face and mouth were painted, her hair was a black fuzz. But she wore a red rose in her hair, her red flowered skirt was full and gay, her thin white blouse was embroidered bright. She was La Fiesta. She was pretty in a pert, child way; he wanted none of her. None of any woman until this business was done. Then he could have one worth having, a sleek one, washed and ironed

29

and perfumed, one he'd find in La Fonda, not on the streets. He said "Hello" and looked away, waiting for her to move on, wanting her to move on.

But she didn't move. She stood there in front of him, looking up at him out of her bold black eyes, laughing up at him. "What's your name?" she asked.

He said, "Sailor."

She giggled and the girl with her giggled. The girl with her had the red rose and the flowered skirt and the thin blouse, the frizz of black hair and the bold black eyes but she wasn't so young. She had a big nose and a big witless mouth smeared with lipstick. Her breasts sagged under the blouse. When she giggled, he looked at her with revulsion. "That's a funny one," she said.

"Is it?" he asked coldly and he looked back at the pretty one, the kid.

She said, "Sailor. That's a funny name, Sailor."

The homely girl said, "My brother, he was a sailor in the war. That is where you get the name Sailor, no?"

"No," he said, and he didn't smile. "I got it because I had trouble with the whole damn Great Lakes navy." He hadn't thought for a long time where the name came from.

"My brother he was in the Army," the kid said. "Were you a soldier, Sailor?" She giggled when she said it that way and her friend giggled with her.

He said, "I wasn't in the war. I had flat feet." It was a lie. The Sen had kept him out of the war. He wanted to get away from the girls but they had him backed against the wall. They saw him shift and they stopped laughing.

"I am Rosita," the kid said. "This is my friend, Irene."

"Pleased to meetcha," Irene said.

Rosita was craning around for something. She found it because she beckoned with her thin hand. "This is my cousin, Pila."

He hadn't seen the third girl until that moment. With the introduction, Rosita diminished her again to the background. There was no reason for him to look in Pila's direction, she hadn't moved, she hadn't spoken. But he looked because he would look anywhere for escape from the scrawny kid and her companion. He looked into Pila's eyes, black fathomless eyes; he saw the stone inscrutability of her brown face. She was square and strong, her face was square, her strong black hair lank about her face. The skirt she wore was bedraggled and worn, her blouse faded, the flower in her hair a joke. She was young, young as the kid, and she was old, old as this old country.

He was frightened of her, the same fright he had felt earlier when twilight was deepening over the little Plaza and the absence of life under the lights and banners a thing unreal. She was unreal, alien; yet she belonged and he was the alien. She, not the kid, was Fiesta; something deep and strong and old under the tawdry trapping, under the gimcracks. Something he didn't understand because he was a stranger.

He knew a frantic urge to bolt, not only from her but from the skinny kid and the homely girl friend. He was saved by the homely one, by Irene. Tired of his disinterest, her protruding black eyes were watching the walkers and she cried out, "Look, there is Eleuterio!"

She pulled at Rosita's arm, moving as she spoke. Rosita called over her shoulder, "Goodbye, Sailor." He looked again at Pila, fearing she wouldn't leave, but she turned without speaking and tagged after them. He took off his hat and wiped his forehead.

Behind him there was a snicker and he turned on the two gangling youths sitting up on the ledge. He didn't have to say anything, the face he gave them was enough. It usually was enough for punks. He was reassured by their scuttling eyes; the withdrawal of scorn.

He walked away. The merry-go-round was still turning although the circle of children was thinner. He could breathe Pancho's sweat this far away. Pancho could find him a room but it would be stained with sweat. It would stink of sweat and chile and stale garlic breaths. He didn't live like that; he hadn't come here to live like that.

He stepped up on the curb out of the way of the street crowd, walked slowly towards the La Fonda cross section. The Sen had to take care of him. Or else. McIntyre ought to be gone by now.

Sailor was going to see the Sen tonight and the Sen could buy the beers.

He walked hard, swaggering his decision, but at the white bank building he stopped and fell back into the shadow. There was a group rounding the corner of the ticket office, a group of swells. They were laughing; they were too gay, satin-and-silk-and-velvet gay, champagne gay; they were a slumming party, leaving their rich fastness momentarily to smell the unwashed part of Fiesta. The Sen was with them.

Sailor stood there, flat in the shadows. He hadn't planned meeting the Sen bulwarked by blooded friends. In all his plans he'd seen only himself and the Sen, alone, face to face. Nothing like this. Anger swelled in him. A big fair fellow in black velvet cavorted by, his arms around a hard-faced bitch in white lace and a small baby-faced blonde in a coral shawl. The bitch screamed, "Hubert, you're divine!" and the baby face snuggled closer. She had a thin chain of diamonds about her throat and she stunk of whisky.

Sailor didn't see the next couple, he saw the Sen approaching and out of anger he stepped out and confronted him. "Hello, Sen," he said.

The look on the Sen's face was worth waiting for. The protuberance of nose, the sleepy dark eyes, the thin lips and brush mustache—he'd watched them in his dreams react just this way. The moment of total disbelief, the realization and the blank masking of all reaction, the groping for customary patronizing sureness. It was all there just as he'd seen it. He'd surprised the Sen.

The weasel face was coming back to life. The Sen hadn't spoken to him and he didn't now.

He spoke to the girl with him. "Go on with the others. I'll catch up in a minute."

Sailor hadn't noticed the girl. He looked at her as the Sen spoke to her. Looked at her and was sickened. For her. He'd never been face to face before with clean beauty. She was young and fair, silvery blonde, and her eyes were blue and clean as sky. She was taller than the Sen, half a head taller, but she had to lift her face to look at Sailor.

When she looked at him he blurred his eyes so that he saw only the starched white ruching of her headdress, the starched white flare of her skirt. She didn't look at him as if he were a bum, her eyes were uncurious, casual.

He knew who she was. Iris Towers. Daughter of the railroad-and-hotel-and-bank Towers. Society page. He didn't know why she'd be with the Sen. He didn't know she was the reason, the why of all; he refused to admit she was that.

"Go on," the Sen said. His voice was rich and tender. The Sen should have been big and handsome for his voice. He was undersized and mean; his voice was a lie. "I won't be a minute." She smiled. "All right, Willis." She smiled at Sailor too before she ran ahead, calling, "Wait, Hubert, Ellie! Wait for me."

The Sen and Sailor watched her until she caught the group at the corner. When Sailor stopped looking after her, the Sen was watching him out of his narrow eyes. His eyes weren't crafty at this moment; they were dull with rage. "What are you doing here?" he demanded.

Sailor said, "Maybe I came for Fiesta." He wasn't afraid of the Sen or the Sen's rage because the tickets were in his hands. There was no reason to be afraid of the Sen. The big shot wasn't on top any more. He said it jauntily, "Maybe I came for Fiesta."

The Sen wasn't amused. "What do you want?" he asked.

Sailor dropped the antics. "You know what I want," he said.

"What do you want?" the Sen repeated.

His voice was as tight as the Sen's. "I want my dough."

The Sen took a breath. "I paid you off," he said. Said it as if he didn't know it was a dirty lie.

"You paid me five C's," Sailor said. "There's another grand due. You offered fifteen hundred for the job."

The Sen wet his thin lips. "I said five hundred," he began, "and I'd take care there wasn't any trouble. There hasn't been any trouble."

"Not yet." Sailor smiled. He waited a minute. "But you'd better come across with my dough. There could be." He stood there, planted on both feet, his left hand out, waiting. His right hand was in his right-hand pocket where it belonged.

The Sen's heavy black brows twitched. His black mustache twitched too. His eyes were nervous, not because of Sailor, the

Sen still thought he was in the driver's seat where Sailor was concerned. He was nervous because the girl was fading from sight. The silvery blonde girl was going away with the fair young fellow and the other big young fellows, the way she ought to.

The Sen hung out his hand, the short nervous gesture of the platform, of the private office. "I can't talk now," he said querulously, "I'm with a party."

"A thousand bucks," Sailor repeated. He was smiling, he was laughing.

Anger bounced up in the Sen. Nothing deep, nothing to tighten the hand on the gun. Just a spurt of mad. "I don't carry that kind of money on me." He implied Sailor should know that. "See me tomorrow."

He was ready to pass but Sailor stood in his way. "Where?" he asked. "When?"

"At the hotel. Tomorrow morning." He brushed by but Sailor's voice caught him before he could run.

"McIntyre's here," Sailor said.

The Sen jerked to a stop. When he looked up at Sailor again the fear had gone out of him. The crafty look had come under his eyelids and under his brush mustache. "McIntyre's here," he repeated unpleasantly.

Sailor gave him his moment. Gave it to him in full. Then he spoke. "He's been here a week," he said. "I only got in today."

He let it lay right there. It was good to watch the snake of fear coiling again in the Sen. The Sen got it all right, same as Sailor had got it earlier. McIntyre wasn't following Sailor.

Words were working in the Sen's mouth but he didn't say any more. He scurried away on his bandy legs. Sailor watched him away. He was playing in better luck than he'd hoped. Mac here. The Sen torn up between trouble and a silver blonde. The Sen couldn't put all his weasel brain on the ball with a blonde taking up most the room. The blonde was important to the Sen. So important he'd crawl over the body of a dead woman to get to her? Revulsion filled his mouth. Iris Towers was too clean to lie in a bloody bed. What would she want with the Sen anyway? What would any decent woman want with the Sen? He had dough; that explained the tramps. Dough and a big name. But Iris Towers had more and better of both than Senator Willis Douglass. Ex-Senator Douglass. Maybe she felt sorry for him, the tragic death of his wife. Easy to see what the Sen wanted with her. He'd married one rich woman but she got old; he was rid of her. He could have a gorgeous blonde now. But he hadn't paid off.

Sailor's hand tightened in his pocket. The Sen would pay off, pay in full. He'd pay off tomorrow, before McIntyre moved in. McIntyre was waiting for something or he'd have moved before. McIntyre would like to know what Sailor knew. If the Sen tried to welch . . .

He heard his own heels thudding above the tinkle of Fiesta. He was by the ledge of the museum again and anger was knots in his belly. Anger at the dirty, cheap, welching Sen. Playing it big, fine clothes, fine car, fine hotels, society blondes. Screwing the price down on a job and then skipping out without paying off. Thinking he could get by with running out on a deal. If Sailor hadn't read the society page, emulating the Sen himself, he wouldn't have known where to collect.

One little note in the gabby society column. "The popular young Senator, Willis Douglass, is vacationing in . . ." Popular with whom? Not with the guys who did his dirty work. Young was a laugh, a belly laugh. The Sen wouldn't see fifty again if he did have a barber who browned up the gray in his hair and beard. Gabby had only one thing accurate. Where to find the Sen. And

Sailor had caught up with the Sen. Because once he'd thought the Sen was big potatoes, once he'd had an idea of being like the Sen, and reading the society page was a part of it.

A thousand bucks. What was owed him. She'd had an insurance policy that paid off fifty times that. If he'd known that beforehand he'd have stuck to the two thousand asking price. Or a percentage deal. The Sen wasn't taking any of the risks; he should pay.

A thousand bucks was small change to the Sen. He'd spend more than that on this Fiesta jaunt, putting up at La Fonda, buying champagne, making a play for Iris Towers. Dressing himself in a black velvet monkey suit. You can bet the Sen didn't ride across country in a stinking bus. A drawing room on the Super-chief was his style.

The knots tightened and envy gnawed raggedly at his guts. All he asked was his due, a thousand bucks. A thousand berries to take across the border to Mexico. A man could live like a prince in Mexico with a grand. Zigler said so.

He'd set up a little safe business of his own in Mexico, making book or peddling liquor, quick and easy money, big money. He'd get himself a silver blonde with clean eyes. Marry her. Maybe she'd have dough too, money met money and bred money. All he wanted was his just pay and he'd be over the border. Not that he wasn't safe; the Sen had fixed it so he was perfectly safe. That part of the deal was on the level. He hadn't trusted the Sen on that; he'd seen to it with Zigler himself.

He wasn't going to be put off any longer. The Sen would pay up tomorrow. He'd pay up or— His head turning, Sailor's eyes met the black stone eyes of Pila. Sweat broke under his arm pits. He didn't know how long she'd been standing there beside him watching him; he didn't even know if he'd been muttering out loud. The fear that sweated him wasn't anything you could put a name on; it was formless, something old and deep. He'd had it once before and the memory of that occasion recurred how, recurred so sharply he could smell the cold washed corridors of the Art Institute. He'd been second-year High and for some reason the teacher had taken the class of mugs to the Institute.

There'd been the granite head of a woman in one corridor. He'd looked at it, it hadn't affected him at all in that first look, just a hunk of stone, a square hunk of stone with lips and eyes chiseled on it. The teacher had herded them by and he'd scuffed along. What returned him to that stone head, he didn't know to this day. But he'd looked backward and he'd returned. As if he were seeing a picture he could see himself, a skinny kid in a limp blue shirt and shabby gray pants standing there staring at an ugly hunk of stone. Until he was as cold as the stone head, he'd stood there. Until one of the guys was sent to drag him back to the class.

He'd known fear, real fear, for the first time in his life as he'd stood there. He'd thought he'd known it before. Fear of the old man's drunken strap, fear of the old woman's whining complaints, fear of the cop and the clap and the red eyes of the rats that came out of the wall at night. Fear of death and hell. Those were real fears but nothing like the naked fear that paralyzed him before the stone woman. Because with the other things he was himself, he could fight back, he had identity. Before her, his identity was lost, lost in the formless terrors older than time.

He had to say something, say anything fast to take that stone look from Pila's face. He said,

"Where are your friends?" His voice came out like an old husk.

"They have gone to the Federal Building."

When she spoke he heard again the shrill, accented voices of Rosita and Irene. Heard them in other painted girls flouncing, giggling by. Pila's accent was heavier but it was a part of her, it was the speech of this land. Her voice was sweet, gentle, almost a sing-song. He knew for the first time that the stone woman was Indian. He knew Pila was Indian.

He said roughly, avoiding her face, "Why didn't you go with them?"

"My father he would beat me."

He looked quickly again at her but there was no emotion, nothing but black eyes in a square brown face. He said, "What for? What's wrong with the Federal Building?"

"They lay with the boys."

Again he avoided her face, her terrible eyes that saw everything and saw nothing. She didn't move. He could see her scuffed black oxfords, cheap shoes, under the bedraggled hem of the limp flowered skirt. He realized now that she was very young.

"How old are you?" he asked.

She said, "Fourteen." She stood there unmoving, her black eyes unmoving on his face. He couldn't tell her to go away and leave him alone. He could but the words wouldn't speak. She had fastened to him as if he were the one familiar thing in this waning scene. He, the stranger. He said, "Come on, I'll buy you a pop."

She didn't say anything. She followed him, walking behind him, to the thatched stand. The old crone was washing up the dishes. "A pop," he said.

He rang the dime on the counter while the old woman uncapped the bottle. She handed it to him. He pushed it to Pila. She didn't ask why he wasn't drinking, she lifted the bottle and tipped it up. She took it from her mouth, rested a minute, tipped it again. Behind the booth, within the park, the merry-go-round spun tiredly; the music was faint. There were a half dozen children still riding this late, dark boys in faded overalls, a girl of about fourteen with eyes crossed together. Pila sucked from the bottle.

He said, "You're Indian."

She lowered the bottle. "I am Indian, yes. San Ildefonso."

"What are you doing here?"

"I came for the Fiesta."

"Did you want to come?"

She laughed at that, her whole face laughed at him. It was startling because he didn't know she could laugh, that she was human. Some of the rigidness left his spine.

"I want nothing so much as to come," she said. "Always I want to come to Fiesta."

He saw it out of her eyes for the moment, the brightness, the music and dancing, the good smell of red chile and the chill of pink pop, the twirling merry-go-round, the laughter and the happiness, flowered skirts to cover old black shoes. He said, "Come on, I'll give you a ride on the merry-go-round."

She set down the bottle. She was reluctant. "Tio Vivo is for children. Only for the children.

Rosie would not be caught dead riding on—"

He said harshly, "She'd be better off caught dead there than where she is. Who's Rosie anyway?"

"She is my cousin. My uncle and her aunt are man and wife. I am sleeping at Rosita's house for the Fiesta." She seemed to think it was an honor.

He was angry without knowing the reason for it. "I suppose she dressed you up in those clothes?"

"Yes. This last year was Rosie's costume. She has loaned it to me this year." She was pleased, proud as punch of the dragging, faded skirt; of the blouse where the reds and purples and greens had run together in the wash. "I have not before had the Fiesta costume."

Remembering the Indian women, he said, "I should think you'd like your own costume better than this." His gesture was back towards the Indian frieze.

Pila understood. She spoke with something of scorn, something of pride. "I do not wear Indian clothes. I go to the Indian School."

They had reached the red palings and words were silent. Her eyes were following the turning horses. The eyes of a child; his eyes looking at a shiny new bike behind Field's window, a bike for kids whose folks could buy them bikes at Field's. He said, "Well, do you want to ride?"

She began to say, "Yes," then she said, "I am too big." She didn't say it with any emotion, she accepted it.

He shook his head out of that troubled anger. "The boss is a friend of mine. He'll let you on if I say so." He studied her face. "Haven't you ever ridden on a merry-go-round?"

She said, "No."

"Is this your first time at Fiesta?"

Again she said, "No. When I was little I came with my family." Her head turned to the Old Museum and back to him.

"But you never had a ride?"

"No."

The horses were moving, slowly, slowly moving, they swayed and were still. The girl with the crossed eyes slid from the green pony and stubbed awkwardly out of the enclosure. The dirty little boys set up a Spanish jabber. Pancho

stood, arms akimbo, talking back at them. "Vaya!" he shouted. "Vaya."

Pila said without disappointment, "It is too late."

"He's a friend of mine," Sailor repeated.

He waited until the boys were shooed away, threatening,
scolding, swearing in spic. Kids like he was once, street kids,
nothing to go home to. Pancho saw him standing there as he
banged the gate. He lumbered over. The night air had dried the
sweat of his shirt. He wiped his fat arm across his forehead. "You
think I have no customers?" he winked.

"Yeah," Sailor said. "You got a customer now." He pushed
Pila forward. Pancho shook his head. "Tonight it is too late.
Mañana. Tomorrow."

"Tomorrow is too late," Sailor said. "Rosita will be around
again tomorrow." Pancho didn't know what he was talking about.
But he knew the dollar that Sailor pulled out of his pocket.

"I am old and tired," he began. "Tio Vivo is tired. Mañana—"

"One ride," Sailor said.

Pancho shrugged. He took the dollar sadly, opened the gate.

"A full ride," Sailor warned. Pila walked to the horses,
put out her hand to one, to another. He saw beyond her the
old withered man encasing his fiddle. He dug for another
dollar. "With music. Gay music." Sailor called to Pila. "Ride
the pink one."

He felt like a dope after saying it. What difference did it
make to him what wooden horse an Indian kid rode? But the
pink horse was the red bike in Field's, the pink horse was the
colored lights and the tink of music and the sweet, cold soda pop.

The music cavorted. Pancho's muscles bulged at the spin-
dlass. Pila sat astride the pink horse, and Tio Vivo began its
breath-taking whirl. Sailor leaned on the pickets. He didn't

know why giving her a ride had been important. Whether he'd wanted to play the big shot. Whether it was the kid and the bright new bike, the bum with his nose pressed against the window looking at the clean silver blonde beyond reach. Whether it was placating an old and nameless terror. Pila wasn't stone now; she was a little girl, her stiff dark hair blowing behind her like the mane of the pink wooden horse.

Four

HE'D NEVER be rid of her now. She stood before him and she
said, "thank you." As if he were a great white god.

Pancho came up behind her. "It was a good ride, no?"

"Yeah," Sailor said. She didn't say anything. Her black eyes
were fathomless on Sailor. He tried to be jaunty. "Come around
tomorrow and I'll buy you another ride. And another pink pop."
He settled his hat and he strode off, to get away, not that he had
any place to go.

He'd been too intent on springing the surprise of McIntyre
on the Sen to remember he hadn't a place to lay his head. All of
his anger flared up again, refreshed, and with it the added fuel of
remembering the Sen trotting off after Iris Towers, leaving him
with an Indian girl in a tart's hand-me-downs. He found himself
in front of La Fonda and he strode inside bumping past the couples on their way out. If his money could buy a merry-go-round
ride for an Indian, it was just as good for a beer at La Fonda.

There was still noise in the lobby and the patio, a scattering
of couples, none of them sober. He walked over to the cocktail
room. It was closed, the door locked. He hadn't paid any attention to the time. He saw now it was past midnight. A dark youth
in a blue smock was wet-mopping the floor. The revelers in the
patio sang mournfully off key.

The clerk at the desk was a woman now, a woman with yellowed white hair and a dyspeptic mouth over her receding chin. He could ask the Sen's room but she'd want to know why. She was the kind who'd call the hotel dick if he told her where to head in. He didn't want any trouble. Not tonight. He was tired, so tired his head was turning around and around like Tio Vivo. He wanted a cold beer.

He was out of the hotel on the darkened street before he faced the truth. He could have called the Sen's room, and with the number in his head, made his way there later. The way he'd planned it before he ran into McIntyre. What had stopped him this time was a girl with clean blue eyes. He was afraid she might be on the same floor with the Sen; he knew the scene the Sen would stage if he returned and found Sailor on his doorstep. He didn't care what the Sen said to him alone, the way things were now he could give it back with change. But he was ashamed to have her witness it, to have her eyes see him as a bum. A dame he'd never seen but once in his life, a dame that was as far away from his touch as the dim star way up there almost out of sight— he didn't want to be a bum in her eyes.

He walked straight on down the street, past the hotel where his bag was stached. His eyes slid through the plate-glass window. There was another guy behind the desk, a tough-looking bouncer. He wasn't the kind who'd take to bums sleeping in the lobby. For that matter there weren't any lobby chairs that he could see. Nothing but pinball machines. He walked on by. He turned and crossed at a drug store and walked on the far side of the Plaza. Dark shops, deserted walk. In the Plaza there were still stragglers. Sitting on the benches and on the circular low stone wall around a memorial slab. On the corner was a deserted garage and he cat-a-cornered across to the museum side again.

But he didn't turn under the portal of the Indians. Up this street, halfway up, he'd seen a neon sign, red and orange wiggles, spelling it out, Keen's Bar. It wasn't closed. He could hear the raucous noise this far away, the sardonic blare of a juke box, the muffled roar of men mixing with liquor, the shrill screams of women mixing with men and liquor.

He didn't hesitate. He walked straight towards the sign. A dump. A dive. There was where he belonged. Not with the swells in their snotty hotel. He wasn't that good yet. Not on the street with spics and squaws. He wasn't that bad off. He opened the screen door of Keen's and went in.

The pack around the bar was yelling over the juke. The air was fog blue with smoke. Every table jammed, the square of dance floor jammed. Everybody drinking, everybody screaming, the only silence a scowling spic waiter, scuttling through the narrow space between tables, a tray on his uplifted paw. There wasn't a chance for a beer here.

Black rage shook him. He hadn't a place to sleep, he hadn't had food, he couldn't even get a beer in this goddamn stinking lousy town. He was ready to turn and walk out when he saw wedged at a table against the wall, McIntyre. In the same silly hat, the red sash. Mac hadn't seen him yet. Mac was watching the dance floor. Sailor knew then that the Sen was here. The Sen and Iris Towers. He took his stance in the room.

The waiter had pushed under elbows to the bar. By some trick he was coming out again balancing his loaded tray. Part of the load was a bottle of Pabst, a cold bottle, the drops of moisture still beading it.

Sailor stuck out his hand and lifted off the bottle. The ape began to sputter out of his warped mouth. Sailor said, "Stow it." He clinked a half dollar on the tray. "Crawl under and get another." He put the bottle to his mouth and his eyes warned the ape what he could do if he didn't like it. The burning ice was heaven in his throat, down his gullet, into his hollow stomach.

He walked off, the malevolent black eyes following him. He took another swig and bumped through the narrow space towards McIntyre. He was himself again. The noise, the smoke, the dirty glare was all part of the usual to him. Even McIntyre, alone, watching, waiting was part of it. He felt good. McIntyre wasn't waiting for him. He shoved on until he reached the wall. Mac looked up at him. Not surprised to see him.

He said, "Hello, Mac. Enjoying yourself?"

Mac was alone at the table which might have been a table and might have been an ash stand with a wooden top put on it to take care of the Fiesta trade. Sailor reached out and swung an empty chair around to the table. Whoever it belonged to could fight it out later. "Mind if I sit down?" he asked and he sat down.

McIntyre had an almost empty glass in front of him.

"How about a drink?" Sailor asked. "Looks like you need a refresher." He took another long drink of the beer, his hands rolling the cool bottle as if it were a woman's body. "If we can get that ape over here."

McIntyre said, "I'll get him." He came near to a smile. "He thinks I'm a cop."

They could smell a cop, those in the half world where a cop meant trouble. You couldn't fool them; they could smell.

Sailor laughed loud. "That's a good one." He drank again. "That's a real one. I was just thinking the same thing myself." He stopped laughing. He was soft spoken. "You wouldn't be here on business, would you?"

His head tilted the way McIntyre's did. He saw them across on the other side of the dance floor. The Sen; the big guy called

Hubert; Ellie, whichever she was, the lace bitch or the baby-face blonde; the two big young guys and Iris Towers. An angel strayed into hell. Part of it but still clean, still aloof from it. Clean and white-starched. Even through the fog he could see the Sen's red nose, red eyes, the way the Sen got from drink. The Sen wasn't having a good time. He was brooding over his glass of Scotch. He had plenty to brood about.

McIntyre was talking. "You wouldn't know anything about my business, would you?"

Sailor kept his eyes on the Sen. He laughed some more. "I wouldn't know if it's business or if you came for the Fiesta."

McIntyre said, "Quite a Chicago contingent here for Fiesta. There's Senator Douglass over there."

"Yeah. I saw him. And Iris Towers."

McIntyre sounded a little surprised. Or he would have sounded surprised if McIntyre could. "You know Iris Towers?"

Sailor laughed out loud. "I know who she is." He tilted up the bottle, drained it. "You don't think a mug like me would know Iris Towers, do you?" He jarred the bottle down on the table. He felt good and cool and warm all at once. His eyes felt bright. He said, "Can you get that ape to bring us a drink?"

McIntyre turned his head barwise. He lifted a finger. The waiter came over swinging his gorilla arms. When he saw Sailor at the table the hate was fresh in his eyes. Sailor said, "I'm buying, Mac, what'll it be?" If the spic ape had a knife under his dirty apron, it was good to be on first-name terms with Chicago Homicide. Sailor wasn't looking for trouble with the locals.

McIntyre said, "The same. Bourbon and water."

"Same for me. Pabst Blue Ribbon."

McIntyre was eyeing the Sen's table again. "Know the rest of the party?"

"Uh-uh."

"That's Hubert Amity," McIntyre pointed out. "Amity Engines. Mrs. Amity's the one in the lace mantilla." The hard-faced bitch. Old man Amity had been one of the Sen's heaviest backers when the Sen was in Washington. A guy with a face like a hatchet. Nothing like son Hubert.

McIntyre went on, "Kemper Prague is the one in the sombrero. The one about to slide under the table." Kemper Prague. Millionaire playboy of the North Shore. Plenty of dirty scandal tainting him. Always hushed up. McIntyre said, "Don't know the others. Must be local talent."

Sailor said and his voice was hard, "I'd be willing to bet they don't have to work for a living." Oh, the Sen had done all right for himself since he left off selling soap and had gone into politics. There'd been his wife's money to get him started. She'd been older than he, ten years at least, but there wasn't any age on her money. He'd come a long way from the little frame house on the South side. Graft and his wife's money, all his now, he'd done well by himself. Only not well enough. Now he was going into the millionaire class. Nothing but the best for the Sen. But he'd welch out of a thousand-dollar debt if he could. He couldn't.

"Wouldn't take that one," McIntyre said. "I wonder what the Senator's after now." He was idly curious.

Sailor could tell him. McIntyre ought to be able to see it himself, he could see her there.

Couldn't McIntyre see her, the white rose, the pale white star?

"Maybe it's the governorship."

Sailor hooted his amazement. "What would he want to be governor for? He's been senator."

"Being governor of the sovereign state of Illinois isn't a bad job." McIntyre was mild. "Not only does it carry prestige, it could be remunerative."

The waiter was sliding in with the tray. He'd brought the beer. He glared at Sailor. "Sev'ty-seex sants," he mouthed. Sailor peeled a dollar, threw it on the tray. "Keep the change," he waved. The ape gave him hate instead of thanks. But the beer was cold. He trickled it into his mouth tenderly. He wiped the corner of his mouth with his knuckle as he set down the bottle.

"I don't think he needs dough that bad," Sailor said. He was thinking of that insurance policy.

Fifty grand. Besides the estate.

"Nobody ever has enough," McIntyre said dryly.

The beer was good but his head was getting a little light. He knew it was time to make a move. He had better sense than to talk to a copper when he was drinking. He wasn't a drinking guy, never had been. That was one reason he'd stayed in the Sen's inner circle. The Sen could trust him not to get woozy and muff things. Strictly a one-bottle-of-beer guy. Two bottles wasn't too much, only he hadn't had anything to eat today. Coffee and a cinnamon roll for breakfast, dry sandwich and coffee for lunch. He'd finish the beer and go. He took another long drink. It was good, good.

"I don't think he'll ever be governor," McIntyre mused.

The Sen was getting up on the floor now. She was getting up too. He was going to dance with her. He was putting his arm around her clean white waist. Sailor clenched the bottle with hard knuckles. He spat through his teeth, "Son of a bitch."

McIntyre heard him. He'd said it under his breath and the juke was blaring the Woody Herman "Apple Honey" and men were bellowing at each other and glasses were clanking and women were squealing and chairs were bumping but McIntyre heard him say it. McIntyre turned his steady colorless eyes on Sailor.

Sailor said, "He'll be governor if he wants it." He laughed just as if he'd not said son of a bitch and McIntyre hadn't heard him.

The homicide detective studied him mildly for a moment then repeated, "I don't think he'll ever be governor." He turned back to the dance floor.

Sailor didn't know what McIntyre was trying to say. He didn't know because that was the way McIntyre was. He never said anything out straight like dumb flatfeet. He let you guess. He could be trying to say the Sen would never be governor because he was going to fry. Fry for the murder of his wife.

Sailor finished the beer. The Sen was still hopping around, his arm clamped around white Iris.

Sailor said thickly, "I haven't eaten all day. I'm going to go get something to eat."

"You can order here," McIntyre said.

Sailor pushed away from the table. "I'm going where I can taste it. Be seeing you, Mac."

McIntyre nodded. "Take care of yourself."

He wasn't drunk, he wasn't even tight but his head was light. He bumped through the aperture. Bumped into one drunk shoving out from the table. The drunk was in fancy pants like the Sen's. The drunk threatened, "Watch where you're going."

Sailor said, "Button your lip." He didn't stop to button it for the drunk, he pushed on out of the dump into the night. He pumped the stale air out of his lungs, pumped in the night freshness. The night was sweet and chill, there was a faint smoke smell in it, like fresh pine burning. He walked back to the Plaza, to the museum corner. The Plaza was dark and quiet, only the circlet of dim colored lights hung over its darkness. He saw deeper shadows under the shadows of the portal. Mounds, blanket-wrapped, shawl-wrapped. The Indian peddlers were asleep, the stuff they'd had spread out earlier wrapped now in big calico bundles like laundry in a dirty sheet. He might borrow a blanket and sleep with the Indians. He put a filthy word into a vicious whisper. He'd never had to sleep on the ground yet.

There was no place to eat on the Plaza. The Plaza was asleep; dark, quiet, asleep. The thatched booths were asleep and the smokestacks which had trickled thin smoke. The shops squaring the Plaza were dark, asleep. The cheap hotel was only a dim light. He crossed into the park and took the path to the right. He hadn't investigated the street that led down away from the square. There could be another hotel. With no rooms. Fiesta, you know. There must be, somewhere, an all-night eating joint. Even hick towns must have some place for night workers to feed their faces. He turned sharp where a street came up to meet this one. He'd walked up it earlier today. He hadn't noticed the restaurant down on the corner, across from The Inca. He hadn't been thinking about food then.

A lighted sign hung out over the sidewalk. He didn't read the big red letters. He read the little blue ones. "Kansas City Steaks." As he read, he saw a couple of men go up to the door and walk in.

It didn't take him sixty seconds to reach the corner. The café was open all right. There were plenty of people sitting around the counter, people in booths. Sailor went in.

He found a place at the counter between a guy in shirtsleeves and a doll in a cheap silk dress. The doll looked at him out of big eyes when he straddled the stool. He didn't look at her. He fixed his eye on the long tall sandy drink in the chefs cap. Kept it there until the guy came over and asked, "What's yours?"

"Couple of steak sandwiches without garbage, side order French fries, bottle of milk."

The guy said, "Rare?"

"And thick." He pulled a cigarette from his pocket and lit it. The doll said in a flat nasal Kansas twang, "What's happened to the pie, Gus?" She said it like she thought she was something cute but she wasn't. She had a face like a rubber doll, round and empty, and a Kansas twang in her nose. She didn't know that her eyes were predatory; she thought they were big baby-blue eyes and that nobody could see what kind of a spirit she had.

Gus said, good-natured, "We're baking it. Keep your shirt on, Janie."

He dumped a glass of water in front of Sailor and a handful of tin to eat with. You could fish your own paper napkin out of the container.

The girl said to the girl beside her, "The service here is getting terrible." She said it to the other girl but she kept the corner of her eye on Sailor. When she started to crawl in his lap, he'd slap her down. Until then he'd ignore her. Though she could probably find him a bed. Trouble was what went with it.

He hunched her out of sight with his shoulder. The guy on the other side of him was shoveling in ham and drinking coffee. He wasn't with anyone; he was like Sailor, all he wanted was food. Sailor said, "You don't know where I could get a room?"

"Naw." He didn't stop eating. "No rooms during Fiesta." He wasn't interested in gab and Sailor didn't bother him again.

You couldn't outrun Fiesta even in a hashery. Across the circular counter were costumes, costumes in some of the booths. Youngsters mostly, blondes and red heads and brunettes with gawky looking guys. Kids with good appetites, with nothing on their minds but having fun; Zozobra is dead, long live Fiesta.

When he was the size of the punk with the ears, directly across, McIntyre had already run him in once for stealing cars. Mac was just a flattie then. They'd both come up in the world quite a ways. He'd always liked Mac. Mac didn't lecture; he said take it or leave it. If you steal cars, you'll do time. What Mac didn't know was that the boys behind the car barns had a better angle: If you don't get caught stealing cars, you won't have to do time. He hadn't seen much of Mac since he moved north. A hello now and then, when you weren't expecting it. Mac hadn't tried to move in. Mac was honest, you could say that for him. He wasn't looking out for a cut. He believed what he told you. You hurt somebody and you're going to get hurt yourself. He was an honest copper, in his mind and heart as well as in his job. That was why the reform commissioner had named him head of Homicide. Now he was out working again.

It had to be something big to put Mac on the street. Something like nabbing ex-Senator Douglass for murder. That silly hat he was wearing might fool some of the yokels but not anyone who'd ever seen Mac at work. Who had ever noticed Mac's quiet slate eyes.

Gus slapped down the thick crockery platter, two open steak sandwiches oozing pink juice on the toast, another platter with French fries. "Coffee?"

"Bottle of milk." His mouth was full already. The potato was too hot. He crunched it, keeping his tongue out of the way.

"Yeah, I remember." Gus opened an ice chest, pulled out the milk.

"Make it two," Sailor said. He didn't wait to cut the sandwich. He bit in big and chewed. He'd known he was hungry but not this hungry. The milk was even better than the beer had been. He finished half a glass while he was still chewing.

He didn't recognize the man with the full greasy mouth, the red-rimmed eyes, the dirty collar line at first. Not until the mouth opened to push in a hunk of bread and meat. He was looking in a mirror. The man was he, dirty, crumpled, his unkempt hair straggling from under his hat down on his forehead, beard shadowed on his chin. He had to find a place to clean up before seeing the Sen tomorrow. He could sleep on a park bench but he must shave, shower, change to fresh linen. He chewed in ugly impotent rage at what the Sen had done to him this day. He ought to be made to pay for the indignities. Five thousand wouldn't be enough to make up for it.

The screen door flopped open and he heard the laughter of an entering group. He was afraid to look, under his eyes he could see the costumes. They passed the opposite side of the counter and he pushed his hat forward over his eyes. After they had passed he looked after them. It wasn't the Sen's party. It was just another group of stay-up-late Fiesta revelers.

He ate faster then. He didn't want to be caught in the glaring light of the hash house by the Sen's crowd. His stomach was bloated when he finished and the cigarette tasted good again, not like an old dry weed. He picked up his check, paid at the cashier's wicket and dived outside banging the screen after him. But the Sen and his party weren't standing there ready to, enter. There was no one on the walk.

From the corner the lights of the Cabeza de Vaca up the street sneered at him. Across, the lights of the little Inca ignored him. Damn them and damn their neon. He'd find him a room better than in those dumps.

He rounded the corner and retraced his way up the slight bill. He turned left and continued down the street. There must be some place with room for him. Book stores, jewelry stores, shoe stores, furniture stores. He walked on in the darkness, the shops growing meaner, the way more dark. Nothing across, a blatant movie house dark, he could pitch a tent in the lobby if he had a tent. Murky bars with muted sounds and sounds not muted, acrid smell of cheap liquor stenching your nostrils. Only a couple of blocks and the street ended. Nothing beyond. Dark little houses, country, vacant fields. Beyond that, mountains. No hotels, no room signs, not even a whore house. Nothing more in this direction and he turned back. He stood for a moment lighting another cigarette, trying to know out of his head what to do, where to go.

And standing there the unease came upon him again. The unease of an alien land, of darkness and silence, of strange tongues and a stranger people, of unfamiliar smells, even the cool-of-night smell unfamiliar. What sucked into his pores for that moment was panic although he could not have put a name to it. The panic of loneness; of himself the stranger although he was himself unchanged, the creeping loss of identity. It sucked into his pores and it oozed out again, clammy in the chill of night. He was shivering as he stood there and he moved sharply, towards the Plaza, towards identity. He heard the pad of walking feet as he moved and he slung his head over his shoulder quick, his right hand hard and quick in his pocket. No one walked behind him. Yet when he moved again, he heard again the soft padding. He had a momentary stab of something like fright, remembering the black hatred in the eyes of the mug waiter. Then he realized. There was no one abroad but himself. It was himself he heard. His short laugh was an ugly, out-loud sound in the dark and the night. He walked on, striking his heels viciously into the broken sidewalk. He wasn't afraid. He wasn't afraid of the spic waiter or of any man who walked. He had never known man fear since the old man had been buried, his strap fastening his pants around his obese middle.

He walked back up the dark street, one block, the second, and he cut slantwise across to the murky bar by the barber shop. Not because he wanted a drink. Because he saw the cadaverous frame of Ignacio, the guitar player, through the smoky open doorway. Because he would find Pancho, and Pancho would find a place where he might rest.

This wasn't a dump like Keen's Bar, this was a dive. A two-by-four saloon with a dirty bar and no fixings. Not even a juke. This was where men, poor men, went to get drunk when the whip of poverty fell too hard for endurance. This was the kind of saloon the old man had hung around whenever he had the price of cheap rotgut. Where the old man had spent the dimes that the old lady brought home for bread. When the old man couldn't stand up on his feet, he'd stumble home and beat the hell out of the kids because there wasn't any bread to give them.

The old man lay in a pauper's grave where he belonged. The old lady lay beside him; it wasn't her fault that she wore out scrubbing floors for bread and left the kids on the street. Some day he'd dig her up; have a white headstone put over her old bones. The girls were drabs, the boys worked for a living. Some living clerks, day laborers. All but him. That hadn't been good enough for him. He'd known what he wanted, money, enough money to go North Shore. No small change. No more stir. Safe jobs. Big pay. He was useful to the Sen because he didn't drink and he looked good in the clothes the Sen bought him. He was a good-looking kid and the Sen liked the men around him to look North Shore. He had good shoulders from boxing; he was quick and tough; he'd done the Sen's dirty work since he was a punk of seventeen and never let the Sen down. The dirty stinking Sen.

A nice white headstone. Maybe with an angel praying on top it. Here lies. He didn't know when the old lady was born or where. Died: Chicago slums, 1936. Rest in peace. The only peace she'd ever known.

He was inside the red murk of the bar and the stench turned his stomach. Rotgut. And marijuana. But he had to find Ignacio, find out where Pancho slept. He went along the bar, craning his head into men's faces, dark, ugly faces, sotted with cheap liquor, babbling in their strange tongues. He went along smelling their dirty pants and dirty shirts, their dried sweat and dung and foul breaths. Until he found Ignacio.

He demanded, "Where's Pancho?"

Ignacio looked at him as if he'd never seen Sailor before. Blank, black eyes, sad drunken eyes in his half-starved face. He said something in Spanish. "Quien es Pancho?"

The language barrier was stifling. More stifling than the foul smell of the dive. "Pancho," Sailor shouted. He remembered then, Pancho Villa was the name he had given the fat man; he didn't know the man's real name. He said, "Your boss. The fat guy. The guy who runs the merry-go-round." He found the Spanish. "Tio Vivo."

The cadaver continued to look at him out of sad, blank eyes.

But he'd been talking too loud and the others at this end of the bar were listening, watching. Suspicious of Sailor's city suit and hat, matted as it was; suspicious of his nose and his eyes and his English-speaking tongue. Suspicious and wary, waiting for Sailor to edge across the line, waiting with knives for him to start something. His fists knotted as the squat man behind Ignacio stumped forward. But the man didn't lash at him, he grinned from behind his snag teeth.

"He say who ees Pancho," the man said, grinning like a monkey. His accent was thick as the red smoke. "He no spic the Englees. He no understand what you say. I taal him." He tapped his wilted blue shirt.

"Listen, you—"

"I am Pablo Gonzalez," the man said. "I speak the Englees. He no speak the Englees. I taal him."

"Tell him I want to know where Pancho is." He scowled quickly. "His name isn't Pancho. He's the big guy. The boss of the merry-go-round. Tio Vivo."

Pablo Gonzalez rattled Spanish at the blank eyes. Sailor waited, hopeful, hopeless. The thin guy was shaking his thin head.

"For Christ's sake, he works for the guy—"

Pablo interrupted patiently. "He does not know where ees Don José Patricio Santiago Morales y Cortez—" his grin was more monkey—"that you call Pancho."

That ended it. He flipped a quarter at the monkey face. "Buy yourself five drinks," he growled.

He got out of the dive fast.

Ignacio was lying. Or the monkey face didn't spic the Englees any better than the guitarist. The barrier of language was even more frustrating. If he could talk to Ignatz he'd find out where the long name was. Pancho had a name like a duke, not like a guy playing the carnivals.

He couldn't talk Spanish and that left him where he'd been before, on the street. Walking up the narrow street, pounding the pavement of a hick town. Standing on a street corner in a dark strange town, with colored lights festooned above his head and grotesque paper masks leering at him.

There was nothing to do about it now but camp on the Sen's doorstep. Give the old biddy at the desk a tall tale and get to the Sen. Scorn in the clean blue eyes of Iris Towers wasn't as important as getting between the sheets. He walked on, past the dark shops, past the dim lighted pane of the hotel where his bag was parked, on to the corner. But he didn't cross to the hulk of hotel. He stayed his steps. Stayed them to a voice in the night. A voice in song.

Through the trees he saw the gentle rocking of a gondola of Tio Vivo. The song came from there, a ragged minor song, lifted into the night. He turned his back on the hotel and he walked towards the little merry-go-round.

Sailor remained in shadow until the song was done. "Adios," the singer sang. "Adios, mi amigo." The sweet voice trailed into silence. But the silence was not the silence of the dark street with the mean shops. The leaves in the trees were rustling and the gondola creaking and the echoes of the sad song were in the ears. Pancho gurgled a bottle to his mouth. He lay sprawled in a gondola, his girth swinging it gently. His hat was on his knees and his bare feet were propped on the seat across. He lowered the bottle, smacked his lips, corked it and laid it in his hat. He saw Sailor then.

"Ai yai!" he cried. "Mi amigo!" His face dented with smiles. His arms flopped open, warm and wide. "Mi amigo! Where have you gone to? Come have a drink."

Sailor unlatched the gate and entered the enclosure. "I don't want a drink," he said. "I want a bed."

"I will share with you my bed," Pancho vowed. "But first we will have a drink." He held up the unlabeled bottle, peered through the glass and beamed. "We will have a drink and another drink. And I will sing for you." He pulled the cork with his teeth, held out the bottle.

Sailor said, "No, thanks. All I want is some sleep." The fat man could sing him all the lullabies he wanted if he'd just show him a bed.

"But no!" Pancho's mouth drooped. His whole face drooped. "You are my friend, no? You are my friend and you will not drink with me?" He looked as if he were going to cry. He'd killed half the pint already. Even without the evidence you'd know that; he was too ready to laugh, to cry, to sing, to vow friendship.

Sailor took the bottle. You couldn't argue with a drunk. He wiped the mouth with the palm of his hand, tipped and drank. Only friendship kept him from sputtering as he set the bottle away. The stuff burned like lye; it tasted like pepper, black pepper. He pushed the bottle back to Pancho.

"Ahh!" The fat man nuzzled it. "It is good, no? Tonight we drink tequila. Not pulque. Not sotol. Tequila. Because it is Fiesta." He drank, corked the bottle and replaced it in his hat. He moved his bare feet. "Be seated, my friend. You think business is not good with me? But tonight it is tequila. That is good, no?"

Sailor slid into the gondola beside the bare feet. He'd like to take off his own shoes. They were hot and heavy after this day. "That's swell, Pancho," he said. The gondola was set in motion as he sat in it. It stirred with the dark, glittering leaves over the square, and the ponies stirred gently as if in sleep. Sailor pushed back his hat and the night was cool on his forehead.

"Zozobra is dead," Pancho said. "Viv' las Fiestas!" He uncorked the bottle and passed it in one swoop. "We will have a drink, no, because business it is good?"

"No more," Sailor said. He stymied the sad face. "Promised my mother when I was a kid. One drink, no more. My old man was a drunk."

Pancho shrugged. "Sometimes it is good for a man to be drunk." He tipped the bottle. There couldn't be more than one drink left after this swig. One more and he'd herd the fat man to that bed. Pancho smacked his lips. He began to sing dolefully, "Adios, adios, mi amigo . . ." His eyes swiveled sly. "Where is the Indian girl?" he asked.

"I left her here," Sailor said. "With you."

"She was most unhappy you leave her," Pancho said.

"I had business."

"Always you think of business." Pancho was sad. Only for a moment. His mouth twinkled. "But it is good business for me you think of business. Hola! I drink tequila."

"You find me a bed and I'll buy you another bottle tomorrow night," Sailor promised.

"With you I will share my bed." Pancho repeated the vow. "I will share my serape. You are my friend. But first another drink." He tipped the bottle but the bottle smile didn't come over his face. "Aaah," he grunted. He tossed the bottle into the shadows that flickered under a tree.

"I'll buy you another tomorrow," Sailor told him again. "Let's go to bed now." He stirred the gondola.

"One moment," Pancho stayed him. "First we drink together." His big hand brought forth in triumph from his hip another pint of the colorless liquid. He grinned as his teeth pulled the cork. He proffered the bottle.

Sailor said, "Remember? My promise."

"It is true," Pancho sighed. "I too have given my promise. Many times." The twinkle bobbed back to his lips. "But this is Fiesta. Tonight we will drink."

Sailor took the bottle. He wasn't a drinking man and this Spanish white mule wasn't a drink fit for man or mule. It was like fire in your gullet. Nevertheless he drank. It didn't matter. Nothing mattered further tonight. If he couldn't sleep, he would drink. There was no reason for him to be alert. He drank, choked, and passed the bottle over to Pancho.

"Bueno!" Pancho applauded. "That is good, no?" He gurgled it, repeated his ritual of recorking the bottle, standing it in his greasy hat. "The little Indian girl . . ." he began slyly.

"Her friends had ditched her." Sailor put his foot on that idea. "I didn't know what to do with her. She was trailing me around. So I gave her a pop and a ride on your merry-go-round. She'd never ridden on one."

"No," Pancho said. His eyes roved across the width of the Plaza to the museum portal where the Indians slept silently. "No." It might only have occurred to him now. "The Indian children they do not ride Tio Vivo."

"Don't have the price?" Sailor asked blackly.

"Maybe no, maybe yes," Pancho shrugged. He passed the bottle. Sailor took it and drank. "The Indians they are funny peoples. They are proud, the Indians. Maybe they do not wish their little ones to be bumped about by the Mexicans and the Gringos. Maybe they do not wish them to be screamed at, 'Get out of here, you dirty Indians.' The Indians are funny. They stay to themselves." He took a philosophic swig. "The Spanish people say that they are proud peoples. Maybe one time, yes. Maybe they come on their horses, a proud peoples, with gold on their saddles. It is said this is true. That is why there is the Fiesta. Because the proud Spanish conquered the Indian. Don Diego de Vargas in his coat of mail and riding in his fine leather saddle on his fine proud horse. That is what they say."

Sailor remembered vague history. "I guess it's in the books," he said. The gondola stirred gently and the dark glittering leaves were a-rustle in the night.

"It is not good to be a conqueror, I think," Pancho said. "The Spanish were a proud peoples when they conquered but they are no longer proud. The Gringos came after and conquered the Spanish. Not by the sword. With business." His lip drooped and he winked at Sailor. "Business it is. Land and hides and wool and the buying and selling of money. That I do not understand. The buying and selling of money. But the Gringo sonnama beetches, they understand it." He took a big happy breath. "They are funny peoples, the Gringos, no? Maybe once they were proud peoples but I do not think so." His nose wrinkled. "No, I do not think so. Proud peoples do not root like pigs for fifty cents, two bits, a dollar, do they? Proud peoples are too proud."

"What about those proud Spanish people of yours?" Sailor asked. He didn't wait for invitation; he reached out and took the bottle from the hat. "Weren't they money grubbers too? Didn't you just say they were rooting for the almighty dollar too?"

"No, no," Pancho denied. "They were not looking for two bits fifty cents. They look for gold—*mucho oro*—the seven golden cities of Cibola. Do you think once there was the seven golden cities?"

"Could be," Sailor said. If going after big dough instead of little made you proud, he'd be pretty proud himself tomorrow. He wasn't listening very hard. The cradle was rocking and the leaves were rocking and there was a quietness in him, a peace in the gentle rocking darkness.

"Maybe so, maybe not," Pancho sighed. "The Spanish was a proud peoples then. But they was not good peoples. They was greedy and selfish and cruel peoples. They do not come with peace in their hearts and love. Love for the sky and the earth and the peoples of this land. They come to steal." His eyes glittered like the dark leaves over the Plaza. "Something happen to them. The land do not like them. They are cruel to its peoples. I am an Indian."

"I thought you were," Sailor murmured. Like Pila. There was a sameness in the big man and the stone girl; he didn't know what it was but he recognized it as there.

"My grandmother was an Apache," Pancho said. "I am Spanish also. The Spanish they are good peoples now. Because they are humble peoples. It is good for them to be humble as it is good for the Indian peoples to be proud. It is the way this land would have it be."

The way Pancho talked about this country you'd think it was some heathen god that must be obeyed. That you had to sacrifice to. Not just a lot of wasteland stretching on and on until the mountains stopped it. Until the mountains uprose, a barrier against the sky.

"What about the white folks?" Sailor asked.

"The Gringos, pah!" Pancho scorned. "They are not of this land. They do not bring nothing to this land. All they want is to take away the two bits fifty cents. Never are they of this land."

The aliens. The ones without existence.

Pancho said comfortably. "I am an Indian and I am Spanish. My grandfather was a Spanish don. That is why I am called Don José Patricio Santiago Morales y Cortez. It is the name of my grandfather. My grandmother was his slave."

"Lincoln freed the slaves," Sailor said. He said it like he was reading from a book, a history book in grade school and outside the window the smoke and grime and cold of a Chicago winter rattled skeleton claws. He went to school because it was warm in school. He'd rather have hung around the pool hall, it was warm there too, but the truant snoops were always busting into the pool hall looking for kids. And the fat guy who ran the pool hall didn't want any trouble with the officers. He peddled reefers under the table and he couldn't afford to get mixed up with the truant officers. He'd push the kids right into the snoops' hands. The kids were afraid to snitch on him about the reefers because they'd seen him kill a man once. Picked the guy up and broke his back like you'd break a stick. He was so fat you wouldn't think he could move so quick or be so strong. He didn't get sent up for breaking the guy's back. Everybody in the place, even the kids, swore it was self defense. The guy was doped and had pulled a knife on the fat guy. Besides the coppers probably knew about the reefers anyhow. Anybody could smell them that walked by. You didn't have to go inside. The same sick smell like in the dive where Sailor'd found Ignatz tonight. The coppers probably got their cut. If he hadn't gone to school to keep warm, kept going even to high school, the Sen wouldn't have picked him out of the bums in the corner pool hall. The Sen wouldn't have sent him to college, yeah, the University of Chicago, for a year and a half. He'd had a good education. He wasn't any bum.

Pancho was shrugging. "Who is this Mr. Lincoln? The Spanish peoples do not know of him. The Indian do not know he has free them. They are poor slaves. After while the Gringos come and say Mr. Lincoln free the slaves. You do not be slaves. You go home now. And you Mexican sonnama beetches you work for us now." He smiled. "You know why you are my friend, Señor Sailor?"

"Haven't any idea," Sailor yawned.

"Because I am an Indian," Pancho said. "And you are good to

a little Indian girl. You do not say to her come to my bed and I will give you a ride on old Tio Vivo."

He didn't say, "I haven't got a bed." He said, "For God's sake, she's only fourteen."

"Does it matter?" Pancho shrugged. "She is older I think at fourteen than the pale lily Gringos are at twice fourteen. But you are a good man. You buy her pop and a fine fast ride on Tio Vivo with music playing. On the pink horse." His smile was wide open, warm. "You do this for her only that she may have pleasure. Not to steal nothing from her. You are my friend." He broke into song again. "Mi amigo, mi amigo, mi amigo, amo te mucho . . ."

"That's fine," Sailor said. He was awake again. The bottle was almost empty. He left enough for one last drink for Pancho. "Let's go to bed, ok?"

"You are also my friend," Pancho said with a sly squint, "because you do not say, "You goddamn Mexican, give this girl a ride or I—" with your hand on the gun in your pocket."

Sailor's hand went quick to his right-hand pocket. The gun was still there, safe. But how had Pancho known it was there? Did McIntyre know? He didn't want any trouble.

Pancho was effusive. "No, no. You are a good man. You pay much money for the favor. For the little Indian Pila to ride on the pink horse. You make rich presents to poor Pancho and to poor Ignacio and poor old Onofre Gutierrez. You make everyone happy for the Fiesta."

"Zozobra is dead," Sailor quoted ironically. "Viva las Fiestas." He laughed out loud. The laugh startled the quivering black night. Nobody had ever called him a good man. Nobody had any reason ever to call him good.

"Thus you are my friend, my primo. I too am a good man. A proud man and a good man."

The old brigand had probably killed a dozen men in his day. Broken their backs like he was breaking sticks.

"Unless you are good you cannot be proud," Pancho said. He lifted the farewell drink, squinted at its meagerness. If he had another pint hidden in the elephant hide of his jeans, he, Sailor, would pop the old devil. "You cannot be proud if you are afraid, hiding in the corners. You cannot be proud if you are bowing this way and that way to the Gringo sonnama beetches. You cannot be proud and be scheming to steal two bits fifty cents. No, no. Only the Indians are proud peoples."

"Sure," Sailor said. "Let's go."

"Because they do not care for nothing. Only this their country. They do not care about the Gringos or even the poor Mexicanos. These peoples do not belong to their country. They do not care because they know these peoples will go away. Sometime."

"A long time," Sailor said, seeing the little shops, the dumps and the dives. It wasn't easy to get rid of the stuff that brought in the two beets feefty sants.

"They can wait," Pancho said patiently. "The Indians are a proud peoples. They can wait. In time . . ."

One thousand years. Two thousand. In time. Maybe it was the way to do things, not to worry about the now, to wait for time to take care of things. What if the measure of time was one thousand, two thousand years? In time everything was all right. If you were an Indian.

Maybe that was the terror the stone Indian generated. In time, you were nothing. Therefore you were nothing. He'd had enough of Pancho's tequila philosophy. Enough of thinking.

"Drink up," he said. "I got to get some sleep. Got business to take care of tomorrow."

Pancho squinted at the small remaining drink. "You promised your sainted mother." He filled his mouth with the tequila, rinsed it from cheek to cheek, savoring it.

Sailor swung his feet over the edge, jumped out lightly.

"Now we will sleep, yes." Pancho sighed. He scratched his belly, wriggled his dirty toes, and put the greasy hat on his head, pulling it down over his ears. He grunted and groaned as he lumbered out of the gondola, stood swaying on the earth. He clapped Sailor on the shoulder. "We will sleep side by side because we are friends. Only the good friends have good talk as we have had this night. Good talk and a bottle to share. Not sotol, tequila! To warm the heart and the belly."

His big hand, his swaying bulk nudged Sailor towards the center pole of the merry-go-round.

"You are my friend," he chanted. He took his hand away, bent swaying over a pile of dirty rags by the pole. He didn't fall, he lurched perilously but it was with a dancer's grace he swooped up one of the rags, stood straight again. "For you my serape," he said. He held up the dirty rag with moist-eyed affection. A long piece of wool, woven of colored stripes that were ravaged by dirt and night into only light and dark. Tenderly he held it to Sailor. "For you, mi amigo. Wrap it about you and you will be warm this night."

Sailor took it. Awkwardly. Reluctant. There was nothing else he could do. Not without hurting the old goat's feelings. He'd hurt plenty of people in his life, sure; but he didn't want to hurt this poor old goat. He took the serape but he didn't wrap it around him. He said, "I'm warm enough. I got a coat, see? You take it. You need it."

"No, no." Pancho shook his head. With the movement he wobbled on his big bare feet. "By your friendship I am kept warm." He stepped aside. "Wrap it about you and he here."

Sailor broke in. "Here? On the ground?" His fist closed on the dirty serape. "You mean you sleep here?"

"But yes," Pancho said. He scowled. "Could I sleep closed into walls, in the bed where many have sleeped, many have died? No, no, no! I sleep where I may breathe, Señor Sailor. Tonight you will sleep with me, no? Where you may breathe and dream good dreams."

For Christ's sake. He didn't curse aloud. For a bed on the ground he'd spent hours listening to a conglomeration of broken English and Spanish, for this he'd drunk tequila, for this he'd endured an old peon's ideas of the world he lived in. To lie on the ground. Like an Indian. While the Sen lay in La Fonda, on clean sheets, in a seven-dollar-a-day bed.

"You did not think I have a room?" Pancho asked anxiously. "You did not think I would trust my little ponies to the thieves in the night?"

He'd never slept on the ground in his life. He'd been poor, he'd been slum poor, but he'd never slept without a roof over his head. He was burned up but when his eyes met Pancho's saddened eyes, he lied. He didn't know why he lied. Maybe the tequila had made him dopey. He said, "This suits me," and watched the happiness seep back into the brown brigand face. "Suits me fine."

Pancho used his toes to push forward a hunk of gunny sack. "That is good, here is the pillow for your head. Wrap the serape about you so." He pantomimed. "You will sleep well, my friend."

Sailor wrapped it about him so. He got down awkwardly as a camel on the earth. He didn't take off his hat when he lay on the gunny sack. Bad enough to be wrapped in this flea-bitten rag. No telling what was on the sacking.

"You are comfortable, no?" Pancho asked. No, he said in his brain and aloud, "I'm fine."

Pancho knelt like a graceful elephant beside him. He made prayer. Spanish prayer. God be with us. The saints preserve and bless us. He stretched himself out on the earth, his arms beneath his head. "It is good to sleep beneath the stars. Goodnight, my friend, he said. He closed his eyes and he was asleep. Asleep and snoring.

Under the stars. The crazy old coot. They were under the canopy of the merry-go-round. Not a star in sight. Ignacio and Onofre were in a room. Pila was in a room. The girls who earlier lay on the Federal Building lawn were in their rooms. The baby face who'd given him the eye in the restaurant was in a room. McIntyre had a room and the gorilla waiter had a room and the Sen had a seven-dollar-a-day room in the best hotel in town. Everyone sleeping in a room, in a bed, except the Indians who didn't care because two thousand years from now there wouldn't be any rooms or any beds or any Gringos or Mexicans to sleep in them. Everyone but the crazy Indians and a crazy old fool who was half and half, Indian and Spanish, and the wise guy from Chicago who thought he was finding a bed by sticking with him.

The ground was hard and Pancho's snores were lusty. The serape scratched and bit. And Sailor's rage against the Sen bit harder, like an aching tooth, scratched like hair cloth. The Sen would pay. He'd pay for all the indignities but he'd pay heavy for making Sailor sleep on the hard ground. Like an Indian. Like a crazy half-breed spic brigand. Like a dog.

The leaves of the tall trees in the park rustled like rain. Afar there were snatches of laughter and aftermath of deeper silences.

The wind was a small cool sound through the shadowed Plaza. Pancho snored. A dog bayed at the loneliness of night; a chorus answered with sharp-toothed barking; silence closed again over night. The silence from the museum portal was deeper than the dark there. No one living could be in that dark, that silence. Maybe that was the secret in stone; the Indians were not living; they were spirits from a long forgotten day, walking the earth, waiting. Waiting in knowledge that they alone would not pass, the excretions of the white man would pass away and they would remain.

The loneness, the lack of identity that had terrified him twice tonight, once in remembering the past through Pila's face, later in that moment of dark and silence on the hooded, unfamiliar street, stabbed again. He rose up, but slowly he sank down again on to the ground. Pancho was there beside him. The wooden ponies were quivering gently. The Plaza was unchanged.

Sleep came into him because he was too tired to allow discomfort to put it to rout. Even the tremble of an unknown fear, the anger at his present humiliation, could not banish it. He closed his eyes, the tightness went out of him. He drifted between the hard earth and the cradle of oblivion.

He was drifting into blissful oblivion when through his closed eyes the gray-white face of Zozobra floated above him. The dead eyes burned, the hideous mouth croaked. *I am evil. I am the spirit of this alien land. Go away. Go away before all good becomes evil. All is evil. Go away. It's going to rain. I'm going to spoil your fun . . .*

He knew he was asleep but he couldn't wake up. He couldn't get away from the obscene floating face. Fire billowed higher, higher, but even fire couldn't destroy the evil thing. He knew he was asleep and then—he was asleep.

PART TWO
Procession

One

He waked to the clangor of church bells. Bright and strong as sunshine they rang in the chill of early morning air. Pancho was rolling on one elbow. His sleep-sanded eyes blinked happily at Sailor.

"It is morning," Pancho announced. He lumbered to his feet, hitching his jeans up over his fat hips. He yawned and stretched and shook off sleep as a dog shaking off water. "A good morning, my friend. Señor Sailor. The little birds are singing songs in the tree tops—"

Sailor glinted at his watch. Not quite six o'clock. They had talked, Pancho had talked, to past three. He muttered, "Church bells," and closed his eyes. He heard the birds as his eyes closed; they weren't singing, they were setting up an infernal twittering din. Clang clang twitter twitter tweet. He pulled the serape up under his chin and grasped for sleep.

When he waked again the church bells were still ringing. Loud and strong but his watch said eight and now the sun lay in bright patches on the green Plaza. Sailor sat up, flung aside the dirty serape, dug under his coat and scratched his shoulders.

Pancho said, "You sleep well, my friend?" He was sitting on Ignacio's camp stool, chewing a doughnut. Sugar frosted his lips.

"Not exactly The Stevens," Sailor grinned back. The big man

75

didn't know what he was talking about. "But I feel pretty good."
He stretched and yawned, breaking off when the two girls crossing The Plaza gave him the eye and giggled to each other. They
were all dressed up in cheap silk dresses, pink and turquoise-blue
silk. They teetered on high-heeled white sandals and they had
dabs of white straw on their black hair. Their mouths were painted. Peasants off to early morning Mass.

Eight o'clock, kids' Mass. The bells would be ringing and the
old lady would nag: *Hurry, hurry, hurry. That's the first bell. You
haven't your shoes laced yet your neck washed yet your coat buttoned
yet . . . you'll be late for Mass, Hurry, hurry, hurry.*

The old man would be shaving, he shaved on Sundays, his
face the color of raw beef. How he could stand on his feet after Saturday night's binge was a marvel to the kids. It slowed
them up on Sundays. He honed the razor on the thick strap and
scraped the gray pig-bristles off his face. Sounded like sandpaper
scraping against itself. *Hurry, hurry, hurry. That's the last bell. Do
you have your prayer book your rosary your penny your handkerchief
. . . you'll be late to Mass. Hurry hurry hurry.*

The kids stumbling on ahead, clumping shoes shined blackly,
faces shined raw with yellow soap. The old lady in her Sunday
black, mincing fast behind them in her Sunday shoes, high laced
black shoes with pointed toes pinching her feet. She'd take off
the shoes when she got home from church, put on the old felt
slippers, one pompom gone, the color they'd once had turned
dirt gray in the soot and grime of a Chicago tenement. The old
man striding along a little in front of her in his black serge, too
tight about the middle; the good suit he'd bought years ago when
he worked at the yards and was an upstanding young fellow. Too
many years ago for the kids to remember. The old man swaggering along like he was the Lord High God of the Universe they

were going to the slum church to pray to, not the old souse who stole the money the old lady brought home for bread, brought home in the wan weary dawn hour after scrubbing marble floors all night. *Hurry, hurry hurry* . . .

The church was only around the corner and they made it as the last bell was an echo, marching down the aisle together, the old man and the old lady and the kids, the eight kids. Eight kids and not enough bread for one. Kneeling together, praying together, marching out again into the cold gloomy Chicago Sunday. The hot sweating Chicago Sunday.

"It's a fine family you have there, Mr.. . . ."

The old man puffing himself up and accepting the compliments on the church steps and the old lady smirking timidly and fingering her worn black gloves. She blacked them with shoe blacking on Saturday nights. The kids standing like clodhoppers with their welts itching under their sawtoothed winter underwear, under their sweaty summer floursacks.

The priest in his stained cassock looking like a pale, pious, nearsighted saint. Saints didn't belong in a slum church; there ought to have been a fighting priest like an avenging angel with a fiery sword. To whack the old man down. To strike the old man and his sanctimonious Sunday smile dead on the church steps.

The pale, near-sighted saint priest and the waxen saintly nuns preaching and teaching about the Lord Jesus and the kids trying to sit still on their blistered backsides and their stomachs crying for want of bread. If you didn't sit still you had to stay in after school unless the nun with the wart was your teacher and then you just got a whack on the head with a ruler. Maybe she knew about the blistered backsides and the welts on the kids' backs, maybe that's why she whacked the ruler on the kids' heads. Maybe she'd been a slum kid before she was a nun. Maybe she whacked them to keep from weeping over them. Slum kids didn't want weeps over them.

But none of that was the reason he quit the parochial school, quit on his own and the truant officer picked him up after four days and took him to the old man and the old man's eyes were like red rat eyes when he took off his belt and slowly moved forward. That was the time he used the knife on the old man. The old man half-killed him and he didn't kill the old man though he wanted to. He cut up the old man and they sent him to reform school as a criminal kid. They didn't do anything to the old man but patch him up.

Reform school was better than home. Three meals a day and you didn't get beaten for no reason. You learned how to steal cars and you smoked cigarettes if you didn't get caught. That was the first time he went to reform school. It wasn't the last time. The last time he didn't stay long. They let him out when the old man died. The old lady cried like a baby, like the old man had been good to her. She wore a mourning veil over her face. It hid her crying and the shiner the old man had given her before he dropped dead. The other kids went to the funeral but he didn't. He went to the pool hall and one day he met the Sen.

The clangorous bells rang out and he scratched himself and watched the stragglers hurrying across the Plaza and up the sun bright street. *Hurry Hurry Hurry*. He didn't have to hurry. The last time he'd been in church was when the old lady died. Cancer, the doc said. The doc should have said she'd just worn out. On her knees scrubbing marble floors all week, on her knees in church on Sundays.

That was why he'd run off from the parochial school. Because he wouldn't get down on his knees every morning, noon, and afternoon and thank God for his blessings. Thank God for the vicious rats in the walls and an obscene old man who beat the hell out of his kids. Thank God for his mother killing herself trying to feed eight kids. Thank God for not enough to eat, for dirt, for shivering winter, for stifling summer, for bad teeth, for pains in the belly, for never enough to eat. Maybe if he was an Indian it would have been all right. He'd have known in time it didn't matter. Poverty, cruelty, injustice were excretions; time would take care of them. You could sit up there on a cloud pillow twanging a harp and laugh like hell in two thousand years. Or stop stoking a fiery pit long enough for a snicker. Screwball philosophy. But old Pancho meant well. He was friendly as a puppy, holding out his sack of stale doughnuts, urging, "Go on. Have something to eat."

"No, thanks," he said. He took off his hat, pushed back his dark hair, settled the hat again. He shook the kinks out of his legs. "I got to be about my business."

"You slept well, no?" Pancho was anxious, chewing the rubbery doughnut.

"Slept fine," Sailor said. "Feel like a new man." Funny thing was he did feel pretty good.

Awake and alive and the air, hot and crisp both, pumping into his lungs. "That is good," Pancho beamed. "You will be back?"

"Sure. Be seeing you." He turned and walked out of the Plaza towards the hotel where his bag better be safe. He was himself again. A night on the ground hadn't changed that. He was himself and all he needed was to get cleaned up, have a cup of coffee, and he'd be ready to face the Sen.

There were, this early, old women in the little thatched booths, building the fires, opening locked cases, setting out the sucker bait, the flimsy yellow birds on their sticks, the canes and the balloons, the black hats with the red and yellow and green bobbles. McIntyre wasn't a bad guy; he'd bought his hat off a booth on the Plaza. He wasn't like the Sen, hiring a dressmaker to fix him up in satins and velvets like a Spanish grandee, price no object, and trying to rat out on a business deal.

Sailor strode across the street, climbed up the high curb to the sidewalk. He went in the hotel. The big shirt-sleeved guy was back behind the desk, looking glum, too much Fiesta. He eyed Sailor. "You didn't pick up your bag."

Sailor leaned his elbows on the counter. "Couldn't find a room," he said. "Had to sit up all night. You couldn't fix me up today, could you?"

"Naw," he growled. But he wasn't mean, he was hopeless. "I got 'em sleeping in shifts now. You know anybody'll give you a shift, it's okay by me."

"Don't know a soul in town," Sailor said cheerfully. "Aren't any of them moving out today?"

"Naw. Nobody's going to budge till Fiesta's over."

"You mean it goes on?" He hadn't read that pink piece of paper crumpled in his pocket. He'd taken it for granted Fiesta was like the Fourth of July or Memorial Day or something.

"Today and tomorrow," the clerk said bitterly.

Sailor echoed the bitterness for the moment. Then he remembered. He'd get his business done and move on. To Albuquerque, El Paso, across the border. He didn't have to stick around here. "Listen," he began. "Look at me. I been in the Plaza all night. I got to see a guy on business this morning. A big shot. I can't go looking like this. I haven't had my clothes off for four days. I stink."

The guy's face agreed gloomily.

"All I want is a shower and a shave." He dug into his pocket. Took out a five. You couldn't offer a hard-bitten Gringo a one.

You wouldn't get any place if you did. This guy wasn't mi amigo; he was clerk-bouncer in a cheap hotel. "You've got a room here. Just let me go wash up in your room. That's all."

The guy eyed the fiver with the right look. "I don't know," he began. "I sleep on shift with the night guy."

Sailor covered the bill in his fingers, began to inch it off the counter.

"He's out having breakfast now," the guy said hurriedly. "If he gets back, I could keep him down here a while." He stood up. "You make it snappy," he ordered. "I'll keep him down here." So he wouldn't have to split. He pushed Sailor's bag out from under the counter. "Come on." He didn't offer to lug it. Sailor picked it up; the locks hadn't been tampered with.

He followed the guy up the steep uncarpeted stairs to the floor above. The guy took a key out of his pocket and unlocked a door just off the head of the stairs. A dinky room with an unmade single bed, men's neckties on the oak bureau, a couple of chairs with clothes flung on them. Nothing fancy but a room and it looked good. Sailor set down his bag easy on the dusty carpet. Not that he cared about stirring up the ancient dust; he didn't want the bag's weight to sound.

The guy held out his hand for the five.

"Sure," Sailor said easy. He started to hand it over but he waited. "Look at this suit." He eyed it himself in the mirror. It looked as if he'd slept in it for a week, in a sticky bus seat, on the ground with leaves and grass and dirt rolling in it. "I can't talk business with a big shot looking like this." He reached in his pocket and took out a one, handed both to the clerk. "You can get it pressed for me."

"It's Sunday," the guy said. But he shoved both bills in his pocket.

"Sure, but this is a hotel." Sailor eeled out of the coat jacket. He carried it to the bureau and emptied the left-hand pocket, a crumpled pink slip of paper, the Fiesta program; a mashed pack of Philip Morris, two cigarettes left; a paper folder of matches, Raton hotel. He slid the gun into his right hand while he fussed with the left-hand pocket. And he kept talking fast. "Hotels got tailors who'll press suits on a Sunday. Wish I could get it cleaned, maybe he can spot it a little." He slid the gun out and under the pink paper and he didn't think the guy saw. He faced him again quick, his shoulders hiding what was cluttering the bureau, unhooked his belt and unbuttoned his pants. "You can send somebody out with it. It won't take long. A guy's got to make a good impression when he's talking over a business deal." He emptied the pants pockets, wadding the handkerchief around the bills so the guy couldn't see the roll. Not that it was anything to bug the eyes out. Around seventy bucks wasn't any fortune. But this buzzard looked as if he'd roll you for a ten spot. Or even a fiver.

The guy said, "I'll have to keep Alfie downstairs longer."

"Not much longer. Shouldn't take long to press a suit. Sponge and press." He went over and hung the dark suit on the guy's big forearm. "You're picking up some change the management won't have to know about." He winked. "Or Alfie?"

"Okay," the guy said.

Sailor stood there on the ugly, dust-drenched rug, his hat on his head, his shirt tails hanging over his blue silk jockey shorts. Until the guy closed the door. He stood there until he heard the big feet slapping down the stairs. Then he moved fast. Turned the key in the lock and left it there. He took off his hat and sailed it at the bureau. It lit. "Jesus," he breathed. A locked door, a shower, a can. All his own. Until the suit came back. He was playing in luck. He stripped off his dirty shirt and dirty shorts, wadded them together, took off his shoes and socks. To get clean again, to scrub.

No wonder he'd been thinking about the old man and the old lady and him a kid. He hadn't been this dirty since he was a kid.

He didn't stop to open his suitcase. He stopped only long enough to grab his gun and he headed for the bath. He parked the gun on the back of the can and he got under the shower, turned it on full force. It hit him like rain in the middle of Chicago summer. Like rain from Heaven. He just stood there for a while soaking it up, the way a tree soaked up the rain.

Butch and Alfie were obliging. They'd left a big cake of pine soap on the wash basin. A bottle of Fitch in the medicine cabinet. He soaped and shampooed and soaped again. He washed away all the stench of the bus and Pancho's serape and lying on the ground like a dog. He stepped out clean. He could have stayed another hour. If he'd been sure Butch hadn't noticed the gun and might get tough if he didn't hurry it up.

He borrowed the best razor, shaved. Borrowed the face lotion and the hair tonic. The stuff must be Alfie's, the day man wasn't any sweet-smelling guy. He carried the gun with him as he whistled back to the bureau. He was clean in the mirror; he looked good. He even washed his pocket comb before combing his short curly black hair.

He whistled as he unlocked the suitcase, threw back the lid. Clean socks, clean underwear, clean shirts. If he'd had any sense he'd have carried an extra suit along. But he'd been counting on a quick finish to the deal and he'd be in Mexico, having linens tailor made. He'd have brought an extra anyway if there'd been room. A suit wasn't as important as the baby. It gleamed dully in the bottom of the suitcase. The sweetest tommy-gun a fellow ever owned. A little present from the Sen two years ago. His baby. He'd never used it; he was too important in the organization to handle artillery. That was for the mugs. But he wanted one and the Sen gave him what he wanted then. It might come in pretty handy now when he started in business for himself in Mexico. A tommy was handy on the Sen's business in Chicago. He rubbed his hand over the stock and he grimaced. At himself. He was like a kid with a toy. But it was a sweet baby.

He picked out pale green silk shorts, dark green hound's tooth socks; a white shirt and a foulard tie of the same green patterned in gray. He was a neat dresser; he'd learned from the Sen. Nothing loud; that was mug stuff. He could look as good as the Sen any day; better, he was young and not a bad-looking guy; the Sen was a little squirt with a weasel face. If Iris Towers bumped into him today she wouldn't look down her nose.

He put on his shorts, his socks and his shoes, polishing the shoes with his dirty laundry. He wadded the laundry in a corner of the suitcase. He was getting ready to lock up when there was a rap on the door.

He froze. Called, "Whozit?"

"Your suit, it is ready."

It wasn't the day clerk; it was an accent. Count on Butch to send it up by a boy, another tip. And he'd take a cut. He said, "Okay," and he slapped down the lid of the suitcase. He took a quarter from his small change on the bureau, pushed the automatic under a handkerchief, went over and opened the door.

The kid was little and brown. He held the suit by the hanger. The suit looked swell.

"Thanks," Sailor said. He gave the kid the quarter, shoved the door shut in his face. He locked it. It was worth a quarter to finish dressing without the big clerk standing around watching.

He looked swell when he was dressed. Looked and felt swell.

He filled his pockets again, the gun in his right pocket resting easy there. It was a small automatic; it looked like a toy but it wasn't any toy. It worked. He lit a cigarette, took a long drag, borrowed Alfie's brush for his hat. A good hat shaped itself up again with brushing. Even if you'd been sleeping in it. This was a good one. Fifteen bucks from the same place the Sen bought his hats.

He locked the suitcase, looked around. Everything the way it had been. Nothing of his left behind. The pink program. He folded it and stuck it in his pocket. Maybe he'd have a chance to read it yet, find out what was going on.

He dragged the suitcase down the stairs to the desk. The big fellow was alone there, glomming. Sailor rang the key on the counter. "Thanks," he said. "Sure was a life saver."

There was some respect in the guy now seeing Sailor the way he looked usually, the way he looked in Chicago. The guy said, "That's all right. Want to leave the grip again?"

"No, I'm taking it up to La Fonda." Sailor said it casual, just to see more respect in the guy's piggy eyes.

"Let me have a couple of packs of Philip Morris." While the guy was getting them out he asked, "Have any trouble with Alfie?" It wouldn't be smart to play it too big here; he might need to ask another favor some day. He might have to come back to this town some day.

The guy put the Philip Morrises on the counter and made change from the half dollar. "I sent him out on an errand," he said. "I got tired of listening to how his wife used to treat him. Before he skipped out. If she was that bad, I don't see why he stuck it twenty-two years. You ought to hear him. Twenty-two years in a doghouse like he tells it."

Sailor said, "Thanks, Butch. Be seeing you." He hoisted the

suitcase and went out on the sidewalk. The Plaza was still quiet enough. Fiesta didn't get started particularly early. It was only a half block and across to La Fonda; a good thing no more. The bag wasn't any lighter than it had been yesterday.

He was almost to the corner when the bells rang out again. Louder now, stronger now, and against their clangor he heard the tinkle of guitar and scrape of violin. He saw them up by the cathedral, the crowds on the church terrace; the people lining the streets. People on the streets as far down as La Fonda. As he reached the corner a brass band blared in a marching hymn. Band and tinkling and the cymbal crash of church bells, all sounding together in Sunday morning triumph. He crossed quickly and set down his bag as the parade rounded the corner. It wasn't much of a parade but he stood on the curb gawking like the rest of the peasants. First the brass band, then maybe a dozen people, men and women, all dressed in dark velvet, wine and purple and black velvet with woven gold chains around their necks. Behind them the queen in her white lace with a crimson velvet cape around her shoulders and the gold crown on her head. The princesses in crimson velvet walked behind, all pretty, dark girls. At the tail end came the court musicians, guitars and violins.

It was like a picture of Queen Isabella's court when Columbus was asking for her jewels. Like a court of old Spain, here in a little village street in the bright hot sunshine, lords and ladies and the royal retinue marching up a little village street to the mass of brown-gray cathedral on the terrace.

The bells rang out and the band played and the court moved in slow regal dignity up the short block. Sailor goggled after them like everyone else, even moving up the street a way the better to gawk. The court stopped at the intersection and from around the corner came another procession. An archbishop in his crimson and white and gold, brown-robed friars following. The bells pealed louder as the archbishop's procession ascended the stone steps, passed slowly up the walk and through the open doors of the cathedral. The royal retinue followed. And the people closed in behind them, poured into the church. The bells stopped and there was a great void of silence in the street. Until the street watchers who weren't going to High Mass broke the void with their little sounds of talk and laugh and movement.

Sailor turned and went in the hotel. He carried his suitcase over to the check room by the closed bar. There was a pretty girl there, black-eyed, black-haired, small-boned. She had a red flower in her hair, a red and green skirt sparkling with sequins, a sheer blouse heavily embroidered in red and green and blue flowers. She smiled, she had a fresh morning look to her.

"Mind if I check this a while?" Sailor asked.

She said, "Certainly," and passed him a numbered check and another smile. Not a come-on smile, a nice clean one.

He smiled back. "It's pretty heavy. Too heavy for you. I'll set it in."

She opened the counter gate and he put down the bag in the farthest corner where it would be out of the way. Where no one would be kicking it around wondering what made it so heavy. He said, "Thanks."

He walked over to the desk, his arms swinging free, sure of himself, swaggering a little. The old hag with the yellowed white hair was gone. The man behind the desk was just a part of the equipment, like in the Palmer House or Stevens. A gent you wouldn't know if you met him on the street five minutes later.

Sailor asked quickly, "Senator Douglass? Willis Douglass?"

The clerk knew without looking. He gave the room number.

Sailor turned around and picked up the house phone, letting the clerk see him pick it up, hear him ask the room number. The switchboard girl wouldn't have needed earphones to get the number; she was sitting on the other side of the desk, only a square pillar between them. If this had been a big hotel with more than one house phone and them around a corner, out of sight, he wouldn't have to go through this hocus-pocus. Heaven help the small-town peasants. Everything was made tough for them, inconvenient. You couldn't have any secrets in a village.

He could hear the ringing and he had a moment's shock that maybe the Sen wouldn't be in at nine-thirty on a Sunday morning. Maybe he'd be dressed up in his velvet panties marching to bells and band into the cathedral for more Fiesta. The Sen in the cathedral was a laugh. Sailor held his left hand tight around the instrument; his right hand, automatic, digging his right-hand pocket. It was another shock after the ringing when the Sen snarled, "Hello."

Sailor cupped his hand over the instrument, spoke silkily through it. "We are sending up a package, Senator Douglass."

He hung up without waiting to hear the Sen start cursing. He would imagine well enough the way the Sen would talk to a hotel clerk who dared wake the ex-senator of Illinois to bring up a package. The smile on Sailor's lips felt good as he cut down the left-hand portal. The portal separated the dining rooms from the patio. There were a couple of people sitting in the patio this early. He wouldn't mind sitting out there himself in a bright-covered swing. At a table under a striped umbrella with a cold beer bubbling. Later. Right now a little business. The smile twisted. He wouldn't waste time standing in the corridor pounding on a door; the Sen would be up and waiting. The good old Sen!

He didn't know the whereabouts of the elevators, he only

knew they weren't in sight in the front lobby so they must be somewhere at the rear. There had to be at least one elevator or the Sen wouldn't have a room on the fourth floor. The Sen wouldn't be climbing any four flights to a room if there were a flock of Fiestas going on.

He turned right where the portal angled into a wider one. Big couches and chairs here and a fireplace big enough to roast a sheep. This one had glass doors opening out to the patio too, and more big potted bushes in the corners. He didn't see any elevators and he walked on to where the right portal met this one. There was a blue-smocked boy with a dark stupid face cleaning the ash trays on a table.

"Where's the elevators, Bub?" Sailor asked.

The boy looked more stupid than ever pointing a brown finger. He didn't say anything.

Sailor followed the finger direction. He wasn't sure the boob knew what he was after; maybe he thought Sailor was inquiring about the can. This didn't look like elevators, it looked like a Spanish palace, dark beams and big rich chairs and on a dark polished table a brass bowl filled with little chrysanthemums. He looked in the open doorway of an immense sunken room, rich and somber, grand piano, red velvet chairs, a fireplace. Opposite the door tiled steps and a wrought-iron balustrade led upwards. He was wondering whether this was up when he saw the check girl leaning against the wall beyond.

"Hey there," he began and then he saw it wasn't the check girl. Another dark-haired, dark-eyed kid; another glittering Spanish costume. He went up to her. "I'm looking for the elevators," he said and in saying he reached that turning and saw the elevator, just one.

She didn't say anything. She giggled soundlessly and stepped into the carved cage. He followed her. "Four," he said. If there was trouble he'd sure played it dumb. She'd remember him and the idiot boy would remember him. The city guy who was bungling around looking for elevators early on Fiesta Sunday. But there wasn't going to be trouble. His hand rammed his right pocket and stayed there.

The girl let him out on four and he waited for her to close the cage and start down before he moved. A carved and painted sign arrowed him in the right direction. His hand was easy in his pocket but it was there all right when he knocked at the door.

It was opened and the lecture started, "I cannot understand why—" and then the Sen took in who it was. "It's you," he said.

Sailor had his foot in the door. He grinned, "Sure, it's me." He pushed in past the Sen and left the Sen to close the door. The Sen was a sight, a scrawny turkey wrapped in a black-and-maroon satin striped bathrobe, too good-looking a robe for an old guy. His face sleep-soiled, his thin hair dripping, his mustache towsled.

"You asked me to come, didn't you?" Sailor crossed the room insolently, knocked a magazine and a newspaper off to the floor and sat down in the best bright yellow chair. The Sen said nothing. "Not bad." Sailor gave the room the eye slowly. It was a big room with twin beds, one of them made up neat with a yellow bedspread tufted in black. The other one was crumpled like the Sen. "I don't have a room," Sailor said. He eyed the good bed with meaning.

The Sen got it. Got it and was needled. He was in good shape to talk business, good shape for Sailor. When the Sen was cold and collected, he was dangerous. He was hot enough now, too hot to talk.

"Couldn't get a room for love nor money," Sailor said. He

leaned back in the chair and pulled out the fresh pack of Philip Morris. He took his hand out of his right pocket long enough to open the pack and put a cigarette in his mouth. He was safe enough. The Sen wasn't packing a gun in his striped bathrobe. Nothing but fists in those satin pockets. "Too bad I didn't know you had an extra bed," Sailor said, lighting the cigarette. "I'd have moved in." He blew the match out with a swirl of smoke. "Guess I won't be needing a room here tonight. I'll be on my way."

The Sen had got words together by now. "What's the idea of waking me up at this hour?" he demanded. He tried to be cold and haughty about it but it didn't wash. He was too mad to do a good job.

Sailor opened his eyes wide, like an innocent guy. "You told me to see you this morning," he said. "Didn't you?" he asked when the Sen said nothing.

"I didn't tell you to wake me up at the crack of dawn," the Sen said out of thin lips. "I expected you to wait until a civilized hour." He started over to Sailor and the right hand tightened in the right-hand pocket. Not too tight, just ready in case. "Give me a cigarette," the Sen said.

"Sure." Sailor passed the pack, kept his hand out to get it back. Wouldn't be the first time the Sen forgot to return a fresh pack of cigarettes. When he was young and wide-eyed and thought the Sen was really the sharpest guy that ever strayed off the North Shore reservation, he'd thought that was class. A guy that couldn't be bothered with such trifles. Yeah, that's what he'd thought. He hadn't known how chinchy the Sen was then.

He kept his right hand firm and his eyes steady on the Sen until he got the deck back. He let the Sen find his own matches. The Sen lit up, his hand shaky, and took a lungful. Then the Sen asked him, cold now but the jitters were under it. "Just what do you want?"

Sailor laughed. The Sen wasn't doing so well when he couldn't think of anything better than that. Sailor could afford to laugh at him. He laughed, "You know what I want, Sen. I told you last night what I wanted." He drew in slow and easy on his cigarette. "My dough," he said not laughing.

"You got paid off," the Sen said.

"I got the down payment." Sailor dragged on the smoke, taking his time. "I got five hundred. The price was fifteen hundred. Remember?"

The Sen said through his teeth, "A thousand dollars. It's a holdup." He scowled and paced. Sailor waited until the Sen stopped wearing out the rug, stepped across the room and looked down his long snout. "If I give you a check for the thousand, will you get out of town today?"

Sailor leaned back comfortable. He was easy as if he was rocking in Tio Vivo's gondola. He said, "No." He waited until the Sen bristled like a porcupine, waited until the Sen opened his mouth, then he spoke before the Sen could. He sounded good-natured. "The price has gone up."

He'd struck sparks with that. He'd known he would. He felt like a million dollars when the Sen's mouth dropped open. "Are you crazy?"

"Not me." Sailor's lips twisted. "Maybe I was once but not any more." He punched it. "I want five grand."

"You won't get it," the Sen snapped.

"I think I will," Sailor said. He squeezed out the butt in the sombrero ash tray. He looked the Sen over carefully and he repeated with quiet emphasis, "Yes, I think I will."

The Sen didn't say anything. There were too many words in

his mouth and he didn't know which to use first. He was too livid to think fast and straight, maybe he had too many things on his mind or too many memories. He couldn't lay the words out precise and nasty the way he'd have done if he were in the driver's seat.

Sailor continued punching. "I'll get it. And it won't be a check. It'll be cash. Five thousand cash." He looked under his eyes at the Sen. "Seen McIntyre yet?"

The Sen's lips were bloodless, like the lips of a toothless old man. "It's blackmail," he said.

There was a spark came into his eye, a nasty spark. "There's laws against blackmail."

"There's laws against murder," Sailor said evenly.

The Sen had the shakes putting out his cigarette, sitting down on the edge of the unmade bed. "What does McIntyre want? What's he doing here?"

Sailor watched him for a minute before he answered. "I don't know," he said. "I haven't talked to him"—the added word was a hot rivet—"yet."

"You were with him at Keen's Bar last night."

He hadn't known the Sen had seen him and McIntyre there. The Sen had been way across the murky red room, the Sen had been with a classy party and the silver-gold girl, the Sen had been drinking too much. But the Sen hadn't been too far gone to spot Sailor with McIntyre.

Sailor said, "Yeah, we had a drink together."

The Sen's mouth curled. "I didn't know you and McIntyre were such friends."

"Sure." Sailor lit another cigarette. The match he struck on his heel made a sharp crack in the silence. "Sure. Known him since I was a kid. One of my oldest friends."

The Sen's adder tongue spit out, licked his dry lips. "What did he have to offer?"

"Nothing," Sailor said. "Nothing at all."

The Sen was forced to press it. Because he didn't know what McIntyre knew or hunched, because he didn't know what Sailor had told the copper. He wasn't really scared as yet because he didn't know what Sailor knew. He didn't have the faintest idea what Sailor knew. Sailor was saving it, hoarding it up for the final punch. The knockout.

But the Sen was uneasy; seeing McIntyre and Sailor together was enough to make him uneasy. He'd have been uneasy enough seeing them together in Chicago. Here in this foreign town it was like whisperings among strangers. The Sen asked, "What did he have to say?" When Sailor didn't answer, the Sen insisted. His voice cracked like dry plaster. "What did he talk about?"

Sailor didn't want to mention her. She didn't belong in this dirty business. But he had the Sen on the skids and he'd use everything to keep him sliding down. "He was telling me about the people in your party," he began. He forced the name out. "About Iris Towers."

The Sen's face went purple. Almost purple. "What right does he have gabbing about her?" He was hoarse with rage.

"Coppers are funny," Sailor said. He sounded like he thought there was a laugh in it. "They think they got a right to be nosy about anybody." He threw it away. "Especially McIntyre."

The thin lips began to weave, to spew whey-like obscenities about the copper. When they stopped for breath, Sailor agreed, "Sure." He yawned. "But you can't argue with the guy in the driver's seat."

That stopped the Sen. It was his own statement, the one he

used to hold the boys in line. You can't argue with the guy in the driver's seat. Not if you want to live.

"It's politics," the Sen said. He began to dance up and down the rug again, his skinny hairy legs sticking out one end of his satin bathrobe, his scrawny neck and weasel face out of the other end. "It's nothing but dirty politics. Because I supported Lennie." He took one of his own cigarettes off the bed table. That calculating look was in his eyes. "I'd like to find out just why McIntyre is here. Who sent him."

Sailor knew what the Sen meant. He'd like Sailor to find out. Another job. All work and try to get your pay out of the chiseling Sen.

Sailor smiled. "I got a pretty good idea why he's here."

The Sen took it up quick. "Why?" His suspicions of Sailor and McIntyre drinking together were sticking out all over him.

Sailor said slowly, soberly, "I think he's looking for the man who murdered your wife."

The color went out of the Sen. It oozed away until he was grayer than the grayness on the old lady's face when she used to come home in the gray tired morning. He came out of it quick enough but the color didn't return, not for a long time. He said, "Jerky Spizzoni killed her."

Sailor's heart was pounding. The Sen couldn't know it, on the face of things he was calm and cool as a cucumber. "Jerky's gun killed her," he smiled.

"What are you trying to do?" The Sen's lips lifted nastily. "You know what happened. You testified—"

Sailor broke in, "It looked good on paper."

The Sen's voice faded out. "What do you mean?"

"There was a little hitch," Sailor said. He went at it just as calmly as if there weren't trumpets blowing inside him. He wished Ziggy were here to see the Sen. He wished he'd let Ziggy come along. Only he couldn't. Because even Ziggy didn't know what he knew. He must have had an idea even then that this was going to turn into something good. For him. Hidden down under layers of subconscious it must have been there waiting for something to knock it loose. Something like having to sleep on the ground in a one-horse foreign town.

Ziggy was going to get a boot out of this scene when they met up in Mexico. Ziggy always got a boot out of Sailor's imitations of the Sen; this one would top them all. It would be even better if the Sen hadn't put in his upper bridge to open the door for the package. Well, he could play the scene as if the Sen didn't have his top teeth in. It would be funnier that way.

"There was a little hitch," he said. "Oh, the boys sprang Jerky that night. Just like you fixed it. And Jerky got it in the back later that night. Just like you fixed it." His lips were thin as the Sen's. "Sure, I know Jerky wasn't worth anything to us any more. He'd gone stir-crazy all right. He'd have sold us out for nose drops."

"What went wrong?" the Sen asked through his teeth.

"You couldn't guess," Sailor said good-naturedly.

"I have no intention of guessing," the Sen gritted. "What—went—wrong?"

"Engine trouble," Sailor said?

The Sen was speechless with fury.

"Happened right after they got away. They were starting back to Chi with Jerky and—engine trouble. Lucky thing though. There was a farmhouse pretty near. So the fellows didn't have to stand out in the rain—remember how it was raining that night?—while they fixed the car. The farmer let them run it in the barn—"

"Why didn't they phone in?"

"The yokel didn't have a phone."

"They could have—"

Sailor interrupted again. "It looked swell on paper. But there were a couple of hours' delay. Too bad you didn't know. In those hours, you called the cops about Mrs. Douglass being killed."

The Sen stood very still. "Why didn't I know about this?"

"The fellows were afraid to tell you." Sailor mock sighed. "They were afraid you might get mad at them."

"Why didn't you or Ziggy tell me?"

"I'm telling you," Sailor said.

He was actually shaking, his skinny little legs couldn't hold still. "Why wait till now? Why didn't I know before I left Chicago? If I'd known—"

"You skipped out too fast," Sailor said reprovingly. "And you didn't leave a forwarding address. Ziggy thought you were in Canada fishing."

"You found me." He was ice cold.

"Yeah," Sailor said. "I found you."

He got dancing mad again. Wiggling back and forth on the rug. "How did you know where I was?"

Sailor laughed. "That's a funny thing. I read it in the *Trib*." The Sen didn't believe him.

"I did," Sailor nodded confirmation. "On the society page. That society reporter must have somebody out here that feeds her the news." He quoted, "*The popular young Senator Willis Douglass . . .*" He shut up without being told. Laughing soundlessly.

The Sen was thinking. Thinking hard. "Does Mac know about this—hitch?"

"May be," Sailor said. "Ziggy and I didn't know about it ourselves till last week," he admitted. "The boys didn't intend to mention it. But the yokel saw a picture of Jerky in some horror mag and came to town." He snickered. "He was going to tell the guys about the crook who'd been in their car."

"You mean he went to the boys, not the police?"

Sailor grinned. "Humpty was sharp that night at the barn. Told the old boy if he ever came to Chi to drop by his hash house and he'd give him a free spread. Saved himself a tip that way." He sobered. "Good thing he's close with his dough. The yokel was set to go to the cops but Humpty stalled him. Then he and Lew came running to Ziggy."

"What's Ziggy doing about it?" the Sen asked quick.

"Nothing." He smiled at the Sen's open mouth. "He told the fellows to give the yokel a yarn about their finding out and helping the coppers land Jerky. He gave them enough dough to show the guy the town with trimmings. Wear him out and send him home." The Sen's mouth hadn't closed. Sailor said coldly, "Ziggy warned the fellows not to let anything happen to the yokel. He didn't want the case blown wide open by another—accident. He told them to take as good care of the guy as if he were a two-year-old kid." He let the Sen soak that in before finishing up. "Ziggy's blown town."

All the Sen said was, "Ziggy's smart." The phone couldn't have had neater timing. It rang just as the Sen was getting back a little confidence. He picked it up and his, "Hello," was normal.

It was the girl. The silvery Iris Towers. The Sen's voice went into its act, the rich sweet tones rang in it. "Yes, this is Willis. Yes, I was awake." He sat down on the edge of the bed and hunched his back to Sailor. "I'm sorry you waited. I've been delayed on a little business matter . . . No, I won't be much longer. I'll meet you in the Placita in twenty minutes." His voice was intimate. "Order me a Daiquiri and save my special chair . . .

Goodbye." He hung up and took a moment to compose his face before turning back to Sailor. He started in just as if there'd been no interruption; and as if he hadn't been craven most of the past hour and a half. He even kept his organ pipes turned on for Sailor. He said, "I don't blame you for wanting to get over the border until this blows over. I take it you're heading for Mexico?" He nodded his head briskly not waiting for an answer. "I'll get the thousand for you. I don't know how, exactly, since you refuse my check. You know I don't carry that kind of money on me. The banks aren't open on Sunday. If you can wait until tomorrow—"

"The banks aren't open on Labor Day," Sailor said. Then shut up, giving the Sen all the rope he wanted.

"That's right, tomorrow is Labor Day," the Sen recalled. "Well, I'll get the thousand for you some way. Come back this afternoon, about five, and I'll have it for you. I have to dress now. I haven't had breakfast."

"Neither have I," Sailor said. He didn't budge. He sat there looking over at the Sen. He said, "I told you the price had gone up. It's five thousand now."

The Sen scowled. "You won't get it." His mouth snapped. "You'd better take the thousand and get over the border while you can. You're in no position to dicker."

Sailor spoke softly. "Yes, I am."

The Sen looked at him, trying to read what he meant, sure that it wasn't what the Sen alone knew; wondering if Sailor had sold out to McIntyre, sure that he wouldn't dare; boring into Sailor's impassive face and getting no answer. He rattled Sailor's words in his brain and couldn't get an answer without asking for it. "Now what?" he demanded.

Sailor said, "I didn't kill your wife."

It was the moment he'd been moving up to and the moment

was worth the feints and thrusts of delay. The Sen stood frozen where he was. He looked really old, shriveled and old. He was in that moment one with the aged violinist of Tio Vivo. There was only a mechanical shell left.

Sailor said, "I shot at her, yes, but I didn't kill her. Somebody else did it." His voice was quiet but distinct. "Somebody was coming. I had to get out fast."

The Sen whispered when he could, "No one will believe you." He shook his head hollowly. "No one would ever believe you."

"Maybe not," Sailor said. "But I can blast things wide open if I talk. And I'm in the clear, I can talk. Whether anyone believe me or not." He stood up and his hand was so tight on his gun, the fingers ached. He had to get out of here. At this moment the Sen would kill him if he could. Kill him with his own hands, not hire a torpedo.

He walked to the door, keeping the Sen covered with his eye and his pocket. The Sen knew what was in his pocket. At the door he said, "I'll see you at five o'clock." He wouldn't come back here again. Not with the Sen having time to plan. He grimaced, "In the Placita. Have the five grand ready for me by then. I don't care how you get it. Bring me the five grand at five and there won't be any trouble."

He opened the door and swung out, closed it, all in one move. As if the Sen were reaching for a gun, not standing there numb and shriveled and old. As he made his way to the elevators, his hand was still cramped until it ached in his right-hand pocket.

Two

HE BUMPED into McIntyre when he turned into the south end of the portal. The end where the big fireplace was. He hadn't noticed before but there were Indian figures blasted on the fireplace. In the same sand color as that head he'd seen in the Chicago Museum when he was a kid. He didn't give them more than a quick glimpse because he didn't want to be reminded of that experience. He had too much on his mind without that.

He didn't know exactly why he'd turned there into the portal instead of walking straight ahead, following the side portal to the front door and out of the hotel. Maybe he'd had some idea of sitting down on one of the comfortable leather couches and getting hold of himself. He didn't know why he should have the shakes. Things had gone his way. It had hit him only after he'd sprung the big news, only when he'd known he had to get out of that room, fast, before it was too late. It had been the way the Sen had taken it, like something dead, like a zombie. He'd never seen the Sen like that before. It gave him the creeps.

The mixed-up part was that he knew why the Sen had been hit that way. It was the girl, the lovely clean girl waiting for him in the Placita. The Sen wouldn't have been scared to point of death otherwise. He'd have been the old Sen, crafty and wicked and smart. The mixed-up part was that he didn't want the

Sen beaten like that; he wanted the old Sen, the one he'd been waiting to kick in the teeth for months, maybe longer. He didn't want to kick the teeth out of a zombie. All he wanted to do now was run, get out of town quick, not even wait for his dough. Maybe that's why he was heading for the couches, to try to put the Sen back together again the way he ought to be, to forget the wizened old man he'd left upstairs.

Because the Sen would put himself back together again. Sailor knew that as well as he knew his own name. And it was up to him to be ready to meet the real Sen, not to carry around the image he had right now in his head.

He was making for the couch when McIntyre spoke to him. McIntyre was sitting on that couch. He said, "Hello, Sailor."

He had to put on an act quick. He had to smile as if the smile weren't cutting his mouth, pull his cramped fingers out of his right-hand pocket and hope McIntyre wouldn't see that they had no circulation left in them. McIntyre who saw everything. He said, "Hello, Mac."

"Been having breakfast with the senator?" McIntyre asked.

Sailor laughed. "Haven't had breakfast yet. Not even a cup of coffee." McIntyre thought he and the Sen were having business together. McIntyre was right but he was wrong. He thought Sailor was here because the Sen had sent for him. It wasn't hard to know what McIntyre was guessing, seeing Sailor coming from the elevators.

He didn't want any trouble from the copper. His alibi was okay and McIntyre knew it was okay. But he didn't want Mac trumping up something to send him back to Chicago. He wanted Mac friendly like he'd been up to now. He might have to spill to Mac yet. He said, "Why don't you come have breakfast with me? In the Placita."

"Make it lunch," McIntyre said, standing up and joining him. It was too quick. McIntyre wanted something. Might be he was getting ready to move in. Might be the Wisconsin yokel had gone to the police after the fellows poured him on the train. But it was done now. He and McIntyre were walking up the postal. Maybe McIntyre knew where the Placita was. Sailor didn't, he only knew that if he'd see the Sen with the girl again, his fight might come back to him. Rage made a man fighting. He couldn't collect off the Sen unless he wore bare knuckles.

McIntyre walked like he knew where he was going. Ambling but direct. Sailor cut his stride to match. McIntyre was still wearing the silly black hat and the red scarf around his middle. But he didn't look silly. He looked more like McIntyre than ever.

Sailor asked, "Where you staying? Here?" He didn't like walking in silence with a cop. "Yes," McIntyre said. "Here."

"Pretty swell rooms."

"Not the one I have." He smiled on that.

"How'd you rate a room here during Fiesta?" The tension was going out of him just by walking with McIntyre. Mac was an easy guy to be with.

"Reservation," McIntyre said.

He was a liar. He hadn't made any reservation in advance. He'd come after he'd found out the Sen was here. But the head of Chicago's Homicide would rate a room. Somebody in Chi would see the Harveys and the Harveys would send word to the Harvey House. Put up McIntyre. Same way the Sen would rate a room.

McIntyre walked to the doorway of the bar, La Cantina. "Want an ice-cold Daiquiri?" Sailor grinned.

"Little early in the day for me," McIntyre said. He went on

in the bar though and Sailor went along. "You drinking these days, Sailor?"

"Not me," Sailor said. "A bottle of beer's my speed." He wondered if McIntyre had been watching him last night. That was one of the dangers with Mac; you never knew when a shadow wasn't a shadow, when it might be a man in the shadow.

McIntyre walked through the bar. They couldn't have had a drink if they'd been drinking men; the bar was shuttered with a scene painted in bright Spanish colors. McIntyre said, "Sunday." He was still leading and they turned into the Placita, the walled Spanish garden. It was set with white tables and the waitresses were in costume, flowered skirts, flower-trimmed blouses. This was Fiesta from the right side of the tracks. On a bench built around an old shade tree there were Spanish velvet men, girls in shimmering Mexican skirts wearing flowers in their hair. There was Iris Towers, her pale hair wreathed in golden roses, her white skirt painted in golden wreaths. He saw her and the church bells began to chime over the peaceful garden. The chimes grew to a paean of triumph, the band brassed into proud sound, guitars and violins plinked merrily. All because his eyes beheld a fair blonde girl under a tree in an old Spanish garden, and she was fair, not what he'd been afraid of after this morning. And the rage was eating him again. And the rage was good but he mustn't let McIntyre know.

The bells and the music were real; the sound of them came louder as the parade passed outside the high wall. This time he was on the right side of the wall where the brightest laughter lay. The Placita began to fill after the music faded, and the laughter and noise were more gay. He and McIntyre had a table in the corner by the far wall where they could watch the entrance, where they could see who sat at each table. McIntyre had chosen it.

They ordered and they were silent, sitting in white wrought-iron chairs side by side where both could watch. They were both waiting for the same man. He came, immaculate in white shirt and white flannels, a bright sash wound about his waist. He was fresh and shaven, his hair combed, his mustache brushed. He was neat and he looked like himself unless you noticed the deeper pockets under his narrow eyes.

Sailor didn't want to talk about the Sen now. He asked, "Ever drink any tequila, Mac?"

It caught McIntyre's attention but not his eyes. Like Sailor's they watched the Sen make an undeviating path to the tree, to Iris Towers and the velvet men and glittering women with her. They watched the welcome of the Sen, the Sen's suave explanation and regret.

McIntyre said, "Never have."

"I tried it last night," Sailor kept on talking as if McIntyre were interested. "Couldn't say no. Funny old duck that runs the merry-go-round insisted. I'm his mi amigo for some reason."

The Sen and his party were seated at the largest table with the Sen making sure that Iris was beside him. The table was near the one McIntyre had chosen, almost too near. Maybe Mac had known it was reserved for the Sen.

McIntyre said, "It's because you gave some Indian girl a ride on Tio Vivo."

Sailor was shot with cold. Mac was keeping an eye on him. Him as well as the Sen. Only Mac couldn't be after him. Mac was here first. Sailor gave a laugh, a short one. "Checking up on me?"

McIntyre spoke mildly. "I just don't want to see you get in any trouble. I don't want anything to happen to the senator."

He'd been checking to see if Sailor was trying to buy a local torpedo to rub out the Sen. That was a good one on Mac. Pancho, the philosophical old brigand, the man of peace. He really laughed at that. His laughter caught the Sen's ears and the head turned quickly, the mean eyes saw Sailor and McIntyre, turned quickly back to his party. Maybe his hand shook a little as he put a light to Iris Towers' cigarette. Maybe his malevolence solidified.

Sailor said, "You don't think I'm looking for trouble, Mac? I'm here for Fiesta like the rest of you."

McIntyre turned his look on Sailor at last. "You aren't here about Jerky Spizzoni?"

McIntyre knew. Sailor was cautious now, cold and cautious. He wasn't ready to talk. He'd play straight if the Sen played it straight. "What about Jerky?"

"He didn't kill Eleanor Douglass."

Sailor acted surprise. He was careful not to overact. "Who did?"

If McIntyre pointed the accusing finger at him he'd have to spill. Mac didn't. It might mean the same but it was the McIntyre way. It didn't require denials. He said only, "I thought you might know who."

"Me?" Sailor was mildly indignant. "You know damn well I was with Leonard Ziegler all that night in the Sen's office going over the tax books." He and Ziggy had alibied each other for that night and the alibi was sound. No one but they and the Sen knew the way out of the building without passing the elevator guy. Through the warehouse on the other street. Or did McIntyre know?

"That's right," McIntyre said. "You're Senator Douglass's confidential secretary, aren't you?"

"Yeah." I was. Until I found out what a lying, chiseling weasel the Sen was. Then I quit. Fired myself. "I didn't even know Mrs. Douglass was dead till you guys showed up that night looking for Jerky."

"Yes, we found Jerky's gun by the body. With his fingerprints on it. Too bad we never got to talk to Jerky."

"Ever find out who bumped Jerky off?"

The waitress brought them their jellied consommé at last. "Coffee right away," Sailor asked. He smiled up at her as if there weren't anything on his mind. "Got to have breakfast before lunch."

She was tall and pert and blonde. She said, "Right away," and swished her flowered skirts at him.

McIntyre began to eat. "Never did. Plenty who might have."

"Yeah," Sailor said. "He double-crossed every gang in Chi." Including the Sen's. But you didn't call the Sen's a gang. They were employees of the Sen. Because the Sen was mixed up with so many enterprises, not rackets. You didn't call the mugs, guys; they were fellows. If you fellows will do this, or that— The mugs ate it up; they liked being fed their pap with a silver spoon.

"But he didn't kill the senator's wife," McIntyre said. "She was dead before he got to town that night."

He couldn't ask how McIntyre knew. How'd you know that? He acted surprised a little more. "You don't mean it!"

"Yes," McIntyre said. "Senator Douglass telephoned the office at ten o'clock. He'd just reached home and found his wife dead. It looked as if she'd surprised a burglar. It looked as if Jerky was the burglar. His gun and his fingerprints on it. It even occurred to us that he might have planned to kill the senator. You know it was the senator's testimony that sent Jerky up."

"Yeah, I know. And Jerky got himself bumped off that night." The blonde poured coffee from a round glass pitcher. "Thanks," Sailor said. He put two spoons of sugar in his cup, stirred it, and drank. Then he started on his consommé. Iris Towers was telling her table something. Her hands were a delicate gesture and her clear blue eyes were like the sun on a blue lake. The Sen laughed just as if there were laughter left in him. When he put his hand on her arm Sailor's eyes snarled again to his soup. "What makes you think Jerky didn't do it?"

"At ten o'clock that night Jerky was just leaving a farmhouse in Wisconsin. He'd been there from quarter of nine on."

Sailor whistled low. The blonde thought he was whistling at her and she came over and filled his coffee cup. He said, "Thanks, doll." He put some more sugar in, stirred it and drank. He said, "Where'd you get that dope? Somebody rat?"

"Strangely enough, no. Mr. Yost, the farmer, talked around to his neighbors and the sheriff heard about it. Sheriff sent him down to Chicago to see me. Nice honest man, Mr. Yost. But slow. If he'd talked sooner about the three men whose car broke down by his farm the night of March twelfth—"

"You found out who sprung Jerky that night?"

"Mr. Yost identified one of them. Johann Humperdink was one of them. The other was probably Lew Barrows. They've both skipped." He was quietly certain. "But they'll turn up again. Or we'll turn them up again."

Humpty and Lew had got away in time.

"You know Humperdink and Barrows, Sailor?"

He finished the jelly soup. "Sure I know them. You know where I come from. I know everybody in the old ward. I've eaten at Humpty's hashhouse plenty. But they aren't friends of mine if that's what you're asking, Mac." He winked at the blonde as she took the soup dishes. Only because he didn't feel like winking. The Sen wasn't paying much attention to the big blond guy telling some long-winded tale to his table. Iris Towers had her eyes breathless but the Sen was wondering what Sailor and McIntyre were talking so much about. The Sen ought to be sitting in. Sailor would have felt better to have him here. The Sen could turn things off better than Sailor ever could. The only reason Sailor wasn't walking out on Mac, telling him to go roll his hoop, was because he'd watched the Sen in action. He'd learned some things.

Sailor said, "I'm surprised Humpty was in on anything like that. I always thought he was an honest hasher. Of course Lew had a little trouble in the past. He was in Sleagle's gang once." He was supposed to know things like that. Not because he'd had a little trouble in the past himself. Because he was the Sen's secretary and was supposed to know the guys who delivered the votes in the old ward.

"I was kind of surprised myself about Humpty," McIntyre said.

That was good. That meant McIntyre didn't know too much about the Sen's organization. "You sure it was Humpty?"

The blonde brought a big smile with the salad for Sailor. He could date her up tonight if he were looking for a blonde.

"Positive identification there. Even if he hadn't skipped to clinch it. 'Gone on a vacation,'" he quoted.

"Maybe he did." The salad dressing was right. Sailor knew about dressings because he'd eaten with the Sen in good restaurants. On the Boulevard. In the swank hotels. The Sen and Ziggy were particular about salad dressings.

"He didn't leave a forwarding address. He entertained Mr. Yost a couple of weeks ago, showed him the town. When Yost saw Jerky's picture in an old true-detective magazine at the barber shop, he took a trip to Chicago just to tell Humperdink the kind of guy that had been in his car that night. Yost didn't know Jerky was dead. He'd liked Humpty, thought he was a nice homey sort of fellow. Wanted to warn him before Jerky did him in, or out, of his store teeth."

"Funny the way things happen." Maybe Ziggy'd been wrong letting the yokel go. Maybe it was better this way. If Yost had disappeared in the city, that country sheriff might have caused trouble and none of them would have got away. As it was nobody was in a jam. Only the Sen. McIntyre was watching the Sen, feeding scrambled eggs mechanically into his mouth while he watched the Sen.

"It is funny. It's what makes police business interesting." McIntyre buttered bread. "You never know what will turn up next." He didn't take his eyes off the Sen. "Humperdink told Yost he'd found out who Jerky was the next day. In the newspapers. His story was he'd picked up Jerky hitchhiking."

"Maybe he did," Sailor said.

"Maybe he did," McIntyre agreed. "Maybe Humpty is on a vacation." He wiped his mouth with the big orange square of napkin. "But Jerky didn't kill Mrs. Douglass."

"I guess you're right there," Sailor nodded. "Somebody did."

That's what McIntyre intended to find out. Who did. That's why he was here. He must have something more than hunch to be here wearing a red sash and a toy Spanish hat. Something more than a fifty-thousand-dollar insurance policy.

"I'd like to meet Senator Douglass," McIntyre said.

"You mean you haven't met him?" Sailor wasn't pretending surprise.

"Not for a long time." McIntyre smiled, a true smile. "They don't send us department roughnecks to interview someone like the senator. The commissioner handled him when Mrs. Douglass died."

The flowered skirts brought a painted menu. "Dessert, sir?"

He wanted dessert but he wanted more to get away. Before McIntyre asked the wrong questions, the right ones. He waited for the cop to answer. McIntyre deliberated. The Sen's party was still at their table and Mac said, "I'll have some peach pie and more coffee."

"Make mine a chocolate sundae." He might as well eat. He couldn't tell Mac he had important business to be about. Mac knew he didn't have a thing to do but walk the streets.

The Sen said something to Iris Towers and she slanted her eyes up at him and the smile on her mouth was the way you wanted a woman to smile at you. The way you didn't want a woman to smile at a murderer; not a young, beautiful, untouched woman.

Sailor said harshly, "I'll introduce you."

"I thought you might." McIntyre was matter of fact.

"I'm meeting him here, in the Placita here, at quarter after five. You turn up and I'll introduce you." Fifteen minutes was all he needed alone with the Sen. If the Sen didn't come through it wouldn't be bad to have McIntyre show up.

"I'll be here," McIntyre said.

The blonde brought the desserts, wrote out the check and put it in the center of the table.

Sailor took it up.

McIntyre said, "Better let me have it. I've an expense account."

"Not today." He could afford to buy Mac a lunch. Mac was helping him to get on easy street. Someday when he had a hotel of his own like this down in Mexico, he'd invite Mac down. Everything on the house. Mac wasn't a bad guy. He wondered if Humpty and Lew were in Mexico. He didn't want to go on with the old set-up. He wanted to be strictly on his own. No cuts. Though Lew was about the best trigger man in the business.

McIntyre said, "Got a room for tonight?"

He didn't want that question. Mac mustn't get a hunch that Sailor was leaving tonight. He said, "Yeah, I'm okay for tonight."

McIntyre finished his pie. He said, "Funny the senator didn't have a room for his secretary last night. It's almost as if he wasn't expecting you."

Sailor put a fiver on the check. Then he had to wait for change. Wait and try to think up answers for McIntyre. The cop was closing in. If he said the Sen wasn't expecting him it was like telling Mac he'd come running to bring the Sen the news about Jerky. If he said the Sen was expecting him, there would have been a reservation for him unless he and the Sen were split. That would mean the Sen expected him to bring trouble.

He laughed it off, repeated the old gag. "I didn't come on business. I came for Fiesta." He lit a cigarette, drew on it, passed the pack to McIntyre who shook his head. "I didn't know you had to make reservations in a one-horse town. I wasn't as smart as you."

The Sen and his party were still at the big table when he and McIntyre went out. They passed so close behind him you could see the hairs on the back of the Sen's neck prickle. The Sen was scared. He should be.

They left the Placita, walked through the empty bar into the lobby. Sailor said, "See you at five-fifteen, Mac." He didn't want to carry the cop with him all afternoon doing nothing. He left McIntyre standing there and walked out of the hotel like he had some place important to be in five minutes. When he got outside he slowed down. It wasn't two o'clock. He had more than three hours to kill. And nowhere to go.

The sun was baking hot on the little street. He walked slowly across to the Plaza. Into Fiesta.

The street that fenced in the square was littered with papers and the remains of food and horse dung and children dragging bright costume skirts. There were kids riding burros and other kids tagging after for their turn. There were two ragged boys in jeans selling rides on a big roan horse. Enough kids waiting on the curb to keep the horse busy till day after tomorrow. The merry-go-round was whirling full speed, the tinkling music lost in the clattering mass of kids pressing against the palings, shouting to be next. Over the heads of the crowd he could see Pancho's muscles bulging, his back aching, sweat bathing him as he endlessly turned the windlass. The counters of the little thatched booths were all jammed. On the bandstand a Mexican band blared through big metal loudspeakers. It wasn't all kids jamming the square, old and young, babies squalling in arms, white beards spitting tobacco on the walks; old women, middling women, younger women gabbing Spanish at each other; gangling youths and painted girls eyeing each other, exchanging provocative insults, working up to night and the lawn of the Federal Building.

There wasn't a place to sit down. Every inch of curb, the concrete wall around the small memorial shaft, even the corner steps that led into the square were packed tight with people. You had to step over them to get back into the street. Sailor stepped over a woman with a baby sucking at her breast, to get out of the stifling square into the street again. To escape the trap of Fiesta. He escaped and he looked back at the box.

At Fiesta. At the crowded little park, hung with faded banners and grotesque masks and colored electric-light bulbs strung on wires. Smelling of chile and pop and dung and cheap perfume and sweat and diapers; chaotic with music and laughter and screams and insults and jabber and crying kids. For this Zozobra had burned. So these people could believe that this tawdry make-believe was good. He slanted through the jostling, careless street strollers and reached the opposite curb, stepped over more people to stand under the portal of the museum. This too was crowded, too crowded to fight through. The costumed and the city visitors, uncostumed—he'd been here long enough to spot the stranger—were blocking sidewalk traffic, bending over the Indian wares spread on the walk.

The Indians alone were not a part of the maelstrom. They sat against the wall, their bright calicos billowing about them, their black eyes inscrutable, ironic. They sat in silence, not speaking unless spoken to, not offering their goods, selling if asked, their brown hands exchanging goods for money with amusement if not scorn. Because they knew this to be make-believe; because in time these strange people did not exist. Pila was once a child sitting here with almond black eyes, inscrutable as her elders and as aloof. Sailor couldn't push through the crowd, he managed to twist back to the curb, to step over the heads of the curb squatters into the street.

He couldn't spend three hours fighting this Fiesta saturated mob. He couldn't spend three hours on his feet. The sun and heat and the lunch he'd put away combined to hit him with the full weight of his weariness. He wanted only to lie down and sleep.

He knew it was hopeless but it was something to do. There was always a chance. He made the rounds again of the hotels. It was to no avail as he'd known it would be. There were no rooms.

There wasn't even a vacant chair in a lobby or on the Cabeza de Vaca porch. The only thing the round trip availed him was, for a brief spell, to get him out of the stench of Fiesta. But he returned to it. With a hopeless kind of fatality, because there was no place else to go, because all directions led to the Plaza.

The streets were whirling louder, faster; on the bandstand a fat black-haired singer blasted the microphones and the crowds screamed, "Hola! Hola!" as if it were good. A running child with remnants of pink ice cream glued on his dirty face bumped into Sailor's legs, wiped his sticky hands there. Sailor snarled, "Get out of my way." A balloon popped behind him and the kid who held the denuded stick squalled.

He had to get out of this. His feet burned and his eyes ached and his nose stunk. If he could reach Pancho, the brigand would know somewhere he could rest. He'd know a cool quiet bar that opened its back door on Sunday. A bar with cold beads on the beer bottles and without any Spanish music. He rammed through the revelers until he was on the outskirts of the solid phalanx surrounding Tio Vivo. Twice as many as before. He was stopped there. Kids were unyielding in mass. Or too fluid. If he advanced past one child, six more cut in front of him, jabbing elbows and knees in him, wiping the dirt of their hands and feet on his neat dark suit. The kids were like ants. They multiplied as he stood there. They were terrifying; he knew if he should be knocked over in their rush, they would swarm over him, devour him without knowing or caring what they did. Pancho was as far away from him here as if he were marooned on the Wrigley Tower.

He turned away, more frightened than angry. If he didn't find a place to rest, he wouldn't be fit to face the Sen at five. And without warning his eyes came against the eyes of Pila. He had the same shock he'd had last night when he first looked upon her. The same remembrance of terror, of a head of stone which reduced him to non-existence. His first quick reaction was to turn away, not to recognize her. But he could not. She was there. She existed. He was the one without existence, the dream figure wandering in this dreadful nightmare.

She was there, in the same bedraggled flowered skirt, the same blouse in which the embroidery had run in savage purple and red streaks. Her black hair hung straight down her back and the red flower was falling to her temple. She stood motionless. She didn't speak to him. But her eyes, black and empty and wise, were on his face as the blind stone eyes once had been.

He said roughly, "Hello."

She said, "Hello." Her mouth had been painted like the mouths of Rosita and Irene but she'd smeared it somehow, pop or hot dog or chile, not man; it stained her face as the embroidery stained her blouse.

He said, "Want another ride on the merry-go-round?"

"No," she said. She didn't offer any explanation but the flicker of her glance at the churning, pushing children was Indian. It was the look in the eyes of the fat calico women sitting silently against the museum wall, aloof, disdainful of the vulgarians who pushed by.

Pila didn't say any more and he started past her, wanting to get away, away from the nightmare and the recurring figure in the dream of this girl woman, of stone made flesh. And then he laughed, laughed harshly at himself for letting a hick carnival get him down. Him, a Chicago mug, getting nerves because a dumb Indian girl didn't know how to talk slick. She wasn't a spook, she was a gift from Heaven.

He went over to her and he grabbed her arm. "You've got a room, haven't you?" he demanded.

She looked up at him blankly.

"You've got a place to sleep, haven't you? A bed?"

She said, "Yes."

He tightened his hold on her arm. "We're going there now," he told her. He began walking her through the crowd, not caring who he bumped or shoved. "How far is it?"

She said, "About a mile."

"We'll take a cab." He pushed her out of the Plaza and Fiesta, towards the frame shack where the pink neon sign had flashed taxi last night.

They were in luck. An old black sedan, dented, scaling, loose-jointed, was pulling up in front.

Sailor knew it was a taxi because the word was stenciled on the door. "Come on," he said.

She wasn't pulling back but he could feel the reluctance pressing through her arm. He repeated, "Come on," and she spoke then. "I cannot take you to this house."

It was he who was stopped cold. Before they reached the cab. He didn't know how much he'd counted on that hour in bed until her refusal sharpened his want. "You can't, can't you?" His demand was ugly. "Why not?"

She stood unmoving where he had released her. Like a sack of flour; like something hewed from stone. She wasn't moved by his anger, neither troubled nor embarrassed nor curious. She repeated without any inflection, "I cannot take you to this house."

"Why not?" he demanded again. "What's the matter with "thees house"? Don't you think I'm good enough—" He began to laugh then. He thought what she'd probably been thinking since he'd grabbed her in the Plaza.

He laughed, "For God's sake, Pila. I don't want you. I just want a place to sleep for a little while." She was as safe with him as she'd be behind the convent wall. He didn't knock up fourteen-year-old kids. He didn't want her; he wanted her bed.

He stopped laughing because of the look on her face, the older-than-time look. It wasn't the look of a floozie like Rosie and yet he knew that if he'd wanted her he could have had her. As easy as he could give her a pop or a ride on Tio Vivo. He was no more important to her than that.

He wouldn't have her on a bet. Because he was uneasy, he blustered, "You don't need to worry about your old man knocking you around."

She said, "My father is at the pueblo."

He didn't know what a pueblo was or where but he knew from the way she said it that her old man wasn't around town. She didn't have to worry about him turning up. It wasn't that bothering her. Not understanding made him mad. He demanded, "Then what's eating you? Let's go."

She parroted, "I cannot take you to this house."

He was really mad by now. He was good enough to buy soda pop for her but he wasn't good enough to take home. He might not look like any prize package at this moment but he was still good enough to go to an Indian shack. He said, "Okay. If that's the way it is. Skip it." He swung away from her up the street, not having any direction in his head, only to get away from a snotty Indian kid who didn't think he was good enough to take home.

He pounded on the broken bricks of the sidewalk, ignoring the presence on the walk of Fiesta.

He walked on, away from the Plaza, anywhere to get away from the gilded muck, from people who thought they were happy because they were all dressed up in ribbons and bobbles, eating hot dogs and chile, drinking pop, listening to plinking music. The smoke of Zozobra's pyre had blurred their eyes; they believed their cry "Old Man Gloom is dead" meant just that, that a word could be fact by the act of being spoken.

He was halfway up the street when she brushed his shoulder. He hadn't known she was following; it came as a surprise, a dirty surprise. He was savage, "What do you want now?"

She said, "I will go with you."

He didn't stop walking. He said, "Scram. I don't want you." He hit his heels harder on the walk, as if he were thumping her. It didn't send her away. He felt the brush of her brown arm against his sleeve. "Beat it," he said.

He might have been talking at the stone woman in the cold corridor of the Art Museum; not to a kid, old and young, on a dirty village street in a sun hot foreign town.

He stopped on the corner and faced her. "Go on," he said, "beat it."

It had been a mistake to look at her. Because looking at her he saw her eyes, her expressionless black eyes. He'd been afraid she might be about to turn on the weeps the way he'd talked to her. He hadn't expected her to look just the same, so terribly unchanged, as if he weren't there. She said, "I will go with you."

He could have threatened her maybe and got rid of her. But he didn't. All of a sudden it didn't matter whether she came along or went away. It had no more importance than that; no more importance than his existence had to an Indian.

He crossed the street and walked on past the filling station, past the big house walled to the eaves, knowing she walked with him, not knowing why, not caring. He cut across beyond the big house, across to the sound of music over by the big building set in an iron-fenced park, the Federal Building. He hadn't meant to go there. But when he reached the walk encircling the park he turned in at the iron gate, set ajar, into quiet greenness. The music somehow went with the quietness. It wasn't good. It was nasal and plaintive, four adolescent boys lying there on the grass, singing in harmony, "Adios, mi amigo, adios . . ." It might have been the song, the song Pancho had sung, which made it sound good in the hot afternoon with the grass smelling sweet and cool under the big trees.

He walked across the graveled paths, away from the music, to a spot alone where the singing was a fainter quiver. He flung himself down on the spired grass. He didn't look at Pila; he knew she was beside him. The sun sprayed through the tree leaves; heat cooled by greenness to a good warmth. He took off his hat and put it over his eyes.

Pila said, "I would not take you to this house. You would not be welcome."

"Sure," he said. "Sure." He'd got it a long time ago. She didn't have to draw a picture. He didn't give a damn now. He was comfortable, a lot more comfortable than he'd be in a flea-bitten adobe dump.

"You would not be welcome because I bring you to this house. Because you come with an Indian to this house."

He shifted the hat, enough so that his eyes could see her although she could not look under the brim shadow at him. "What they got against Indians?" he demanded. "They're Indians, aren't they? Your uncle and aunt?"

"My uncle, yes. He marry with a Spanish woman—Español—my aunt she is a Spanish woman. She, her people, do not think the Indians are so good as the Spanish people. If I take you to this house they will say you are a friend of a dirty Indian."

"To hell with them," he said. Zozobra was dead and everybody was down on the Plaza acting like they were all friends, Spanish and Indian and Mexican and Gringos. But the real Indians were sitting under the portal of the museum and the rich Gringo sonnama beetches were safe behind the garden walls of La Fonda and the Mexicans were remembering they'd once been the conquerors of this land and there wasn't any brotherhood between them even if it was Fiesta. It didn't mean anything to him; he was an outsider who'd wandered into this foreign land; all he had to do was finish his business and get out. He wasn't losing any sleep over Pila and her folks.

He pulled his hat down over his eyes. "How come you're staying with them?"

"It is very good of them to let me stay with them for the Fiesta."

He couldn't tell if she was sarcastic or not, her voice didn't have any inflection. Nor her face.

He didn't bother to look.

"I must cause them no trouble. It is good of them to let me stay there." She was repeating what someone had told her. "I have not been so lucky before. I must not bother Rosie."

Drowsiness was green all around him, green and grass-smelling and sun-warm. Her light voice and the singing of the lazy boys all blurred together.

There was no period between waking and sleeping. He slept. Nor was there a period between sleeping and waking. He woke.

He pushed away his hat. Pila was still sitting there, cross-legged beside him. She might not have moved in the interval.

The sun had moved. It slanted low over the lawn. He yawned, "What time is it?" He looked at his watch. Four-thirty. The gun was hard in his pocket.

He had slept and he was revived. She had watched over him while he slept. He sat up, punched his battered hat in shape. "Thanks. I needed that." He could finish the job now.

He stood up and stretched. A dash of water in the face, comb his hair and he was ready for the Sen. Maybe not as spruce as he'd be on Michigan Boulevard but his hand was just as steady. He said, "Come on." They walked out of the park.

Pila said, "You slept so long you missed the parade."

"What parade?"

"The De Vargas parade. It is a big parade. I could hear the horses and the music."

He scowled, "Why didn't you go to it?"

"You were asleep," she stated.

"What the hell—" he began.

She said, "I did not want you to be alone while you sleep."

He shook his head. "Did you think something might happen to me?" She didn't know he carried a gun. "I can take care of myself any time."

Her voice was soft. "When I am in a strange house I do not like to be alone while I sleep."

He shut up. Feeling a little queer inside. Because she'd said it, said he was a stranger, said he wasn't he in this strange house. That he couldn't take care of himself in this alien world. He needed a guardian, even if it was just an Indian kid.

They could see the Plaza from the street they took, hear the muted music, the human sounds over it. They scuffed through litter, walking the last block in silence. When they reached the museum he stopped her.

"You can't go with me now," he said. "I got business." He felt good. Because he'd been wrong thinking she was hostile to the stranger; she was his friend. "Meet me later at Tio Vivo and I'll buy you a flock of rides." He felt better than he had since he boarded the bus in Chicago. "If the deal comes off I'll buy you anything you want. What do you want more than anything else in the world?"

She said solemnly, "A permanent wave."

He was still laughing as he swung away from her, cutting across the Plaza, to the hotel, and to the Sen.

Three

I⟨T WASN'T⟩ more than a few minutes past five when he came up from the men's room. He'd washed up, brushed himself off as best he could. He didn't look as if he'd been sleeping in the park. The patio was filled but quietly; a few, not many persons milled in the lobby. He started towards the Cantina. Started and didn't dare turn aside when McIntyre rose up to meet him. Mac hadn't any business being here yet. It wasn't time for his appointment.

McIntyre said, "Hello. You're early."

"A little." It hadn't occurred to him that Mac would be here waiting. He didn't know what to say to the cop. He couldn't tell him to beat it until his own private confab with the Sen was done. He had to carry Mac with him. Not knowing if the Sen would join him if he saw the cop there. Not knowing how he'd get rid of Mac for the necessary moments alone.

"Going in now or wait for him here?" McIntyre asked.

"Might as well go in," Sailor said. He laughed a short one. "Maybe he's still in there."

McIntyre followed Sailor this time. He said, "He isn't. He and his party left about two o'clock."

McIntyre was watching close. Watching the Sen as close as he was watching Sailor.

Sailor asked wryly, "You been counting noses in the lobby all afternoon?" But he wanted to know.

McIntyre said, "No. I took a nap."

Were McIntyre's eyes knowing? He couldn't tell. Did McIntyre know he'd been sleeping up on the Federal lawn?

He asked ironically, "You haven't been doing Fiesta?"

McIntyre chose the table again. Not in line of the entrance this time. Around in back of the tree where the Sen would have to look for them. And finding them couldn't act as if he hadn't seen them. McIntyre was smart as hell. He even chose the chair he wanted, putting Sailor's back to the entrance, placing himself where he could glimpse anyone coming in. But the branches of the tree hid his face.

"I caught a bit of the parade," McIntyre said, "but I decided to skip the Chocolate. Not that it didn't sound peaceful but the fashion show with it—" he shook his head. "I didn't think a guy like me would be any asset." He smiled. "Mrs. McIntyre will be mad at me for missing it."

He'd never thought of McIntyre having a Mrs. McIntyre. He'd never thought of McIntyre having any life but on the Chicago streets. Like a dog. Smelling out trouble, trotting after trouble, digging up old bones of trouble. Until the commissioner boosted him to a desk and a leather chair. Where he could rest his nose and his feet, send other cops out to follow trouble.

Sailor said, "I didn't know you were married."

"Eighteen years," Mac said. "Have one girl in college this year."

The waitress who came to the table wasn't pretty or young; her mouth wore tired lines and she didn't care that they weren't ready to order. She left the table and stood with another waitress by the open-air fireplace. The pert blonde wasn't around.

Sailor said, "Sure you don't want something?"

"I'd take a drink. This Sunday law is a hindrance. To a working man."

"I could use a beer." Then he grinned. "Thought you were here for the show."

"That's right," was all McIntyre said. "What did you do this afternoon?"

"Took a nap," Sailor said like Mac had said.

McIntyre didn't ask any questions. As if he knew where. But he didn't know if he too had been sleeping. Sailor didn't want Mac to know. He didn't want to have to explain that he hadn't been laying with an Indian girl; that she had tagged after him, that was all.

There were a few parties in the Placita, drinking parties. None of the Sen's crowd. The parties had brought their own bottles; the men pulled them out from under the tables like in prohibition days. The waitresses brought setups. The Sunday law evidently didn't cover drinking, only selling of drinks.

Sailor said, "I wonder if he went to the Chocolate." He could see the Sen's greedy eyes watching dressed-up girls trot by. No. The Sen would be watching Iris Towers. No one else. But his eyes would still be greedy.

"No. He went to Tesuque to a private affair."

It surprised him again, that McIntyre was keeping that close tabs on the Sen.

"The Van der Kirks' ranch," McIntyre said. "They came over during the war and stayed. Not poor refugees. Diamonds."

Not poor if the Sen were there. The Sen didn't visit the poor. He used them. For his dirty work.

"Will he get back in time?" Sailor wondered aloud before he realized it was out loud.

"I think he will," McIntyre said. "I think he'll be anxious for you to tell him what I was talking about at lunch."

Sailor pulled in his belt. "I can't talk to him with you sitting here."

"I'll tell him myself," McIntyre said without inflection.

If he could only bust open McIntyre's head, see what was inside it. If he could only lay out those little squares, like lottery tickets, each one labeled with a name and a thought and a plan. Was his name on the winning ticket, the losing ticket; or was it the Sen's? He couldn't ask McIntyre; he could only sit tight and wait. And make talk.

"How many kids you got?"

"Two girls and a boy." Talk suited McIntyre. He too had to wait.

McIntyre would live in a suburb, Evanston probably. A nice house, maybe white pickets, maybe a green hedge. A green lawn and trees and flowers; Mac cutting the grass on a summer Sunday, shoveling snow off the walks on a winter morning. Mrs. McIntyre in a tiled kitchen fixing him and the kids good dinners.

"Patsy, the oldest, she's the one in college. University of Chicago. Molly, she's the pretty one, still in High. She wants to be a criminologist." He smiled at memory. "Ted's only twelve. Eagle Scout this year. Scouting's a good thing for boys."

"So is being born in the right part of town," Sailor said.

McIntyre said quietly, "I was born four blocks from where you were, Sailor."

He hadn't known that. Long as he'd known Mac, he hadn't known he came from the old ward. His mouth twisted. "How did you get out?"

"Not any easy way." His eye was on Sailor.

"You think I came out easy?"

Mac didn't answer that. He said, "I joined the force when I was twenty-one. That was twenty years ago, twenty years last spring." He kept his eye on Sailor. "It isn't easy pounding pavements summer and winter. Lots of work, little pay in those days." His mouth tightened. "What I grew up with down there, from the time I was a kid, made me want to make the world better, not worse."

Sailor said belligerently, "Your old lady didn't scrub floors, I bet. I'll bet your old man wasn't a drunken sot."

"My mother worked in a laundry. My father in the yards. No, he wasn't a drunk, Sailor." His eye was steady. "I've wondered often why with what you went through, you didn't grow up feeling like I did. Wanting to make things better, not worse."

"I've made them better for me," Sailor bristled.

McIntyre didn't say anything. He just looked until Sailor moved his eyes, pulled out his cigarettes. Sailor said to the cigarettes, "I don't owe the world nothing. It never did anything for me."

McIntyre said, "I've heard a lot of you say that. It's always seemed to me you were blaming the world for something missing in you."

"What are you trying to say?" Sailor scowled.

"The world doesn't care much what happens to us. Least that's the way I've always figured. Like this table." He flattened his hand on the painted metal. "It doesn't care if you bump your shin on it. It doesn't even know you're around. That's the world. The way I see it." He lifted his hand and looked at the palm as if the paint had smeared it. He had a broad hand but his fingers were thin. "It's up to you what you are. Good or bad. You get the choice. You can do anything you want to with yourself. You can use the world"—again he touched the table—"or you can break your toes on it. The world doesn't care. It's up to you." He smiled faintly. "Seems I tried to tell you that a long time ago, Sailor."

Sailor said out of his scowl, "Maybe you think I chose to be starved and beaten when I was a kid."

McIntyre's eyes saddened. Briefly. "I guess kids can't choose. Not while they're kids." Then he looked straight into Sailor. "But when you're old enough for choice, it's up to you. The right way or the wrong way. Good or bad."

"You think I chose wrong." Sailor was casual, drawing on his cigarette. "You think I shouldn't have let the Sen help me out? Send me to college. The U of Chicago like your kid. You think maybe I ought to have pounded the pavements like you instead of letting a good guy help me out." The Sen had been a good guy once. Sailor wouldn't be where he was today if the Sen hadn't given him a lift.

McIntyre said, "There's a lot of old stories, might be true, about a man selling his soul to the Devil."

Sailor jerked back his head and laughed. A good long laugh as if it were funny. Mac just sat there. And it wasn't funny. The Devil could look like the Sen. The Devil didn't have to have red horns and a forked tail and a red union suit; he could have a big snout and a brush mustache and wear the best clothes in Chicago. The Sen was a devil. If Mac knew half what Ziggy and Sailor knew, he wasn't just shooting off his mouth. Sailor said, as if it were still funny, "As long as you're preaching, Mac, what about God? He's supposed to take care of us, isn't He? That's what they used to tell me at school. God'll take care of you."

Mac said, "I don't know." He spoke slowly, like he was thinking it out. "Maybe it's like it says in Scripture. You can choose between God and the Devil. Good or bad. Right or wrong. It's written that way, more than once in The Book. I'm no preacher, Sailor. You know me better than that. But I see a lot of the wrong way. Makes a man think. The only way I can see it is that maybe God doesn't want those that choose the Devil. The Devil's own they used to call them. Maybe He withholds His hand, waits for them to turn to Him. To decide to go right, not wrong." He added it so quietly he might have still been thinking. "Want to tell me where the senator was the night she was killed?"

It was like something not real, sitting there in the quiet walled garden with the sun slanting through the crooked branches of the old green trees. Something in a book, Mac talking about God and the Devil and right and wrong. With a funny hat on his head. Not preaching but talking like a preacher only straight, a man to a man, not set up high in a pulpit talking to too many people and most of them not listening. Most of them having a Sunday-morning snooze. Then Mac said it and he was a copper again. A smart copper, catching you off guard. Only when he said it his face put on its mask suddenly and Sailor looked where he was looking. The Sen was there. The Devil in a white shirt and white pants and a red sash. And a vicious look that went from his eyes so quickly you wouldn't believe it had been there.

The Sen was looking for Sailor and he was caught by the eyes of Sailor and Mac before he could act as if he were looking for someone else.

He tried not to be caught. He nodded as if he were greeting an acquaintance. Sailor spoke fast, knowing he had to grab onto the Sen before he faded out for another night. Even knowing how the Sen would be when they were alone, he spoke. "Hello. Thought you weren't coming," he said.

That was when the viciousness fleeted through these narrow dark eyes.

McIntyre took it over fast. He said, "I hope you don't mind my intruding, Senator. I asked your secretary if he'd give me an introduction to you."

The Sen was caught. He stood there while Sailor said, "This is Chief McIntyre, Senator Douglass. From Chicago too." As if the Sen didn't know.

The Sen sat down then, as if he were brittle, as if he might break if he sat down in the white metal chair. But his tongue was smooth the way it could be. "I've heard a lot about you, Chief. Seems strange we'd travel across the country to meet, doesn't it?" His smile was right.

"Yes," McIntyre said.

"I'd offer you a drink but the bar's closed. As you know, doubtless." He took his cigarette case and passed it. McIntyre took one. Sailor didn't. He wasn't offered. "You here on business, Chief?"

"Partly," McIntyre said. He accepted a light from the white-gold lighter. The lighter that never sputtered, that always made a good pointed flame.

The Sen touched it to his own smoke. He acted surprised. "A little far from your bailiwick, isn't it? It must be important for the Chief of the Bureau to handle it."

"It is important," McIntyre said. "It's about the death of your wife."

The Sen didn't show any surprise. He just looked properly solemn. Solemn and a small bit touched with grief. He didn't say anything. He could act; he was good at acting. But when he was acting, he wasn't safe. He was too sure of himself, on top. Sailor didn't like it. He kept his eyes under his lids on the Sen.

He could keep them there because the Sen wasn't paying any attention to him. This was between the Sen and McIntyre. The Sen finally put surprise and curiosity into a question. "Really?"

"Yes," McIntyre said.

"But—" The Sen touched ash to the tray. McIntyre didn't help. The Sen had to go on with it. "I thought you did a splendid job in solving her tragic end so quickly."

"We thought so too," McIntyre said. "But Jerky Spizzoni didn't kill her."

The Sen looked properly shocked. He could have said a lot of different things then but he didn't. He was smart. He waited.

"That's why I'm working," McIntyre said. "I'm looking for the man who killed her."

The Sen took that and mulled it. He said, "It's hard to believe. The commissioner was sure—"

"New evidence," McIntyre cut in. "Spizzoni didn't get to town that night until after she was killed."

"The gun—The fingerprints—" The Sen acted innocent as hell. He fumbled as an innocent man would.

"Somebody had Jerky's gun. With his fingerprints still on it. It was smart," McIntyre admitted.

He didn't know how smart it was. Ziggy had taken care of that. Visiting day. Ziggy had told the Jerk somebody wanted to buy his gat; to put a price on it.

Jerky had handled that gun every day before he was sent up. When he was shipped, the Sen had made sure the gat was tucked away in a clean handkerchief, that no one else touched it. Maybe the Sen had known then. Maybe that was why Jerky had been sold out.

"Have you any leads?" the Sen asked.

Mac took his time. "I wouldn't exactly say we had," he admitted. "I thought maybe you could help us out. Maybe you knew something that might give us a lead."

The Sen shook his head. "I wish I could." He put out the cigarette, half-smoked. "As I told the commissioner that night, I knew of no one who wished harm to my wife. She had no enemies. She wasn't a woman who could ever make an enemy." His eyes looked moist. When his voice made music that way, he could turn on the waterworks. "I appreciate your coming so far to tell me of this, McIntyre. I'd like to go over it with you more thoroughly." His wristwatch was bold and expensive, a platter of gold that looked like platinum. "Right now I must dress for an engagement. Perhaps after Fiesta, or are you leaving before then?"

"I'm staying for Fiesta," McIntyre said. "Might as well as long as I'm here."

They were both getting up and Sailor got up too. He followed them out of the Placita, through the dim bar into the lobby. He didn't know what they were saying, he tagged like a mongrel. In the lobby they were bowing goodbye. The Sen said, "Sailor will give you any information you need about that night. He knows the details. We've been over them often. In fact I don't doubt he knows more than I about the death." That was the undercut. There might have been others. "You'll excuse me now."

He wasn't getting away with this run-out, not if McIntyre's whole bureau were standing with fixed attention. The dough was to be ready now. He wasn't going to get away with not paying off.

Sailor said, "I'll go up with you while you dress." The lips pulled back over the Sen's teeth but Sailor continued, "There's some stuff to go over." And his hand was cold and hard in his right pocket. He wasn't afraid. The Sen wouldn't dare pull anything in the room right now; not with Mac knowing the two were going up there.

The Sen said brusquely, "It can wait till later."

"This is new stuff," Sailor said. That did it. Because the Sen didn't know what Mac might have let out at lunch. He couldn't take a chance. "You'll excuse us then?" he asked McIntyre.

"Yes," McIntyre said. "I'll see you later."

The Sen's skinny legs were ill-tempered. They pecked the portal flagstones. Sailor swung easily at heel. Neither spoke until they reached the elevator, had to wait for the descent of the cage.

The Sen said, "What else did he have to say?"

Sailor didn't answer because the elevator was down and some swells in blue-white hair and a lot of glitter were coming out. They had a speaking acquaintance with the Sen and he put on the platform manner automatically. He could always do it. Give him an audience and it didn't matter what was knocking him out, he performed. As soon as he was in the elevator, behind the little elevator girl's back, he put it away. But he didn't repeat the question, not until they were on the fourth and outside his room. Not until he had put in the key and was pushing open the door. "What else did McIntyre have to say?"

Sailor stood behind him while the Sen picked up the two telephone message slips off the rug, read them before folding them tight in his palm. Sailor walked when the Sen did. The Sen went over by the telephone table. Sailor took the good chair, settled in it, his hat on his head, his hand comfortable in his pocket.

"He was wondering about the insurance."

The Sen forgot the telephone. His black eyebrows were a tight angle. "What about it?" he demanded.

"Nothing," Sailor said. "Just wondering. Maybe he'd like to know how long you had that policy on her. That fifty grand."

The Sen sat down slowly. On the edge of the bed. "So that's it," he said. He read the messages again. One he slid in his pocket, the other he held in his hand. As if it were warm and living, a warm white body.

"I don't know," Sailor said. "I don't know what the angle is. All I know is he's looking for the guy who killed your wife."

The Sen's eyes were mean little slits. "He doesn't have to look far."

"No, he doesn't." Sailor kept his look steady on the Sen. Steady and with meaning.

The Sen shifted his shoulders. "You'd better get off to Mexico. Right away. I can let you have five hundred now. I'll send you the other five hundred when the banks open—"

Sailor laughed at him. Laughed hard and harsh. "It's five grand, Sen," he said. "Not five C's." He was suddenly mad. He'd had enough waiting. "Don't you have it yet?"

"No, I don't." The Sen got mad too. He was like the old Sen when things didn't suit him. "The banks are closed. I can't pick five thousand dollars out of thin air. Or even one thousand. You'd better take the five hundred now and get out of here. Before Mac finds out you're the one he's looking for."

Sailor's mouth was easy. The words came out of it easy. "I didn't kill your wife."

He liked the way the Sen's mouth opened. Like a fish. He liked the fury that stiffened the fancy white shirt. He even liked hearing the Sen's voice grate across the space between them. "You tried that one last night. If you didn't kill her, who did?"

Most of all he liked his own soft answer. "You did."

The Sen wasn't shriveled with fear yet. Because he didn't know yet what Sailor knew, how much he knew. He thought it was an accusation, no more. He thought he could afford to pull his lips up in a sneer. "You won't get anywhere accusing me."

Sailor said, "I think I might. If I told Mac the whole story." He lit a cigarette, let smoke snort out of his nostrils. "Jerky wasn't the only one whose plans hitched that night."

The Sen didn't know of knowledge yet. But he burned. "You mean you had car trouble too? You were late?" He didn't believe it. He was refusing to believe it.

"Uh-uh," Sailor said. "She was." He let the Sen have it now, have it both barrels. Now was the time. "I got there the time you told me. Storm and all. I did it just like you said, pulled things around to make it look like a loot. And I had the lights out when the taxi drove up outside. Just like you planned it."

He was remembering it as he spoke. Not with any emotion, like something he'd seen in a picture show sometime. Kind of a dull picture. The Sen's library there at the front of the house, books and couches and a desk. French doors opening out to a little yard. He'd come in the French doors like the Sen told him, they were easy to open. His hands gloved. Good gray suede gloves, soft, expensive. He'd pulled out papers from the desk, opened the wall safe. Like he was Jerky looking for blackmail and maybe a haul of easy dough.

"I had Jerky's gun all ready to let go when she came in. Only she didn't get there the time you counted on. I guess she couldn't get a taxi for a while account of the storm. She came in just like you said she would, front door, with the key she hooked. Only she hadn't hooked a key; it was hers. She wasn't Jerky's dame. She was Mrs. Douglass."

The Sen's mouth was so thin, the brush mustache hid it. He opened it only a slit to speak. "And so you killed her by mistake.

But I protected you. I knew you never would have shot her if you'd known. It was an accident, a bitter accident."

"That's what I thought, then," Sailor said. Carefully he lit another cigarette from the stub of the first, not moving his tight right hand from his pocket. "There was a big slash of lightning right after I fired and I saw I'd made a mistake. An awful mistake." He pulled in a lungful of smoke remembering the dread moment. The tall gray-haired woman, the horrified surprise on her face as she fell. "I didn't know what to do." Letting out the smoke fogged the small mean figure sitting there on the bed, sitting like a mummy not a man.

"I didn't know what you'd do. I started over to her, to see if I could do anything for her—" The remembered moment was stark again. "I heard a car come in the drive. I dropped the gun. And I got out quick."

The Sen said again angrily, "I took care of you. I didn't mention you to the police. What's the point of all this?"

"The timing was wrong. You got home too soon. That was your car. I was outside the window."

The Sen's rigidity was electric.

"She wasn't dead. She was pushing up, trying to get up. You picked up the gun and let her have it. You had your gloves on."

The Sen began to curse him, to curse and revile him with obscene eyes, a toneless throat. But the Sen didn't move. He knew he was covered by Sailor's right-hand pocket.

Sailor waited until he was quiet. "I'm no killer," he said. "I never killed anyone only in self defense. You knew you couldn't hire me to kill your wife. You needed a triggerman. But you didn't dare put one of those fellows on anything that important. I believed your bull about getting rid of Maudie Spizzoni before she landed us all in the Federal pen. I thought about it like it was self defense. She wasn't any good to anybody. Even so I wasn't a killer. I didn't want even to kill Maudie cold like that. I wouldn't have done it only for the chance to do something on my own. Only for the dough." If Mac hadn't talked like a preacher . . . "All right, so it was wrong. I shouldn't have said I'd do it. But I didn't know it was your wife you wanted killed." His teeth were bare. "And I didn't kill her!" He caught hold of himself. "All I want is five grand and you won't ever see me again. Mac won't ever find out what you and I know."

The Sen snarled, "It would be your word against mine."

"Mac's not looking for me," Sailor said. "He's looking for the guy who killed your wife. The guy that got fifty grand for killing her." He said harshly, "Five grand isn't much."

The Sen didn't know what to say. There wasn't anything he could say, he was caught. The way all the fellows hoped and knew he'd be caught some day. But none of them ever thought Sailor would be the one to catch him. Sailor never thought so.

"After all I've done for you." He'd turned on the music in his pipes. "Taking you out of the gutter. Educating you like you were my own—" The phone spoiled his art. Interrupting as it had earlier today. It rang short, then long. The Sen looked at it the same way Sailor was looking at it, as if it had no business sounding. As if its intrusion were insolent.

The Sen reached out a withered hand. He said, "Hello," and was silent. Sailor knew who was calling. The hopelessness that came over the Sen was the hopelessness of the damned. Even her voice couldn't help him at this moment. He listened silent. When he spoke his voice was dry, old. He said, "I'm sorry. I'll be down right away. I'm sorry, Iris." There was no caress in the name. He replaced the phone.

Sailor said, "Well."

The Sen moved unsteadily. Standing up from the bed, standing there as if he were a blind man in an unfamiliar room. Sailor's hand gripped tight in his pocket. But the Sen only began to unbutton his shirt. He said, "You've got to give me more time."

Sailor was silent.

"I promised my friends to go with them to the Procession. I have to dress and shave." He might have been talking to himself, telling himself what was on his mind. "Dress and shave." His eyes wavered across to Sailor. "You've got to give me more time." He was querulous as a child. "The banks are closed. Tomorrow is a bank holiday. Labor Day. I can't do anything until Tuesday."

Sailor stretched up from the chair. He was as sure and cold as steel was cold before a hand hotted it. "You got friends," he slurred. "You're a big shot. You're Senator Douglass." His voice cracked like a whip. "I'll give you till midnight."

"I can't—" The Sen was going to whine.

Sailor cut him off. "Midnight. By Tio Vivo"—he translated—"the merry-go-round." Pancho for bodyguard in case the Sen came out of his trance. "I don't want Mac in on this any more than you do."

He walked sharp to the door while the Sen was pulling off his shirt. While his claws were caught in satin cuffs.

"I won't go to Mac unless you want me to." Sailor gave the Sen a sudden grin as his left hand turned the knob.

The Sen's lips moved. He forced the word through them. "Guttersnipe!" It was more evil than the obscenities had been.

Four

HE WOULD have sat down in the lobby. On a comfortable brown
leather couch. Only he saw a Spanish hat with bobbles there.
It wasn't Mac but he remembered Mac. He walked out of the
hotel. He didn't want Mac around him tonight. While he was
watching the Sen. The Sen wasn't going to run out on him this
night. The Sen wasn't going to get by with any monkey business.

He took his stand outside the display windows, next to the
entrance arch. There were painted tin platters in the windows,
kids' chairs with red and blue roses daubed on them, a hideous
wooden saint holding out a bleeding wooden hand, a couple of
fat yellow painted pigs. A hodge-podge for the La Fonda rich
guys to take back to civilization, to remind them of the Fiesta
visit in a foreign country.

He could stand there; no one cared. There were people standing all over the streets, leaning against shop windows, tired of
making merry, tired of the music and the dance and the gimcracks, tired of a three-day Feast before the second day was done.
Tired, just tired. In the feet and the eyes and the guts, leaning
like warm wax against the windows and walls. The Plaza spun
on in its tawdry tinsel cage. But it was tired too, the children's
voices on the merry-go-round were muted, the violin and guitar
were faint music, even the leaves on the tall trees were still. Ev-

erything was quieted in the weary twilight. He could stand there as long as he wanted waiting for the Sen. With no one paying attention, no one knowing him, no one caring that the man in the rumpled suit with the hat pulled over his eyes was holding a gun in his pocket.

Before the bells began to ring, he saw the shawled women moving towards the cathedral. He saw the gray stone mass of the cathedral overshadowing the little street, the purple clouds piling behind its squat towers, the black-shawled women and the children dangling from their hands, the church yard filling with men and women and children, quiet and dim as ghosts. Sunday night. Vespers and benediction. The old lady used to slip off and go to vespers when things weren't too tough at home. The old man never went. By Sunday night he was sitting around in his dirty stocking feet, bloated with beer or red-eyed with whisky. The kids wouldn't go to vespers, all the kids in the neighborhood went to the movies on Sunday evenings. But the old lady wanted to go, and she'd come home looking rested, almost as peaceful as she did years later when she was dead.

When the bells began to ring the cathedral doors opened like a kid playing church-and-steeple with his hands. Standing there Sailor could see into the lighted nave, see all the way to the altar with its burning candles. He didn't know vespers were part of Fiesta, not until the Sen came hurrying towards the church. He almost missed the Sen in the depth of twilight and him watching the shadows gathering on the church terrace. He might have if she hadn't been beside him.

He followed the pale white froth of her skirts. Even as he followed he didn't believe they were heading for the church. Catching the Sen in church would be like catching the Devil in a prayer book.

He almost didn't keep on when they walked up the steps towards the open doors. He hadn't been inside a church since the old lady died and he didn't want to go in one again. A lot of pious talk, a lot of praying, a lot of that turn-the-other-cheek, love-your-enemies stuff. Nothing about how to get out of a Chicago slum into the Gold Coast. He'd learned that in a pool hall. The church had never done anything for him.

But he followed. He wasn't going to lose sight of the Sen. The Sen didn't know Sailor was trailing, there were too many in the church yard besides him. The Sen went on in as if he weren't something to be exorcised with holy water. Sailor let some of the crowd go first. When he got inside, his eyes found the white mist, the silver-gold hair, down in front with the wine velvets and gold chains. The black velvet beside her was still the Sen.

Sailor slid into a back pew where he could watch them. The cathedral was big and tall and wide, dim even with its lights. It looked old and sanctified. It wasn't packed but it was pretty well filled. A lot of fancy costumes, yet it wasn't all Fiesta. There were the mourning women in their black dresses and black shawls. There were men in old jeans and blue work shirts; and old men in their Sunday bests, their netted brown faces peaceful under their white heads. There were brown children kneeling rigidly, like wooden images.

He didn't pay any attention to anything but the white-and-silver girl down in front. She belonged here; she was like something holy, like one of the altar candles, like an angel. He didn't pay any attention to the altar. There were priests up there chanting the litany; their white-and-gold benediction vestments draped over the red velvet chairs. There was a choir of seminarians singing. Singing the responses. Their faces were foreign like the town; brown Mexican faces, somber, and their voices, unaccompanied, were like a heaven choir. He didn't care about that. He hadn't come here to pray; he'd come with a gun to keep his eye on a rat. He wasn't going to be sucked in by holiness. He kept his mind and his backbone rigid when the golden censers swung the musk-scented smoke, when the organ and choir blazoned together the *O Salutaris Hostia*. He got on his knees only because everyone else did, because he didn't want to be conspicuous. Even the Sen was on his knees down there in front.

He didn't know why the dim perfumed cathedral didn't belch the Sen out of its holy portals.

But looking down the long aisle to the lighted altar, up to the high vaulted roof, he did know. The church was like the stone of its walls, like the stone of the woman. It was too strong, too fast, too great to be aware of a small crawling thing like the Sen. The Sen was dwarfed to unimportance, he was without identity here.

God on the high altar could strike the Sen down in his mockery of prayer. God wouldn't. God had infinite patience. He had infinite mercy. He had infinite justice as well. The finality of Justice. Someday the Sen would pay.

The choir's voices lifted in the *Laudate* and everyone rose. It was over. Sailor was ready to get out quick, to take his stand near the door, shadowed, to watch the Sen and the girl leave. But a monk in brown robes was speaking from the altar. Something about the formation, Sociedad this, Sociedad that. The ushers were passing candles. The Sociedads were lifting painted satin banners on golden poles. The church bells began to ring out above the organ. Outside a band faltered into a hymn.

Sailor slid over to the side pew. A pillar protected him from the eyes of those moving up the aisle. The old men and the little children. The rich and the poor. The alien and the native, the magnificent and the black shawls. The monks and the choir and the Sociedads, a slow-moving, silent procession to the open cathedral doors, out again into the night. Candles flickered like fireflies from all the vasty corners of the cathedral. When the Sen and the girl passed, Sailor moved up the side aisle fast. But he couldn't follow. He had to wait to press into the line; balked, impatient, he had to wait. By the time he reached the open doors he had lost the Sen, lost him completely in this, the Procession to the Cross of the Martyrs. The town had been blacked out, no neons, no shop fronts, candle flame alone, flickering from the hands of those who walked to the cross. Down the long street rounding the Plaza, he could see only the twin lines of moving light in the unaccustomed depth of dark. The silence was deep as the dark; silence deeper than the choir chant, the somber hymn of the band, the tinkle and strum of the tamed Mariachis breaking their hymn against the brass, the shuffle of feet. No voices.

Sailor fell in with the right-hand line, his lighted candle in his left hand, his right hand where it belonged. He didn't know when his candle had come to light. As in a dream he remembered a Spanish voice speaking while he had been blocked in the side aisle. Beyond that no memory.

He maneuvered forward in the line because he knew how, because he'd trailed men before and in Chicago crowds. Snaked forward until he saw the white girl again, in the left-hand line, forward. The width of street separating, and the dark. The Sen was behind her.

The slow procession wound the Plaza when even the garland-colored bulbs that crowned Fiesta were dark. Around the square, turning up the wide lightless street where last night the cacophony of Keen's Bar had smeared the night. Those doors too were dark, shuttered. Up the street, past small wood fires burning at the intersection, to circle a park and its dark massive building. The Federal Building park where the girls and their chosen had lain last night. Deserted now. Another narrow street lit by small fires and candle flame, a bridge ahead, across it the pinpricks of light winding up a hill, clusters of candlelight atop the hill. Against the sky, a wide white cross. The sky was blue black as the night, the stars were distant, flickering like the candle flames. Across the band of naked horizon a zigzag of lightning ran through far violet clouds. And a wind came up as out of the lightning, wavering the candles.

Sailor couldn't see the Sen as he toiled up the hill but he could see the misty white skirts. He kept his eye on the skirts. The Sen's velvet was blacked out in the night. He wouldn't lose the Sen if he watched Iris Towers.

He hadn't known there would be such a crowd until he too reached the top of the hill. This wasn't just for church people; this was Fiesta and everybody of Fiesta was there. He'd lost the skirt and he had to push through massed humanity before he found its whiteness again. There was a brown monk standing up in front of the cross talking through the loudspeaker. Talking of an ancient vow. The vow Don Diego de Vargas Zapata Lujan Ponce de Leon had made when he reconquered the ancient pueblo of Santa Fe. The old unforgotten vow.

Sailor didn't care about old vows, about old Spanish and Indian wars; he'd lost the girl in the shifting of the dark, candle-pricked mass. He edged quickly towards where he'd last seen white and again the veil of it fluttered behind a blurred wall of man shapes. As he shifted to keep the white in his view, someone's elbow caught him under the shoulder bone. He growled, "Watch where you're going," but his words were broken by a sword of lightning cutting the sky. In the flash he saw the face of the girl in white. It wasn't Iris Towers.

Impotent rage filled his mouth and with it the pain thrust. A shaft of pain under his shoulder. With the pain the lightning of fear. He dropped his lighted candle as if it burned. His hand went slowly under his coat, touched the pain and returned to sight. The hand was wet with blood. He'd been knifed. He swiveled slowly, ready to kill, his trigger finger itching to kill. Behind him were the brown listening faces of grave men and women, their eyes lifted to the monk at the white cross. They hadn't seen who'd jostled past in the crush. You didn't turn around and catch a knifer wiping blood from a blade. Only a dope would expect that.

Only a dope would seek in the quiet brown faces a face with secret triumph on it, with the laughter of hate distorting it. Would, with the pain thrumming now, stalk the silent circle of faces for a face. Sailor's hand gripped the gun and the force opened the slant wound. He felt the flesh pull apart, felt the slow trickle of blood. Whoever had cut him, behind him in shadow stood the Sen. This was the Sen's answer to Sailor's demand. He should have expected it. He should have known the Sen wouldn't wait to bring out his killers from Chicago; he'd use the local thugs. Every town had its killers; the Sen knew how to find them. The Sen knew all the root paths of evil.

He had to get away from here, before someone noticed. Before someone got officious and stuck him in a hick hospital, before the police got nosey. He swung his eyes again to the white skirts; it was still the wrong girl. The Sen and Iris Towers were lost in candlelight and darkness and a sermon at the Cross.

He made his way warily out of the crowd, alert to danger in back of him, at his side. If the lightning hadn't cleaved when it did, rocking him forward in the shock of the wrong white skirts, the knife thrust would have been deep and true. It wasn't meant as warning; the Sen didn't give warning. Death in the back; a gun for Jerky, a knife for Sailor.

If the lightning hadn't cleaved when it did, he would have killed Eleanor Douglass. The Sen's own hand had had to kill. Because of rage in the heavens. The Sen wasn't going to get a chance to take care of this failure. Sailor was clear of the crowd now and he scrambled down the stubble of the hill, no longer a target, hidden by the hill. He wasn't bleeding much; not enough to be weakened. All he needed was a patch and he'd be ready to meet the Sen. That was the only thing he wanted, to meet the Sen face to face.

At the foot of the hill he looked back upward. Nothing stirred but candles in the wind and the mockery of white skirts. He walked on over the bridge, down the dark street where the bonfires flickered into reddened ash. The sky was lit again with lightning and in the distance thunder threatened. The monk's voice, distorted by microphone, followed him.

He walked on, not too fast, not wanting movement to harry the pain. Around the dark circle of the Federal park, shying at the few couples he met. The heavy trees held in their boughs the glitter of candles from the hill but were lost as he went on, lost with the echo of the metallic voice.

Shadow and silence rested heavily on the Plaza. Under the portal were the mounds of Indian women, their cigarettes reddening the dark, fading, glowing. He didn't know who might be hidden among them. He cut swiftly across the square and headed towards Tio Vivo. Only then did he realize this was the haven he sought. Pancho would fix him up.

The square was as deserted as if the ghostly hand of Zozobra had smote it. But the way was small and he was outside the faded red palings, the locked fence. He cursed then. The unease he'd experienced the night before on the dark unfamiliar street ran in his veins. That quickly it came, the feeling of one lost, alone in an alien deserted world. He cursed it away, shaking the padlocked fence, fearing to climb over its height lest the gap under his shoulder widen.

Lightning flickered again in the hidden sky, and with the thunder rumble, the deeper thunder.

He wasn't alone; under the canopy Pancho snored.

He called out, his voice too loud in the silence. "Hey, Pancho. Pancho!" He didn't expect to wake the sleeping hulk; he was afraid to shout too fully, afraid of the shadowy silence. But the snore choked in Pancho's throat and the man rose up, alert as an animal stirred from sleep. "Who is it? Who calls Pancho?"

"It's me. Sailor. Let me in."

Pancho groaned up from the earth, scratched his belly and his lank black hair as he plodded to the fence. "It is Sailor. Waking a poor old man from his little rest. *Pancho! Pancho!* Waking a man from his slumbers, por que?" He unfastened the gate, grumbling as if he meant it, his face a caricature of sleep, his eyes awake, lively.

"I need some help." Sailor walked through the gate, waiting within for Pancho to fasten it. "Que pase? You have another muchacha for whom I must wear out this old arm?" He had turned again to Sailor and the jest went out of his mouth. Out of his merry eyes. "Por que?" he repeated but it was a question to be answered now.

Sailor asked, "You know any doctors? One that doesn't ask foolish questions?"

"Doctors. For what is a doctor?"

"Somebody scratched me."

Pancho's eyes were pinpoints. "The police?"

"They aren't in this. They aren't going to be. What about a doc?" He was impatient. The pain was slitting him.

"The police are not looking for you?"

"For God's sake, no," Sailor snarled. "They don't know anything happened. Somebody stuck a knife in my back while I was up there watching the show—"

Pancho had interrupted lazily, almost happily. "It was a knife."

"What'd you think scratched me, a pin?"

The big belly joggled. "You are so funny, my friend, the Sailor. A pin?" He went off into fat giggling anew and the jut of pain under Sailor's shoulder twisted. The black eyes slit soberly at the rage gnarling Sailor's lips.

"Perhaps I think the gun in your pocket met with a friend, no?" He was reassuring. "The police will not bother about a knife. Certainly no. A gun, yes. A knife, it is nothing."

Sailor gritted the words. "What about the doc?" The old brigand would stand here gabbing until the Plaza filled up again, until there were eyes to notice a wound in a dark coat. He'd stand blatting until it was time for him to crank up the merry-go-round. And Sailor biting on pain, pushed around by a bunch of kids, bleeding away the strength he needed to take care of the Sen. He put it all into the question, "What about the doc?"

Pancho hitched up his pants. "You come with me. I will take care of you, my friend. You need not be disturbed." He unlocked the padlock, carefully locked it again after them. "We will be back before the sermon it is over. The little abuelita will make you good like new." Thunder cracked his words. He shuffled his feet a little faster. "Yes, we will be back soon enough unless it should rain." He eyed the sky. "A little rain and the sermon it will end more quickly." He shrugged. "But no one will ride Tio

Vivo in the rain. I do not think." He smiled complacence. "Besides it does not rain in Fiesta. Not often. Zozobra is dead. It will not rain."

Sailor walked beside him. He didn't give a damn about rain or sermons, all he wanted was someone to fix him up, fix him enough that he could meet the Sen tonight. His lips pulled back from his teeth. Maybe the Sen thought he was dead by now. Maybe the Sen meant to be awfully surprised when he showed up at midnight and no Sailor met him. He could see the Sen looking for Mac in the hotel lobby, wondering to Mac what had happened to Sailor. Snickering that Sailor was probably lying with a girl and had forgotten to show up. It was the Sen who'd get the surprise. Sailor would be there.

He hadn't attended the way Pancho was leading. Any more than he'd been listening to what Pancho was saying. The streets away from the Plaza were dark; Sailor recognized nothing until Pancho said, "This is where we go." Familiarity was shock. For they stood on the dark alien street where he had strayed the night before. Returning here now was the fearsomeness of a bad dream. A dream of wandering in a labyrinth, of being unable to escape from the murky maze, of returning over and again to this unknown yet terrifyingly known place. Pancho's big hand was on the closed wall. He said, "Come. This way, my friend."

He did not see the rejection on Sailor's face. The dark masked all but shape. Pancho opened a gate in the wall, bent down and squeezed through. Sailor moved after him. If this was the trap, and it was a trap, he could not refuse to enter. The whole town was a trap. He'd been trapped from the moment he stepped off the bus at the dirty station. Trapped by the unknown, by a foreign town and foreign tongues and the ways of alien men. Trapped by the evil these people had burned and the ash had entered into their flesh. That evil the Sen had seen and known and used. In Chicago he wouldn't have had a knife in his back; he would have been alert to Sen treachery. Now he was following a brigand into a box from which there was no escape. Only by shooting it out. The Sen would be waiting inside. There was no way to surprise the Sen; Pancho's bulk crunched loud across the sandy courtyard towards the small lamp shine at the rear. No way to walk quietly after Pancho, only to grip the pain and the ready gun. Pancho knocked at the low door, stooped to enter. Sailor, his temples wet, followed.

The Sen wasn't there. It must have been part of the bad dream to expect the Sen in this dump.

He must be running a fever. Pancho was his friend, mi amigo; the Sen couldn't buy Pancho away from him. He must have been nuts.

Pancho saw his face. He was gentler. "You are afraid? Do not be afraid. A knife it is nothing. I have many times been scratched with the knife. It is nothing. Nada!"

Sailor said, "I'm not afraid." He couldn't explain why he wasn't afraid now. He couldn't tell Pancho he'd been nuts. He looked at the room. A low room, rigidly clean, rigidly barren. An oil lamp on a bare wood table, bare wooden chairs; a bench of plaster, part of the wall. There was a small fire, piñon scented, in the little fireplace. A gaunt crucifix above it. The woman on the low stool before the fire was older than time. Shriveled, scant hair more colorless than white, her brown scalp shining bald through it—she sat there without words, without life, even in her eyes. Her gums mouthed a cigarette, as brown, as withered, as lifeless as her face, as her needle-thin arms. Pancho crooned over her. In Spanish; Sailor heard nothing but the repeated abuelita; the pantomimic cuchara, cuchara mas grande. He could catch the drift of it; Pancho was describing a great knife battle. But he wished Pancho would stop performing and get the old lady to fetch the doctor. He hurt.

Pancho turned back to Sailor. "It is all right," he beamed. "The little abuelita will take care of you. Let us now see the scratch."

Sailor stepped back. "Wait a minute." Suspicion webbed his face. "Where's the doc? I want a doctor."

Pancho's whole body grieved. "For why you want a doctor? I bring you to the little abuelita. She will take care of you. Because I ask it. Because you are my friend."

He didn't want a witch woman mumbo-jumboing over him. He wasn't a spic; he wanted a doctor. He wanted to be fixed up.

Pancho's grief quivered his lip. "You do not wish the abuelita to help you? She knows better how to take care of the knife cut than any gringo doctor could ever learn to know." His eyebrow cocked slyly. "Besides the gringo doctors might tell the police."

The pain was cutting hard. Something had to stop it quick. Pancho was probably right; the old witch would know all about knifings. She hadn't moved; she hadn't even appeared to understand what Pancho had said to her. Sailor reluctantly let Pancho help him slide off the coat. He unbuttoned his shirt; it was Pancho's hand that eased it away from the wound. Pancho turned him to the fire where the old lady could see the damage. If she was conscious. If she was anything but a grass-stuffed dummy, set before the fire to dry.

Pancho gave a rumble of joy. "It is nothing! Like I say, nada."

The croak was the old woman. "Nada." It must be her dirty spike of finger probing the pain.

Sailor cursed between his teeth.

Pancho danced about to face him. "A scratch. A pin. You were right, my friend. Nada!" He beetled his brows into Sailor's face. "You do not worry now about the abuelita? Look!" He ripped off his dirty shirt. His big finger jabbed the scars on the grimy sofa cushion of his chest. He turned his back, feeling for the welts. "This one," he jabbed. "And this one, how deep! But always the abuelita fix me up good like new."

The finger had stopped, only the fire heat licked at the sore. Sailor hadn't heard her leave the room; he didn't know she was gone until she returned with no more sound than a ghost. She carried a dirty wadded handkerchief. He watched her spread it on the table, watched her old twig of a finger pry into the stuff there, brown and withered old weeds like herself. Herbs! A knife in his back wasn't enough. He had to come to an old herb woman to get it fixed.

Pancho scoffed. "You are not afraid. You are a man." Thunder quavered across his voice and the lightning flickered like firelight across the room.

"No, I'm not afraid," Sailor denied. But the jumps in his stomach shook his muscles. He wasn't afraid of anything where a gun was good. But a gun wasn't any use now; you couldn't turn a gun on the germs of a witch woman and her seed bags and her spittle. You could only stand and take it, take the leap of pain, take her grunts and Pancho's encouraging, "Now it is good. Muy bueno. You will lie down and sleep, tomorrow you will not know there was an arroyo under your shoulder."

"Sleep where?" he scoffed. Pancho was helping him on with his shirt.

Pancho rubbed his big nose. He scrubbed at it and as if the thought sneezed out, he cried, "But where? Here with the abuelita. Always she has a room."

Sailor stopped him. "Thanks. But I can't go to bed. I'm seeing a guy later. Business deal. Give me a hand."

Pancho eased the coat on him. "It would be better you sleep—" He shut his mouth at Sailor's decision. "Okay," he said cheerfully. "You do not have to sleep. A bottle of tequila—that is as good as sleep." He directed. "Give me a dollar for the old woman."

Cheap enough. One dollar for a first-class infection. But the pain already was easing. He handed over a rumpled dollar to Pancho. He stood at the door while the two of them gibbered Spanish, Pancho's loud and bright, the old woman's a mutter. He waited, watching the lightning run with the wind across the barren patio. Waited until Pancho said, "We must go. We are now late."

He followed to the street, the dark, silent, known and un-known street. Walking into the whirlpool of wind towards gim-crack music and flowered lights. He asked, "What about the tequila?" as they breasted the bar of Un Peso. A burning drink would put the bone back into his spine.

Pancho slapped his pocket. "Why you think I need the dol-lar?" he gurgled. "The little abuelita has the worthless son. He brings from Mexico the best tequila."

"You mean you didn't pay her for fixing me up?"

"For that, it is nada," Pancho shrugged. "Who would not help a poor traveler who has been hurt?" His lips pursed. "Quien sabe? It might have been the worthless son who sharpened the knife."

"What for? Why would a guy I've never laid eyes on want to knife me?"

Pancho said gently, "Why you carry a gun?" He didn't want an answer. They were entering the Plaza, the Plaza with lights again garlanding it, with music strumming the whirling pink and green and purple horses; with the wind gyrating the smoke from the chimney pots of the little chile booths. He remembered how long since he'd eaten but he didn't want food. He didn't feel up to food. The couples, the men and women and children and sleeping babies over tired shoulders were seeping into the Plaza. The prize package which had held vespers and procession and sermon at the cross was consumed. They were buying another box of cracker jack now. Fiesta Sunday evening on the Plaza. In the bandstand the Conquistadores in their shapeless old-fashioned uniforms blared out of tune into the loudspeakers. The lights above the bandstand blazoned the faces circling it, the faces as still and remote as they had been in church or on the hill. In the distance was thunder.

Pancho said, "We are a little late. It does not matter. Ignacio can make Tio Vivo lively enough. Not so good as me. But good enough till I get there."

He lumbered over the paths; Sailor let the big man break trail. Outside the palings, Pancho pushed through the children to the fence. "Vaya, vaya, chiquitos! Out of my way, you little scrubs." His big hand lay on the gate.

Sailor touched his arm. "Mind if I sit inside for a little? To get my breath?"

Pancho's head thrust around, quick and anxious. "It cut deeper than we think?" He scowled. "You come inside, yes. You must rest. You should have this night a bed."

"I'm okay," Sailor grunted. "I can't go to bed until I get my business finished."

He went inside with Pancho. The string-bean Ignacio wound the crank while the old man made thin music on his old fiddle. Pancho spouted Spanish at both as his great hands took over the windlass. Ignacio plucked quickly at his guitar. The music quickened. Pancho sweated and heaved and Tio Vivo became Uncle Lively anew.

There was no place to sit but on the ground, on the bunch of dirty blankets that was Pancho's bed. Sailor let himself down before he fell down, he was light-headed as if he'd just got out of a hospital bed. The earth was good and solid to feel. He lit a cigarette and leaned on his good elbow. Then he lay back, his head crooked on his good arm. Above and around him Fiesta spun and sang and made laughter. He knew he was drifting away from it, knew and didn't care. It wasn't his Fiesta. These hicks thought it was something special. They should have seen the Chicago World's Fair. That was a show. He was thinking about the World's Fair when sudden panic came upon him and he fought to hold to this small tinkling square. He wondered in his panic if he were dying, if he were drifting out of this unknown into a vaster unknown. But he couldn't hold on; whatever purpose the witch woman had in her withered skull, it was stronger than he. The fog of blackness closed Fiesta away.

Five

HE MIGHT have been conscious the entire time he lay under the blackness. He heard the sound of Fiesta the entire time or thought he heard. And he thought he heard roar of thunder and splash of sheeted rain; he thought Zozobra's evil ghost had returned to spoil the fun.

All of this was in the dream, if it were dream, and he a mite floundering through the storm, trying to push through the blackness to the tinkle of music and shimmer of flower-like lights which grew beyond. When he fought most furiously he found he could open his eyes and he was lying where he had lain, on Pancho's dirty blankets. The merry-go-round was motionless, save for the sway of one gondola, the one where Pancho sprawled contemplating his own bare toes.

Sailor sat up, brought his wrist quick to his eyes, remembering as he moved that he should move warily. But there was no sudden pain, no pain at all but a vague smarting under his shoulder blade. The herbs weren't half bad. And it wasn't yet midnight, only a bit after eleven. He stretched up to his feet, picked up his hat from the earth, dusted it and set it on his head.

"Hola!" Pancho said. "You feel better, my friend?"

"Feel fine." He swung over to the gondola, leaned on it. "Business over early?"

"For me. The little ones must get some sleep. Tio Vivo does not stay open late like the saloons and the movie pictures." He removed his feet for Sailor to sit down. "Besides there was a little shower."

He hadn't dreamed. The wetness of rain smell was in the night. Sailor said, "I'm hungry. I don't know when I've eaten." Besides there was nothing to do in this dump to kill time waiting on the Sen but eat and sleep.

The bandstand was dark and only a drift of people was left wandering under the heavy wet leaves of the tall trees. In the street, there in front of the museum, a group was singing. "Ai, Yai Yai Yai," they sang, and they danced while they sang, a country dance, lively as Tio Vivo. Their laughter scrawled across the quiet Plaza. Behind them, against the museum wall, was the dark frieze of the Indian women and children, scornful in their immobility. *Ai, Yai Yai Yai* . . .

"How about a little food, Pancho?" There was time before the Sen.

"I think yes," Pancho said happily. He stuffed his feet into the dust-colored shoes, let the frayed laces dangle. "We will go to Celestino's booth. His wife, she makes the most fine chile on the Plaza."

Sailor had meant food, a steak and French fries, maybe a piece of cherry pie to top it. He didn't say anything. Maybe he was too tired to walk farther than the nearest thatched booth. As if Pancho held to his hand, he followed the brigand. Pancho was smarter than he. They could keep an eye on the merry-go-round, could see any stranger who approached it.

They sat on a wooden bench, sat in a welter of smells, garlic and onion and chile and cheese, coffee, fried beans and garlic and chile. Pancho bellowed flowery compliments at the woman behind the counter by the hot coal stove. She was big and billowing, black-eyed, black hair bound with a kerchief, a white apron, specked with chile red, over the billows. Sailor knew Pancho was being flowery from the toss of her head and the flirt of her black eyes. She wasn't young, her breasts were big with suckling, her arms were soft and brown but muscled like a man's. And her eyes were bright as a girl's. She was giving Pancho good as he gave her. He turned good nature to Sailor. "For me and you, my friend, Juana has fix the finest of enchiladas. And frijoles with the best chile."

"And coffee," Sailor said.

"And coffee. Fresh tortillas she will make for me, and for you because you are my friend. I tell her we do not want the slop she feeds the touristas. We are hungry men." He drummed his fists happily, sang in echo, "Ai yai yai yai . . ."

Sailor said, "You get around, Pancho."

The big man giggled. "I have known Juana since we were little fellows. And that Celestino, that no good. Drinking sotol with Ignacio when he should be washing the dishes for his good esposa. He is my primo, is Celestino. Primo—how you say—my cousin."

"You get around," Sailor repeated.

Pancho growled content. The woman's hand slapped the thin, round, white-and-blue tortillas.

She sang, "Hoopa, hoopa, hoopa—" Her bare hand flipped over the tortillas on the hot range.

"Maybe you can find out who knifed me."

Pancho's face was round and innocent as a baby's. And as sad. "I should know that?"

"No," Sailor denied. "I'm sure you don't know anything about it." He insinuated, "But maybe talking around the way you do, you'd hear who did it."

Pancho shook his head. "It is better you do not know. All this killings, they do no one good."

"I'm not going to hurt him," Sailor protested. He spoke slow truth. "I just want to ask him one question. Just one." Pancho's eyes were curious. "Who paid him."

"Don't you know that?" Pancho asked with disbelief.

"Yeah, I know." His hand dropped to his pocket, to the reassurance of steel. "I know but I want the guy to tell me. I want to hear him say it."

The woman set the bowls before them, red as fire, hotter than the flames of hell. The first mouthful scorched Sailor's throat, steamed his eyes.

"Take it easy," Pancho warned. "With the tortilla, so!" He folded a spoon of muddy blue, shoveled up chile and beans, opened his mouth. His face glowed happily. He had a spic throat for spic food.

Sailor stuffed white tortilla into his burning mouth, swallowed coffee. He took it easy after, hungry as he was, hungry enough to eat a horse, a raw one. But not hungry enough to burn up his mouth and throat and stomach with food tasting like lye. This wasn't chile and beans on Randolph Street. He took it easy and the devil food became good to eat. Enchiladas, with cheese and raw onions smothering the egg; tamales, the corn husks steaming; the bleached white kernels of posole. Pancho slathered everything with the chile gravy; Sailor went warily and the heat of food began to warm him, to fill the hollow curves of his insides. Pancho shoveled gluttonously into his mouth and the big woman leaned her big arms on the counter and smiled on the big dirty man.

When he was gorged, Sailor lit a cigarette, drew deep and good, shoved the pack at Pancho. "How about it?" he asked.

Pancho said, "Muchas gracias." He offered the pack to the woman before helping himself. She said, "Muchas gracias," and her smile was crimson velvet.

Pancho smiled back at the black-eyed woman. Pancho was in a familiar place with the comfort of a woman who spoke his own sweet tongue, his belly distended with the foods of his desire; the sweet sad singing, faint across the wet-leaved night, turned into lullaby by his own peace. Sailor dwindled into a loneness more intense than his dream; he was the wayfarer, the stray, the lost. He flipped away the butt, gathering his loneliness into a hard ball of anger. He stood, dragging bills from his pockets. He flung them on the counter. "Let's go," he said. He'd been knifed, he had the hand behind the killer to meet within the hour, but Pancho could dally with an old dame and ignore his needs.

Pancho, with a final burst of Spanish, a flowery doff of his battered old hat, lumbered after him. The brigand wiped the palm of his hand across his mouth. "It was good, muy bueno, no?" He unlocked the gate enclosing Tio Vivo, made for the gondola. He settled there, an elephant of a man, rubbed off his shoes and belched garlic.

Sailor leaned against the pole. He couldn't sit down; his nerves were too quick. He stood with his back protected, in an angle where he could watch the corner of La Fonda from where the Sen would come. If he came. He'd come because he thought Sailor was cut down.

There was a shape crossing cat-a-corner from the hotel. Sailor's eyes pried into the night. But it wasn't the Sen. It was a bigger man and he turned and passed the botica on the corner. Sailor's hand relaxed.

Pancho sighed. "When first I see you, you are alone and a stranger. I welcome you, the way it is the Spanish people welcome a stranger. My house is poor but I make you welcome. My house is your house. I give you my friendship. Perhaps you too will give the friendship." He sighed again. "Why did you come to Fiesta with a gun in your pocket?"

"I didn't come to your lousy Fiesta," Sailor flung at him.

Pancho's eyes were sad. "Ai yai," he keened.

Sailor grimaced but his mouth tasted bitter. "Maybe I got a gun so I'll stay alive. Maybe you might figure it that way. Sort of looks like I was right, doesn't it?"

It was past midnight. The Sen ought to be coming. But the street was dark. Even the hotel corner was deserted. The Sen wasn't coming. The Sen thought he'd taken care of Sailor; he didn't have to come. He thought no one would know there was to be a meeting at the Plaza tonight.

"Ai yai." Pancho grieved. "You are too young to die."

"That's what I think," he swaggered. "That's why I keep a gun handy." He'd have to go after the Sen again. With a handy gun. This time he'd get the dough. Even if he had to rough up the Sen, he'd get it. Time to leave this dump while he was still healthy. Healthy enough to leave. He tilted his hat.

Pancho came out of his sorrow. "Where do you go, Sailor?"

"Business."

"It is late." The old guy was scared for him. "Better to wait until tomorrow. Mañana. We will drink tequila and then we will sleep. We are tired. Tomorrow the business."

"I'm not tired. I feel fine. You drink the tequila." He'd never felt better. Now was the time. When the Sen wasn't expecting him. "See you later."

"You will come back?"

"Sure. I'll bring you a present." He'd give Pancho a fin, maybe a C note when he got the dough. For caring what happened to him. For fixing him up tonight. He'd give it to him just to see the guy's brown eyes get as big as moons. "Don't wait up," he laughed. "I may be late."

Under his breath Pancho said, "Vaya con Dios, Sailor."

The hotel lobby was quiet, quiet as a hotel lobby in a hick town that had never heard of a Fiesta. The night clerk didn't even look up from his ledger. The blue-smocked kid mopping the tiled floor looked but he didn't care. The news-and-cigar stand was shuttered with a steel fence. Sailor passed it, walking down the dim right-hand portal towards the elevator. At the far end of the portal someone stirred on the dark couch.

Sailor's hand caught the gun tighter, pointed it through his pocket. The voice of McIntyre came from the darkness, the ordinary voice of McIntyre. "I'd almost given you up."

His hand dropped the pocket into place before McIntyre could notice. "What's the idea?" he asked.

"I've been waiting for you a long time." Mac's voice was a little tired. "I'd almost given up. Thought maybe you weren't coming." He stepped quietly as a shadow to Sailor's side. "Ready to talk yet?"

Sailor made something like a laugh. "I might. A little later." He nodded his head towards the elevator sign.

Mac took his hand off Sailor's arm. "I wouldn't go up," he said.

When a cop like McIntyre said he wouldn't do something, said it like that, it was better to agree. To pretend to agree. Not to snarl: what the hell is it to you? The way he wanted to snarl it. He'd waited too long for the Sen to see it his way; he was ready for the showdown and McIntyre had no business sticking his snoopy nose into it.

Sailor set his jaw. "Why wouldn't you?"

Mac was casual. "I'm interested in keeping you on your feet."

"For a witness?"

"Could be."

He couldn't bolt to the elevator. He couldn't knock Mac out and get away with it. He had to stand there with frustration tying him in knots. Until he could get rid of Mac.

McIntyre said, "After tonight, I should think you'd like to talk."

"What about tonight?" he demanded.

"Sort of a close shave, wasn't it? If it had been a gun, someone who could shoot straight . . ."

He hadn't seen Mac. Not in the church or the procession or at the Cross of the Martyrs. He hadn't seen anyone; only white skirts and the brown mass of faces. He hadn't had his eyes open. He demanded, "How do you know about it?"

Mac said, "I'm interested in keeping you alive, Sailor. You and the senator both." He ran his eye down Sailor's coat to the right-hand pocket.

"Who stuck me?"

Mac shook his head. "The local police have him. For being drunk. A kid with a record. He isn't important." He touched Sailor's arm. "Come on up to my room. I've got a bottle. We can talk it over where it's comfortable."

He had better sense than that. Letting Mac feed him booze, loosen his tongue. But it was a way to get rid of Mac. Go up for a drink, then say goodnight. Get to the Sen.

He said, "I don't drink."

Mac said, "I do. And I need one."

He went along. Not back to the elevator. To the front staircase, up a long flight, down a long dim corridor. This was a hotel room, just a hotel room, nothing grand and Spanish like the Sen's.

Mac said, "Found a room yet?" He flung his hand towards one of the twin beds. "Get comfortable. Take off your shoes. Maybe you'd like to bunk here tonight. Be more comfortable than lying on the ground."

He scowled. Mac even knew that, knew he'd slept wrapped in Pancho's dirty serape. He ignored the bed for the stiff armchair. Fat chance he'd sleep with a dick. Talk and drink until you were tired enough to say anything, to spill. He wasn't going to spill until he got his hands on the money. If he didn't get the money, he'd talk. He lit a cigarette and threw the match on the rug.

Mac poured himself a slug. "Want to change your mind? Should think you'd need one after tonight."

"No, thanks. Strictly beer."

Mac said, "I prefer rye." He carried his tumbler to the bathroom, filled it with water. He came back and he wanted the chair. He wanted Sailor on the bed relaxed and himself in the chair. Sailor had outsmarted him there. Mac sat on the foot of the near bed holding his glass. "I prefer Irish, matter of fact. They didn't have any downstairs." He switched off the conversation. "Why does the senator want to rub you out?"

Sailor was flip. "Maybe he doesn't like me any more." This wasn't going to be hard. Mac was too tired to keep it up long. His eyes were wrinkled; when he took off the silly hat and hung it on the bed post, his head sagged.

"Why didn't he rub you out in Chicago where it would have been easy?"

"Maybe he liked me then."

Mac took a swallow of the drink. "What are you holding out for, Sailor? You'd be safer if you told me about it. Didn't you discover that tonight?"

Sailor looked at the smoke coming out of his mouth. "You're trying to tell me dead men can't talk?" He shook his head. "I've known that a long time, Mac. That's why I'm staying alive. I like to talk. When I got something to say."

Mac rubbed the sag of his forehead. "I might be wrong." He sounded a little surprised at the idea. "Maybe it's you who doesn't want the Sen to talk."

Sailor's eyes slit. He'd better go carefully: Mac was smart; Mac was used to making guys talk. He didn't need a rubber hose to do it. Not Mac.

Sailor said, "You could find out easy enough. Why don't you just up and ask him?"

Mac didn't say anything. He looked down into his glass as if it were a wishing well, not a bathroom tumbler half-full of rye and lukewarm water.

Sailor drew up his lower lip. "He's too big a guy, isn't he? You got to pick on somebody more your own size, don't you? You can't ask questions of a big shot like the Sen."

"I can ask them when I'm ready," Mac said. He took a drink out of his finger-smudged grail and then, he lifted his eyes to Sailor. "You could help me get ready a lot quicker."

Sailor let out a laugh. "You mean me work with the cops."

Mac ignored him. "What I can't understand is why you're still holding out. Unless you're expecting a bigger cut."

Sailor held his breath. Mac knew too much. He had to be

guessing but he guessed too much. His breath oozed out regretfully. "Now, Mac," he said. "You wouldn't expect me to rat on the Sen. After all he's done for me."

Mac's quiet eyes just looked him over. From his hat with the twigs and dirt on it, down his crumpled suit to his dusty shoes. Sailor's knuckles were tight. Mac wouldn't have looked at him that way in Chi. Sailor was the best-dressed, best-looking guy in the Sen's outfit. Mac knew it. Mac had no right looking at him as if he were a bum. As if the Sen had made a bum out of him. Mac knew this was temporary. Mac was trying to needle him. He held on to the palms of his hands and he laughed. "He's been like a father to me. He's been my best friend since I was a punk."

"Loyalty is the last thing I'd expect from you, Sailor. I knew you had ambition and a kind of pride." He shook his head. "If you'd used them right—" There was a lot of gray through Mac's hair. His hair wasn't as thick as it was when he'd first picked Sailor up for stealing cars. "But I didn't expect loyalty. The others have run out. Or been run out. I don't know why you're sticking."

He didn't know and Sailor covered his small triumphant smile. He didn't know how much Sailor had on the Sen. That's why he had Sailor up here, trying to find that out. Sailor said, like he was still the wide-eyed goofball he once had been, "He's been good to me. He took me uptown."

"There's just as much bad uptown as downtown. I guess you know that. Maybe there's more. It's just hidden better."

"You ought to know, Mac," Sailor said. He tipped his chair and pitched the cigarette butt out the window. "You're always digging for trouble." He let the chair down. "You look all in. I'd better run along."

Mac yawned. "The Sen's gone to bed. I wouldn't bother him." He yawned again. "We had a long talk tonight. He's tired out."

Sailor didn't quiver a muscle.

"He won't run out. Iris Towers isn't leaving for another week."

Her name didn't belong in Mac's mouth with the Sen's name. She was a white angel. Mac should know that if he was so smart.

"He doesn't feel so good tonight. Better wait till tomorrow." Mac was serious. Sailor cocked his shoulders. "Maybe he'd like me to cheer him up."

Mac looked up into Sailor's eyes. Sailor wouldn't look away because Mac's eyes weren't saying anything. They were colorless as water. Colorless as Mac's voice. "He'd like me to believe you killed his wife."

Rage was red in Sailor's brain. He began to curse and then he broke off because he wasn't sure. This could be Mac's trap. To make him talk. To make him spill. His tongue was thick. "I didn't—"

Mac interrupted, "I'd hate anything to happen tonight to make me not believe that. Better wait till tomorrow."

Six

HE DIDN'T have to leave the hotel. When he got to the foot of the stairs he could turn to the right. He could go to the Sen's room. He could squeeze the dough out of that skinny neck. He could knock it out of that weasel snout. He didn't have to use a gun.

The lying, double-crossing, skunking Sen. How did he expect to make that stick? Sailor's alibi was set. Set by the Sen himself and the Sen's brain man, Zigler. How did the Sen expect to break it down without giving himself away?

The Sen could do it. He could make up a yarn that would sound as true as if it were true. That was the kind of brain the Sen had, twisting lies around it and making them true on his oily tongue. Mac wouldn't believe that crap. Mac was too smart. Mac knew the Sen had done it himself. Mac could know if Sailor would talk. He ought to march right back up the staircase now and tell Mac the whole story, just like it happened. Mac would take care of him if he'd talk. And Mac would know who was telling the truth. Mac was too smart to believe the Sen's lies.

If he would talk. He could put the Sen where he ought to be. In the hot seat. Where he couldn't ever get at Iris Towers. If he'd talk. He was going to talk. He was going to tell Mac the whole thing, just what happened that night. It wouldn't put him on a spot; he'd be state's witness. The only witness. He and the Sen and the dead woman. No one else knew.

He'd talk just as soon as he got the money. He wasn't going to give up that kind of money. He needed it; it belonged to him; he was going to have it. What was owed and what he deserved above it. Five thousand dollars. The most he'd ever had at one time. Peanuts. He should have asked ten. The dough wouldn't do the Sen any good where he was going.

As soon as he got the money, he'd walk right back to McIntyre and spill. The Sen had crossed him; he deserved nothing better than the cross in return. He deserved a lot more than that. And he'd get it.

Sailor was at the foot of the stairs and he itched to turn right. Only trouble was if he did, and he and the Sen had it out, he was mad enough to do something dangerous. That's what Mac was warning him about. He mustn't kill the Sen, even in self defense. He mustn't do anything to make Mac believe he was a killer. Cool off first, see the Sen tomorrow early, hard and sure of himself. He turned left, out of the hotel.

Out on the street. The night cold closed around him. Cold enough for frost, on the earth. And he had nowhere to go. No place to lay his head. But on the earth. He shoved his hands in his pockets and hunched his shoulders. There should be a warm room, a soft enough bed. He shouldn't have to sleep in the dirt another night.

He didn't have to. He could have a room at the old witch's. He could have one of Mac's beds. He could even yet go wake up the Sen and sleep with his elegance. He was returning to Pancho out of choice. Better an old blanket under the cold sky with the warmth of Pancho's heart thrown in. With the safeness of a friend. He set out to the corner. In the deserted silence of the night his steps were loud, too loud. It was as if he were the only person left alive in an empty world, as if his clangor were disturbing the sleeping dead. He scudded across to the Plaza, wove through shadows to the red palings. Pancho's face peered over, little anxious lines netting his brown eyes. His smile rubbed them out.

"You are back. I hear you coming."

Sailor went in through the gate. "Did you think I wouldn't be?" he grinned. He went first, bunching his shoulders against the knife cold while Pancho wound the chain over the lock.

Pancho sighed, "I do not know. Who knows when a man goes if he will return? The good God has brought you back." He didn't lumber over to the gondola. He went to where the blankets were spread out. The serape, the best blanket were folded for Sailor. Pancho wrapped himself in the tattered one and lay himself upon the earth.

Sailor said. "I brought myself back. What were you worried about?" He wrapped himself in the serape, lay down beside the brigand. "I don't need that other blanket. You take it."

"It is for you, mi amigo." Pancho pulled it over Sailor, as if he were a little kid who'd kicked off the covers. "My fat, it keeps me warm," he gurgled.

Sailor lit two cigarettes, handed one over. "Did you think somebody was going to take another crack at me?"

Pancho sighed deep in his fat belly. "I do not know but I am afraid when you leave tonight. It is not good to go looking for a man when there is anger like was in you then." He sighed to his toes. "But the good God has taken care of you. When you leave me I say a small prayer that you will return unharmed." His voice smiled in the darkness. "And you return safe to me."

Sailor watched the thin blue swirl of smoke rise from his

mouth. It was good to rest with the heavy woolen robes warming him, and the cigarette good under the cold stars. He mocked gently, "I wouldn't expect you to go in for the holy stuff, Pancho. Not with all those knife scars you carry around."

Pancho said, "When I was young, sometimes there is a little trouble. Not bad trouble because the good God, He takes care of me. Should I not now say gracias to Him that He takes care of me?"

"I don't know." Sailor let the smoke slowly out of his mouth. "I stopped praying a long time ago."

"But one does not stop praying," Pancho stated.

"I stopped. It wasn't getting me anything. It didn't get my old lady anything and she was always praying. Nothing but work and more work and death. I don't know what she was praying for but it didn't get her anything."

"Maybe she pray for you," Pancho said slyly. "That the good God take care of you."

Maybe she had at that. It would have been like her. Even to pray for the old man. She wouldn't have prayed for herself. She never asked anything for herself. What had it got her? What it got anyone who didn't look out for himself first.

"Now that she is gone to Heaven," Pancho said comfortably, "maybe you better start praying the good God take care of you."

Sailor laughed. "I'll stick to my rod, thanks. I know what'll take care of me."

Pancho sighed down deep. "Then I will pray for you."

Sailor laughed louder. It was funny. Everybody preaching at him. A cop and an old brigand. If the Sen started preaching, he'd bust a gut laughing. He snickered, "I sure never sized you up as a Holy Joe, Pancho."

"Holy Joe, I do not think I know this," Pancho said in dignity. That meant he was offended.

Sailor said quickly, "I don't mean anything. You're a good guy, Pancho. You're my amigo."

"I am not so good," Pancho was comfortable again. "But it is good to be good. Maybe it does not fill the belly or warm the heart but it is good. It feels good." He crunched on the earth turning his bulk over. "A man wishes to die in his bed, I think. Even if he has no bed, no more than a serape under the stars. It is more comfortable that way." He propped his chin on his big fist. "It is in the Good Book, I think, if you live by the sword, that is the way you will die. It is not good to live by the gun, I think, Sailor."

"It is if someone is gunning for you," Sailor said flatly.

"But why? What have you done someone should wish to kill you? A young man like you?"

Sailor said out of his thought, "I haven't done anything. Nothing but want things better than they were. I only wanted what others had—I didn't want to be poor like my folks, like everyone around me. I wanted things better than that."

"What is for you, will come to you." Pancho's sigh shimmered like the dark leaves overhead. "The way of the poor it is hard. It is better not to be poor. If you must be poor, it is better to thank God for it. Better than the gun in the pocket, I think."

"Maybe no one ever kicked you in the teeth."

"Ho, ho, ho," Pancho laughed. Like that: Ho, ho, ho. "I have not been kicked around? A poor native not kicked around?"

"What do you do about it?"

"When I was young," Pancho said solemnly, "with the hot blood, you understand, there are the knife scars which you have seen. But now I grow old. I am at peace with everyone."

"Even with the guys that kick you around?"

"Even with the gringo sonnama beetches," Pancho said cheerfully. "When I am young I do not understand how it is a man may love his enemies. But now I know better. I think they are poor peoples like I am. The gringo sonnama beetches don't know no better. Poor peoples."

The Sen wasn't any poor peoples. He was a stinking rich bastard who would welch out of a two-bit deal. Loving him was like loving the Devil. Even the Good Book didn't tell you to love the Devil. Sailor said, "You're a good man, Pancho. You've been good to me. When this deal of mine comes off, I'm going to pay you back."

Pancho said, "With the Spanish peoples, there is no pay between friends. If this deal does not come off, my house is your house. I am your friend."

Pancho was a good guy. He meant it. He'd take Sailor home with him and they'd hoe the bean plot or whatever you did with beans. No thanks. He wasn't going to be trapped in this wilderness; the deal was coming off.

Sailor said, "Don't worry. The deal is coming off. Tomorrow." He yawned. "And I'll buy you the biggest case of tequila in town."

Pancho's voice was beaming. "That is good, Sailor. Tequila too is good for a man's soul, I think."

PART THREE
Baile

One

ON THE third day there was shouting and squeaking and whin-
neying and barking, laughing and crying and squealing and
singing. Sound heralded the morning. The morning of the Fiesta
children. When Sailor pushed open his eyes the children were
seething in the Plaza. Children with painted cheeks and flow-
er-decked hair, in glittering red-and-green skirts and long full
Indian calico skirts, in velvet trousers and cheesecloth britches,
children playing Navajo and Mestizo and Spanish señora, Mexican peon and Mexican charro and Spanish caballero; children
everywhere laughing and crying and shrilling their voices into
the sun.

Children in the streets striding horses and burros, children
leading dogs and cats and ducks and lambs and tiny sisters, a
child with a parrot perched on his shoulder, a child dragging
a little red wagon in which rode one goldfish in a bowl. Children swarming over the walks and the curbs, climbing into the
bandstand, running and pushing and swirling like dervishes.
Only the red fence kept Sailor safe from them. The kids pressed
against the palings, shouting, demanding Tio Vivo.

Old Onofre sat like a slab of wood on his camp-stool, his
fiddle across his knees. Sat there as if he didn't know the horde
was threatening the gates. Ignacio smoked a twisted brown cig-

arette, his guitar at his feet. His face didn't like kids any more than Sailor did. Pancho wasn't around.

Sailor flung off the blanket, shook himself out of the serape and pushed to his feet. The hard floor of the earthen bed left him, after two nights of it, full of kinks. His shoulder hurt. He settled his hat, pulled down his coat jacket. Wrinkled, dirty, unshaven, his tongue sour with last night's garlic, stoned by the jeers in the mouths of the ragged Mex kids outside the gate. Without being able to translate their tongue. He muttered, "Shut up, you little bastards." He didn't need them to tell him he'd have to clean up before he could see anyone today. He'd have to have a clean shirt, clean linen. His suitcase was where he'd left it, in the check room at La Fonda. He was ashamed to go for it, ashamed to walk into the hotel looking like a derelict.

He put a cigarette in his mouth, lit it. It tasted dead. There was no use asking Ignatz or the old man about Pancho; they wouldn't know even if they could speak his language. He brushed off the dust from his trousers and stalked to the gate. If any of the kids gave him a dirty look he'd slap them down so fast they wouldn't ever forget it.

His approach quieted them. In a fearful way. Their eyes, the battery of their unmoving eyes, lay on him as if they'd never seen a Gringo before. Flat black eyes, hundreds of them watched his hand unfasten the gate. Their silence heightened the whirl of noise in the streets outside the Plaza. Their silence was more menacing than any words they could have flung. He walked through the gate, banging it after him, fastening it. He got away from the kids quick; they let him pass. As soon as he had passed, their gibberish rattled again. He walked on fast. Kids weren't hypocrites. When the copper showed up they were like statues, hostile-eyed, withheld breaths. The older folks cranked up smiles or words, but not the kids. The old folks pretended that Fiesta made all a oneness in the land, Indian, Mexican, Gringo. The kids didn't hide their knowledge of the enemy among them. They were too smart.

The raw sunlight hit his eyes as he left the green shade of the Plaza, left the squawking kids parading their pets, pushing and yelling and slamming their sticky hands against your only suit. Yesterday dozens; today hundreds of them. He didn't know where to go next. He must pick up his suitcase. The thought of lugging it winced his shoulder. And after he picked it up what would he do with it? No Turkish baths in this two-bit-fifty-cent town. He walked down the street, passing the hotel where he'd bummed a bath and shave yesterday. The same shirt sleeves were leaning on the cigar counter. He didn't think it would work again, the guy had a snarl for a face this morning. Maybe he didn't like kids either.

It wasn't a good idea to try it again anyway. The guy might start wondering how the slick-looking fellow of yesterday morning had changed back into such a bum. He might wonder out loud. Sailor walked on and turned in at a café. Coffee would help him out.

It was a glossy place outside but inside it wasn't more than any hashery. He sat at the counter, ordered. The food wasn't good when it came, it was strictly hashery, but he ate it, drank a second cup of coffee. He felt better. He didn't look any better. The mirror over the cigarette machine showed him that. He fed in coins for Philip Morris, lighted up and went out on the street. The smoke didn't taste so bad after the coffee.

He could go to Mac. But he couldn't take his suitcase up to Mac's room. Mac would find a way to have a look in it. Mac wouldn't like the baby inside it. He'd get wondering. He'd get chilled up. Besides he didn't want to talk to Mac. He was mad enough to spill. He'd better stay out of Mac's reach until he had his gab with the Sen.

The Sen's last chance. He was a boob to give the Sen a chance after last night. He was a boob, yes, but he needed that dough. His roll had sunk and there wasn't anyone in Chicago to send him more. Ziggy in Mexico. Humpty and Lew, God alone knew where. The Sen right here. The Sen had to pay up. It wasn't a question of what was due any longer; not the way it had been. It was getting to be a matter of need.

He walked aimless, on down the street, past a men's store, a little one; past a five-and-ten, drug store, grocery store, Penney's, end of the block. He could buy a change of clothes; razor, tooth brush and stuff. But after he bought them, he had no place to use them. He turned around and walked back up the street, back to the squealing Plaza. Tio Vivo was spinning. On the circular bandstand a brass band had moved in; a little kid with a reedy voice and a cowboy hat sang into the mike. Kids were still swarming everywhere.

He walked to the corner, ducking the ones coming out of the corner drug store dripping ice cream cones and greasy popcorn. He crossed over to La Fonda, only because there weren't kids there. He wouldn't go in; he wouldn't dare go in looking like this. If the Sen saw him now he wouldn't pay up a thin dime. Not without real trouble. He cursed the big hotel, cursed every room in its terraced bulk. All those rooms and baths, and he couldn't borrow one long enough to look like a human being. Long enough to get the scum off his teeth. He walked on by, muttering his helpless anger.

He felt the hand on his arm and his own right hand jammed his pocket before he looked down. It was a kid. A dirty little kid, a pipe-stem kid in colorless jeans and a torn shirt. He'd got away from the Plaza of kids and one came tagging him.

"Get the hell out of here," Sailor said. He bumped off the thin brown hand.

The kid said, "Don José he wants to see you." The kid's black eyes were too big for his face.

"Who the hell is Don José? What does he want with me?"

"Don José he wants to see you," the kid parroted in his spic accent.

He was ready to tell the kid to tell Don José where to head in but it came to him in time. Don José was Pancho Villa; Don José was his friend. Maybe Don José had miracled a bathroom with a shower.

He made sure. There could be another Don José; somebody the Sen had dug up who could thrust a knife straight. "Where is he?"

The kid rattled. Don José was at Tio Vivo and the kid was going to get a free ride for running after Don José's friend if he caught up with Sailor . . . Sailor tossed a dime. "Have one on me," he grunted.

"Gracias, Señor! Gracias." You'd think he'd thrown the kid a grand. The thin dirty face flashed a quick smile before the kid's bare brown feet cut out across to the Plaza.

Sailor cut across too. So he wouldn't have to pass La Fonda again. There were clean people coming out of it. He knew Pancho hadn't uncovered a bathroom. By his smell he knew Pancho didn't bother about soap and water and a scrub brush for his teeth. But something must be up. Pancho wouldn't have sent for him if something wasn't up.

He had to wade through the anthill of kids to get to Pancho. Even then he wouldn't have made it to the fence without stepping on a mess of them if Ignatz hadn't noticed him and signaled Pancho. It must have been a signal. At least after the flip of greasy black hair, Pancho's eyes searched over the heads and his warm anxious smile found Sailor.

Sailor had to stand there until Pancho finished winding up Tio Vivo. Like he was some kid's old man. He looked around for Pila but she wasn't there. Too early for the older gang.

As the merry-go-round began its unwinding, Pancho lumbered over to the palings. "Vaya, vaya ustedes!" he yelled at the kids. And something about mi amigo. He must have told the kids to let Sailor through. They weren't willing but he could nudge his way forward.

"What's up?"

Pancho wiped away his face sweat with the sleeve of his shirt. "It is the abuelita. She wants you should come to her."

"What for?" He was suspicious. A payoff. Or the cops. Asking questions. Questions he wasn't going to answer.

"It is to fix—how you say—the shoulder."

"My shoulder's okay."

Pancho shook his head. "You must go, my friend. You do not wish poison to set in. You must go to her."

It felt all right. A little stiff but nothing sore about it. He didn't want her poking and pushing around it again. Yet he didn't know what she'd done to it. The weeds and herbs might have to be changed or there'd be infection. He couldn't know, he'd never gone to a witch doctor. The Sen had the best doc in town for Sailor, not even a political one, the time Sailor had cut his arm. On a broken windshield.

He asked, "You'll go along?"

"How can I go?" Pancho rolled his eyeballs and his hands. He didn't have to explain. Right now the kids were like savages, ready to break down the barricade if Tio Vivo didn't hurry up and spin again.

"I don't know where she lives," Sailor told him. He was ready to give up the whole idea, glad to give it up. He wouldn't die of blood poisoning this soon; he could see her later when Pancho was through working; when he'd tended to his business.

"Lorenzo will show you the way. Lorenzo!"

It was the same kid, the same dirty little bag of bones. Pancho rattled Spanish at the kid, threats and promises. The kid rattled back just as fast.

Sailor said, "Come on. I'll give you another dime." Get it over with. Maybe afterwards he could borrow the abuelita's bathroom and get himself cleaned up. Maybe there'd be a razor around he could borrow too. He pushed away from the fence, through the kids. Lorenzo tagged after him.

After they were clear of the Plaza he asked, "You Pancho's kid? Don José?"

"Oh, no!" Lorenzo said. And after a moment, "Don José he is my uncle." He was proud of it. Don José was the most wonderful man in the Fiesta of Children. The man who owned Tio Vivo. He was more important than the Sen had ever been.

"You know where you're taking me?"

"Si." The word came long drawn from his lips. "The abuelita," he explained, "she is my grandmother. Abuelita is grandmother. In Inglis-speaking."

Sailor's eyes opened. "Pancho's mother?" The small dried up twig, mother to big fat Pancho? "Pancho. Don José."

"Oh, no!" The kid was amused.

"But he's your uncle?"

"Si." Again the "e" sound dragged out. Again the kid was proud.

He didn't care about Pancho's family relations. He'd just been making conversation, to keep from walking in silence. Because he didn't want to go back to the old crone but must go. It was so ordered.

They went on down the narrow street. He recognized the house though he hadn't before seen it by daylight. Flush on the street, the blank wall of the gate closed. The kid stopped at the gate. "You geemme a dime now, Meester?"

His hand was out, his eyes scooting back up the street to where Fiesta flourished. "You take me to her house," Sailor said. "That's the bargain."

The kid didn't want to waste the time. But Sailor didn't want to cross the alien courtyard alone, stand alone outside the door. The kid pushed open the gate and Sailor followed, ducking under the frame. Ducking in time to keep from cracking his head, remembering how Pancho had bent down to go through the gate last night.

The kid ran across the barren sandy patch of the courtyard to the door. Sailor crunched after him, regular steps, just as if he didn't feel funny about coming here. He wasn't scared the way he'd been last night; he just didn't like coming. He didn't belong in this kind of a setup. He was a city guy, used to the best after he met up with the Sen. He'd have the best again, too; splitting with the Sen was going to make things better not worse. He was going to get that wad and do better on his own. Mexico City was just as swell as Chicago. Better, Ziggy said. It wasn't grimy or too cold or too hot and there were flowers blooming everywhere. It was going to be like a wonderful dream only it would be real.

"You geemme a dime now, Meester?"

He said, "Sure." He'd like to keep the kid along until he was safe out of here but he didn't have the heart. He been just as hungry-looking and dirty himself once when a dime looked big as a grand. He dug in his pocket. "Sure," he said. "Here's a quarter. Keep the change."

"Gracias, Meester!" The kid bowed. The quarter made his eyes bigger than ever in his ragged little face. He stuck it in his jeans and skipped. Sailor knocked on the abuelita's door.

There was some kind of sound from inside that might have meant come in; he went in. The old woman was by the cold fireplace but she wasn't alone. On the wall bench were two other dames. One as old as the abuelita, older, her black shawl pulled over her thin white hair, her hands clutched on her cane. It wasn't a real cane, it was the dead twisted branch of a tree. She bent over it, her lips mumbling without sound. The other woman was younger, there was a familiar look to her but she didn't look like anything. Her face was dull, only her dark eyes had any living quality. She wore rusty black, like the old woman, the shawl pushed back over her dark hair. Her breasts were big with milk, her hands work-knotted as his mother's had been. He knew then what was familiar in her; she was the hopeless face and sagging shoulders and defeated flesh of all poor women everywhere. He wanted to bolt. Even in this small way he did not want to be pushed back into the pit of the past. The pit he believed he had escaped forever.

The abuelita said something. It was in her own tongue and the thongs of helplessness wound tighter about him. The woman from whom he had turned his eyes said in her heavy accent, "She say take off your coat."

He looked at the abuelita. Her claws pantomimed it. He turned an almost frantic look towards the old crone and the work woman. They had not moved. They weren't going to move. They had come to see the show. Or they'd come to gossip by the cold hearth and this was all a part of the everyday at the abuelita's.

He took off his coat, began unbuttoning his shirt. Unbuttoned it slowly, feeling naked, ashamed. He hadn't known shame since he was a kid, a cowed kid taught shame by his mother's old-fashioned scruples. In the Sen's world nobody thought anything about taking off his shirt before strangers. The Sen did half his business while he was dressing.

Sailor didn't try to track down his queasiness; shaming the shame, he pulled off his shirt and stood there as if he were naked, not merely half-naked. Fear had returned to him, atavistic fear; he was helpless before three witches. It was this which had delayed his hand; before their incantations he needed all the protective barriers of civilization, even a dirty shirt. He knew now the root of his hesitancy in coming to this house; a fear of the primitive, root fear of the alien and the strange which had been threaded through these three days. He was a city man. The city didn't have to be Chi. He'd been in Detroit and Minneapolis and Kansas City, once to Philadelphia; he was at home in any of them. He wasn't a foreigner on city streets. But this place wasn't civilized. Behind the strangeness, lay the primitive; this land was too close to an ancient past. He would not be caught in its caves; he would get away before he was buried, before the stone woman turned him to stone.

He swaggered, "Okay, Grammaw, how does it look?" He was shivering as he had last night, unable to control the shakes, even before she laid her lifeless fingers on the place of the knife.

He smelled of the earth and Pancho's serape and unwashed sweat, his breath smelled of stale garlic. He was unclean and he knew himself to be. Yet he had to stand there naked in his

filth while she wadded and mumbled and pried and smelled him.
While the other witches watched with obscene eyes.

He took it she was satisfied by the mumbling, by the little
shakes of her head. He took it she was finished with him when
she began tucking the little packets of twigs back into her dirty
handkerchief.

"Got a place I can wash up?" he asked.

She didn't know a word he said but the younger woman did.
"You wish to wash?"

"Yeah." He gathered up his shirt and coat. She led him
into the kitchen, a big old-fashioned kitchen with a coal stove
warming it. The table and chairs were old and ugly; green-and-
red-and-yellow plaid oilcloth was tacked on the table top. She
poured water from a tea kettle into a tin basin, cooled it from the
tap, set it on the table. She put a broken cake of Ivory beside it.
Then she went away.

No bathroom. Outhouse in back, you could see it from the
kitchen windows. Some way to live. Even if you were a bunch of
old witches. This one was back with a clean towel for him. He
said, "Thanks. Gracias." They'd have him turning into a spic if
he stayed around much longer.

She sat down on a wooden chair and he saw she'd brought
needle and dark thread. She was mending the tear in his coat.
He didn't have the nerve to do a sponge bath before her. Just
his hands, but he washed them as if they were embedded with
grime. Kept washing them, hoping she'd get out and let him
splash his face. She didn't. He dried his hands, took up his shirt.

She said in a heavy accent, "If you wait a minute, I will mend
your shirt."

He gave his head a shake. "Thanks. Haven't time." He wanted

to get away fast. From his mother mending his broken clothes. He hadn't worn patches since he left home. He wasn't going back to patches. He'd throw these clothes away. Tomorrow. He was awkward with the shirt, the new dressing burning his shoulder; she came over to him and helped him.

He said again, "Thanks. Gracias," even as he withdrew from her. She helped him with the coat. Her hands were work-veined like those of slum women.

He could get out now. Almost as dirty as when he came, and his shoulder jumping when it hadn't hurt before. He strode into the front room, handed a dollar to the abuelita. She'd probably have to split with her big fat nephew who'd brought him here when he'd wanted a doc and no questions asked. He'd be out of this town by night, with his dough. Pick up a plane in Albuquerque and be in Mexico City tomorrow. Get him a real doc there. Get him a new suit. Tomorrow night he and Ziggy would be sitting in the best hotel ordering champagne. Toasting the Sen, the late, unlamented Sen.

Two

IT WAS past ten-thirty. He couldn't waste any more time. He didn't want the Sen to skip out on him. The Sen had seen him without a shave before. The La Fonda swells could turn up their noses; they wouldn't when he had that five grand in his pocket. The Sen didn't have any choice after last night; he knew he had to pay up or Sailor would hand the noose to Mac. He knew Sailor wouldn't be taking any more of the stall. What the Sen didn't know was that choice had been eliminated; he was going to pay and swing both.

The Plaza was strumming, music on the bandstand, music on twirling Tio Vivo, strolling musicians on the paths. Chimney pots smoking, costumes glittering, voices lifted in laughter and singing. Sailor didn't enter the square. He walked on up the street, crossed to La Fonda. He paid no attention to those coming out or those entering with him. He walked right on in. The lobby was seething this early, like a convention, a convention of fancy-dressed actors. There was a lot of noise coming from the bar. In the patio the sun and the fountain, the geraniums and the striped awnings of the swings and umbrella tables were like something on a stage.

Sailor didn't waste time, he made for the house phone, called the Sen's number. He could hear the ringing, over and again, no answer. He clapped down the phone. The Sen didn't get up early; not unless he was running out. Maybe he'd told them not to put through any calls. Sailor strode to the elevator, rode up to four. His knock on the door was the only sound in the empty corridor; he tightened the hand in his right-hand pocket while his pounding shattered silence. But there was no answer from within.

He went back to the elevator, put his finger on the buzzer and left it there. The Sen was probably in the Placita having his morning cocktail and coffee. Dressed up clean and white, using his voice tenderly on Iris Towers' clean whiteness, fooling her with soap and water and a razor and his rotten sweet voice.

The pretty little elevator girl didn't say anything when Sailor got in. Didn't give him hell for hanging on the buzzer, the way a Chi yahoo would have done. And get his teeth broken for it. The elevator slid down in silence. He left it in the same silence, walked up the portal, seeing no one. He couldn't go out in the Placita after the Sen, not until he was clean. He turned downstairs to the barber shop. It looked swank as the hotel but there were only two operators and both chairs filled. He walked through the room, out to the street and across to a shop that looked like any barber shop. He didn't have to wait; the customers of this one weren't steaming out hangovers, they were dancing in the streets.

"Shave and shine," Sailor said.

The fat, bald barber wasn't gabby. Maybe he wanted to close up and get out into the streets too. The job didn't take long. Sailor looked a lot better already.

The biggest men's store was closed, Labor Day; but the little one further on down was open. He bought a blue shirt, a pair of socks and shorts. He started back to La Fonda but he changed his mind on that. Somebody might get officious; all Sailor needed right now was a bastard to get officious. There'd be trouble. He didn't want trouble; he was saving that for the Sen.

He went to the bus station, changed in the can, wrapped his dirty laundry and checked it in a locker. He looked okay. He looked swell. He could sit in La Fonda all day if he wanted to. Sit there until he caught up with the Sen. He went back to the hotel. It was noon now. He pushed into the Cantina. The Sen wasn't there. Hundreds of costumes were cramming the cocktail room but no Sen. He edged and shoved through to the Placita. The head waitress was crisp as her white dress. But polite. She said, "I haven't a table right now."

He could tell that. He said, "I'm just looking for a friend. Thanks." He counted faces. And he saw hers. Delicate, fine, her silver-gold hair tracing the shape of her face. There were white flowers in her hair; her dress was white peasant stuff, the blouse cut low off her golden shoulders. The mucker, Kemper Prague, was pressing against her shoulder but he couldn't touch her. She was clean as sunshine; the other women looked as if they'd been soaked in rum all night, their eyes haggard, but she was clean. The men looked like hangovers, young men, not an old weasel among them.

Sailor moved his eyes clockwise across the tables, counterclockwise back again to hers. The Sen wasn't there; he wasn't in the Placita. Sailor could have walked over to her table, it was only a few paces. He looked a lot better than the guys she was sitting with. She wasn't a princess or an angel from heaven; she was Iris Towers, a Chicago girl. The same as any other Chicago girl only her father was a big millionaire. He could walk right over and ask it courteously like he'd learned from the Sen. "Do you know where I could find Senator Douglass?" She'd be polite too because she was brought up that way. She'd tell him where the Sen was. She'd know. He stood there and her head moved and he was looking into her eyes, her clear blue eyes. She looked at him. But there was no recognition; only that a man was standing there looking at her. He turned on his heel and left.

He didn't care whom he elbowed getting out of the Cantina. He saw no one, only the fact that the Sen still wasn't there. There was the jingle of sleigh bells, the thud of drums, as he stepped into the lobby. And a crowd blocking further exit, a solid half circle moving in to where four Indians stood, Indian men, painted, feathered, looking like Indians should, like Indians in a book. Two were naked but for the bells on their wrists and ankles, the beaded breech clouts, the gaudy circles of parrot feathers decorating the clouts before and behind. Their braids wound with ribbons, a few feathers in their hair. The other two men wore bright shirts and blue jeans, moccasins on their feet, silver and turquoise beads and belts. One thudded an enormous tapering drum, almost waist high, hung with feathers. The second began to chant as Sailor moved into the circle, and the naked Indians were dancing. Pawing and thudding the floor, bells ringing, feathers shimmering, naked muscles tight under lean brown flesh. The dance ended as sharply as it began; the singer was silenced, the dancers circled bell-like, quietly; the drum was a muffled roll.

It began again with the high-pitched call. With hoops now, a dozen or more thin willowy hoops in the dancers' hands. Wilder than before, shivering their bodies through the hoops, bent double through the smallest circles, their feet beating incessant with the drums, the bells jeering. The Sen ought to be here. The Sen liked to go back to Chicago and tell about the fancy things he'd seen.

Sailor's eyes quickened about the massed circle. Across was McIntyre. Mac's eyes were watching the Indian dancers, not scanning the crowd for the Sen or for Sailor. That meant Mac knew where they both were. That meant Sailor could find out about the Sen.

Another dance. A warrior dance, the dancers lunging at each other, without warning letting out startling whoops. It made him jumpy. Then it was over, the dancers jingling away on soft feet, the drum beating away into silence. The crowd broke, speaking silly things to exorcise the spell.

Sailor started around the outskirts, to come on Mac by accident. His step faltered. He picked up his stride again; he didn't want to think about that. About the Indian faces with no expression; even when they war-whooped, no expression. Like the Indians in the street and under the museum portal. Under the brown stone faces, this violence. Under the silent wastes of this land, their land, what violence? The fear, the unknown fear was rising in Sailor but he set his steps hard, pushed it down. And Mac wasn't around.

Sailor went down the right-hand portal, crossed the lounge, looked in the New Mexican room and the dining room. No Sen. No Mac. He could wait. He didn't have anything else to do. More comfortable here than walking the dirty streets. He was in luck for once. Somebody moved off a leather chair right in the middle of the lobby, across from the desk. Nobody could come in the side door or front door, nobody could leave the bar or go to the desk without him seeing. He'd like to try the house phone again; it was over there, the Sen might be on the other end of it. But the Sen's room had been too empty and he didn't want to have to stand up all afternoon for nothing.

He lit a cigarette, nice hammered-copper ash tray at hand. If he only had a beer, he'd be more comfortable than he'd been since he blew in. He rested, comfortable, in the chair. Only his eyes moving, watching left and right, not seeming to watch. He didn't need to keep his right hand where it usually was. There wouldn't be any punk stalking him in the center of La Fonda lobby.

"Looking for the senator?"

He lifted his eyes easy. "Hello, Mac. How's Fiesta?"

Somebody got up from the couch next to his chair, as if they'd been holding the place for Mac. Mac sat down.

"Viva las Fiestas," Mac said. Even he was turning Spanish like his hat and sash.

"Sure," Sailor said. He wasn't going to be in a hurry to talk about the Sen. Mac wasn't apt to get too far from the subject. "When you going back?"

"Maybe tomorrow," Mac said. He wasn't gabby this afternoon. He was taking things just as easy as Sailor. "When you going back?"

"I don't know," Sailor said offhand. It sounded too much as if he were waiting for orders from the Sen, and he added, "I haven't made up my mind yet."

"You're going back?" Mac didn't have any expression on his face.

"To Chi?" Sailor shouldn't have sounded amazed, even to his own ears. But he was. The idea of Mac thinking he wouldn't be going back to Chicago. He couldn't wait to get back. Back where you knew what to expect, back where there were lights and buildings and shows and people—and life! He woke up. He wasn't going back. He was going to Mexico. His laugh wasn't good. "What made you ask that?"

Mac was calm as ever. "I thought maybe you weren't counting on going back."

"I can't wait to get back." State Street, Michigan Boulevard, North Shore, The Stevens, the Palmer House, the Lake, the cold wet wind off the Lake. Field's and the Athletic Club and the Trib Tower and Ziggy's office right about next door. Ziggy's office was closed up. For good. Sailor wasn't staying in this dump anyway. He was going down to Mexico City and it was a city, a swell city. Ziggy knew; he'd been there. Sailor didn't say it again, not out loud; there was only the echo in his ear: I can't wait to get back.

There were other places as good as Chicago. Plenty of them. He took a deep drag off the cigarette. "I thought you'd be waiting for the Sen."

Mac said, "I think he'll be leaving tomorrow."

He wasn't sure the way Mac said it, whether Mac had found out all he wanted and was taking the Sen back with him or whether the Sen was running out and he was just tagging along. The Sen wasn't going to wait for Iris Towers, or he'd changed her plans. The Sen didn't like Mac's breath warming his neck. He didn't know Mac would be plodding behind him waiting for the break. The Sen's time was running short. Sailor was the break. The Sen would settle today or Sailor would give Mac what he wanted.

He asked it casual. "Where is the Sen today? You seen him?"

"He's sick," Mac said.

Mac was trying to catch Sailor off guard. That's what he was doing sitting here, popping out with stuff you weren't expecting, with that dead-pan face of his.

Sailor didn't even move his little finger. He just laughed. "What's the matter with him? Too big a night?"

"I don't think that's it. Not all of it." Mac threw another fast one. "How's your shoulder?"

"Fine." The Sen wasn't in his room. Unless he was holed up there not answering the phone, not answering the door. Unless he was that sick. He wouldn't be that sick with Iris Towers likely to be outside the door, on the other end of the phone. "It was only a scratch," Sailor said. "Some guy must have made a mistake."

"Yeah, it was probably a mistake," Mac droned.

He could be meaning the guy was a poor judge of distance. He didn't know about Sailor ducking just at the right time. That was one thing even Mac couldn't know. When lightning would flash. "What's the matter with the Sen?" He brought it back.

"I don't know. Just not feeling too good, according to Amity. You ready to talk yet, Sailor?"

"What about?" He was just as noncommittal as Mac. He'd play it Mac's way. But he knew where the Sen was. Mac had told him that much. Not that Mac knew he'd been giving out. Sailor should have thought of it before; it was one of the Sen's favorite dodges. Holing up in another guy's room when he didn't want anybody to know where he was. When he'd come in from Washington unexpected to do a little business. Holing up in Sailor's apartment.

The Sen might be in Amity's. He might be in Iris Towers' room, lying on her bed, sick because he was worried, because things hadn't gone his way for once. Because Sailor had roughed his game.

"Where were you the night of Mrs. Douglass' death?"

A quick pitch but the same old question. Sailor was gentle.

"Why, Mac," he said. "You know where I was. I was down at Ziggy's working on the books. We worked there till your boys came in to tell us about the tragedy. We never left the place."

"You never left the place."

"You know we didn't, Mac"

"I'm not asking about Zigler," Mac said. "I'm asking about you."

"For God's sake, Mac. You know every step I took that night. You sat in on the testimony."

"You never left the place," Mac repeated.

His own lips were as tight. "I never left the place," he lied with emphasis. It was kind of funny swearing to a lie now and maybe by evening telling Mac the truth. Mac wouldn't think it funny; he was used to it. Mac would know it was all in the game. "You're not trying to pin that rap on me, Mac?"

Mac said, "I don't pin raps, Sailor. I'm after Mrs. Douglass' killer."

"You're not after me."

"Maybe not."

"You're not." He'd talk this much. "If you were you wouldn't have been here ahead of me. You'd have been trailing." He explained Mac's own moves to him. As if Mac didn't know what he was doing. "You didn't get here first because you knew I was heading this way. I didn't know it myself until the day I took the bus."

Mac didn't answer him. Not straight. "What happened between you and the Sen?" He wanted the answer to that one. Something different in the way of asking.

"What do you mean?" Sailor sounded as innocent as he wanted to sound. Let Mac take the lead here. Until later when he spilled the whole business. But as he spoke they came out of the Cantina, Kemper Prague and the lovely Iris Towers. They gave Mac his question.

"It wouldn't be his new friends?"

They didn't come across the lobby. They went out of sight into the left-hand portal. Going up to see the poor sick Sen. The hidden Sen. Take him a drink. Or an aspirin. Or a satin white hand for his aching head.

Sailor was short. "No." He couldn't say that he and the Sen were the same as ever with the Sen accusing him to Mac last night. That was too raw. That was why he'd spill everything to Mac once he collected. He had to collect first or Mac might take the Sen away before Sailor had his chance.

Mac said mildly, "I didn't know. See you later, Sailor," and he was gone. No excuses, just gone, down the right-hand portal. To ride up in the elevator with them. To find out where the senator was holed. Beating Sailor to it. And the Sen's new friends, his rich society friends wouldn't even notice the quiet man in the funny Spanish hat and sash. Any of the old organization would. Not one of the old organization who wouldn't spot a cop on sight.

He was too restless to sit there longer. The Sen wasn't going to come out, not until he thought he was safe. Mac would find out where and Sailor could get it out of Mac later. He could, if he had to, make a deal with Mac. Promise the story if he could have fifteen minutes with the Sen alone first. That was all he needed. He could cut it down to ten.

He might as well eat lunch. Not here where they'd soak you; he'd go back to the Kansas City steak house. Eat his kind of food. Fool around a little, have a cold beer later, get back to the hotel around cocktail time. If he couldn't get to the Sen by that time, make the deal with Mac. One thing sure; he had to get out of town tonight. If he didn't, Mac might see to it that Sailor turned back to Chicago tomorrow. He'd have to say he was returning with them tomorrow and pull a sneak tonight. After he'd told Mac the truth.

The momentum of music and color and motion, of sound and smell had increased on the Plaza. Fiesta was revolving to climax, as if by moving faster and faster the end might be delayed. As if accentuation of its gayety might delay the return to tomorrow's dull everyday.

Sailor walked in the street, it was simpler than being pushed off the high curb by the sidewalk crowds. Past the corner of Tio Vivo, Pancho sweating at his toil; Ignatz and Onofre plinking and plunking mechanically. Past the thatched booths, past the chile and the pop and the cardboard canaries swinging on their willowy rods. Past the balloon man. Stepping aside for the burro carts and the horses with their costumed riders, past the corner where strolling musicians sang to little clusters of listeners.

"Hello, Sailor."

She giggled when she said it, giggled and blocked his way. It was Rosie, with the paint on her mouth and cheeks, the invitation in her black eyes and in the twist of her immature body. She was arm-linked with a different girl today, a girl lush as the flaming roses in her hair, a girl with rippling black hair and swelling breasts and wide hips. A girl with a dirty neck and a gum-chewing mouth and wide beautiful eyes.

"Looking for Pila?" Rosie giggled.

He said, "No," and started by them.

"I bet Pila she is looking for you," Rosie said.

He'd push her out of the way, the little slut, if she didn't move. Her and the exquisite slattern with her. He made another attempt to pass.

"I bet she is looking for you to say goodbye," Rosie giggled.

He stopped. "Is Pila going somewhere?"

"Yes, she is going." She evidently couldn't talk without the silly giggle.

"Where?"

"She is going home," Rosie said. "Her father he has come to take her home. Back to San Ildefonso. They are Indians." Her giggle went up and down again like the shrill of a flute.

"I know it," he said brusquely. "When is she going?" He owed her a pop or another ride or a permanent wave. He'd promised her.

Rosie shrugged. "I don't know when," she sing-songed in her accent. "Maybe tonight." He'd been interested; she hadn't expected it. She'd thought he would laugh at Pila too. He wanted to knock the frizz off her head, knock the paint off her mouth.

The slattern put her slow black eyes into him. "Muy macho," she slurred.

Rosie remembered her then and perked up. "This is my friend, Jesusita. 'Sita, this is Sailor I was telling you about."

Jesusita said, "Hallo." With the same look.

If he was going to be here, time on his hands, he might stick around with these two. He might give the slattern a knowing eye. She'd be worth a trip to the Federal Building. But he was getting out. He didn't need to fool around with slovenly dames; he'd have his pick in Mexico City.

He said, "Tell Pila I want to see her before she goes," and he moved quick, past them, out of the Fiesta square, covering the quarter block and turning the corner to the steak house. He didn't look back. He didn't know if Rosie had any intention of passing on the message. Nor if Pila could get away from her old man for the last afternoon of Fiesta on the Plaza.

He walked on fast to the restaurant. It wasn't crowded this time of day. If Pila was staying over till tonight he could treat her to the permanent wave. With the Sen's money. He'd have it tonight. He had forty dollars left and a pocketful of change. Not much. Not enough to take care of Pancho and Pila like he wanted to. Enough for now. He'd been saving money, sleeping and eating and doctoring with the natives. If anyone had told him before he left Chi that he was going to move in with a spic carnival operator and play Lord Bountiful to an Indian kid during Fiesta, he'd have told them how nutty they were. If anyone had told him he was going to take in a Fiesta he wouldn't have known what they were talking about. Travel was sure broadening, he didn't think. That was just another of the Sen's crummy ideas. Maybe it was broadening if you had your dead wife's fifty grand to splurge with.

He paid the check, stuck a toothpick in his mouth. Outside he threw away the toothpick. The Sen had taught him better. He walked back up the street, taking his time. That was all he had to do now, waste time. Until five o'clock. It wasn't quite three.

Three

THE CLOUDS had piled up over the cathedral, not storm clouds, big white ones, soft and thick as marshmallows. The sun was hot, the sky a burning blue. If he had a room, he'd go take a nap. When he got to Mexico City he'd get the best room in the best hotel and sleep for a week. He'd lay in the bathtub for another week.

He didn't want to go back to the Plaza but there wasn't any place else to go. Unless he went to La Fonda and sat in the lobby. And talked to Mac. He'd never run into Pila in La Fonda lobby. He wanted to tell the kid goodbye. He wondered how much her permanent wave would cost. It wasn't her fault the Sen had ratted again last night. She'd look like hell with a permanent wave.

He wandered up the street, automatically ducking the kids, his ears filled with cacophony of noise, music and jabber and singing and laughing and crying, all kinds of noise mixed up into one big Fiesta noise. He wandered on up to the corner where Fiesta was most noisy, where Pancho made Tio Vivo gallop a lively course. Pancho was a funny guy. He didn't have anything to be happy about but he was always happy. He didn't care about getting any place. He didn't care where he slept or what he hung on his back or what he put in his stomach.

A funny guy. Sailor wondered what Ziggy would make of

Pancho. Ziggy studied guys, figured them out. Sailor went around in back of the merry-go-round, leaned against the fence. The kids weren't on this side. They crowded in by the gate. He could watch Pancho without Pancho knowing it. Watch the big muscles swelling under the sweaty shirt. He couldn't figure Pancho out. Working like a ditch-digger for nickels. Not for nickels, to make a bunch of kids happy. Maybe that's why Pancho was happy, because he was making other people happy. Even making an amigo out of a stranger. A funny guy.

While he was leaning there, he saw Pila. She was on the other side, in back of the kids, watching Tio Vivo. He didn't know her at first. She wasn't in the costume; she was wearing a plain blue dress, the kind kids wore in orphanages, white collar on it, big buttons down the front of it. Her hair hung in braids; she looked like the little kid she was. He went around to her as quick as he could push the mob of kids aside, came up behind her.

"I'll buy you a ride on the pink horse," he said.

She turned slowly. "No. My father he is waiting for me. To take me home."

"I'll buy you a pop. A pink pop." He took her arm. "You can take it with you, drink it on the way home." He pushed her through the crowd, out of the park to the pop stand. He rang down the dime for the bottle.

Pila said, "Rosie, she say you want to see me."

He put the pop bottle in her hand. "Yeah. About that permanent."

Her eyes didn't leave his face. The eyes of the kid in front of the bike window. Not hopeless, simply without hope.

"How much would it cost you?"

"For three dollars, Rosie she can get a permanent."

Things were cheaper in the sticks. The dames the Sen knew paid twenty bucks in Chicago.

He grinned, "It's a deal." He took the bills from his pocket, peeled a five, added another.

She looked at the money in his hand but she didn't touch it. "Go on, take it," he said. "I promised you, didn't I?"

"It does not cost this much."

He put the bills in her small brown hand. "After you get it, you'll need a new dress, won't you?" He looked down at the orphan shoes on her feet. "And some shoes."

"My father—"

"You don't have to tell your old man, do you?"

She crumpled the bills into her pocket, pushed her hand down on them. "Thank you." She didn't grin and jump around like Lorenzo. If somebody had handed Sailor the red bike out of Field's window, he wouldn't have jumped around. He'd have stood there looking up, saying, "Thank you," like he hadn't any other words in his heart.

She said, "I must go to my father."

"Sure." He swung along beside her.

She was clutching the pop bottle to her blue dress.

"I don't know what you want a permanent for," he said. Making conversation. Just wondering.

She looked at him. Like he was the Sen. "Then I can come into town and go to work. Like Rosie. Rosie gets five dollars a week cleaning houses. I can clean better than Rosie, I learn at the Indian school. At nights Rosie goes to the picture show and to dances—"

The bright lights of the big hick town. A permanent and a new dress and working out like Rosie. Meeting the boys after dark. Next year the old man wouldn't count. Laying with the boys on the Federal Building lawn. Like Rosie.

"Listen," he said. He grabbed her arm and she almost dropped the pink pop but she caught it, clutched it more tightly. "Listen," he said. "Don't you do it. You stay where you are. Stay at the pueblo. Get yourself fixed up if you have to but you stay there. With your own people. Find you a guy there, a good guy. One your old man likes. You don't belong here, Pila. You're too good to be like Rosie." He didn't know what he was talking about. Old Mother Sailor. He didn't know why he was afraid, why he was warning her off. She'd do what she wanted to. But he could try.

"Don't forget what I'm telling you. Stay where you belong." He was trying to tell her. "Fiesta only lasts three days. After that Zozobra isn't dead any more." Maybe she'd get it. Maybe she'd think about it. He didn't say any more. They were at the end of the museum portal and she turned to him.

"Goodbye."

He wasn't to go any further with her. He got it. He watched her cross the street, watched her walk down to a pickup truck in front of the Art Museum. She climbed in the back of it. There were already a bunch of kids in it and a couple of women with calico shawls over their heads. One of the two men against the side of the truck must be her father. The two looked like all the men around here, old jeans, old shirts, battered hats. Lean brown faces. They both climbed in the front of the truck. Sailor stood watching while the truck backed out, shook and clanked on its way. She didn't wave goodbye; she didn't know he was there watching. She was drinking the pink pop.

He'd tried. He didn't know now why he'd given her ten bucks. Ten from forty left thirty. Not much money to go on. Maybe he thought she'd be his lucky piece. Maybe he was paying off the look in her eyes, the look that scared him. Because it knew too much, it knew what had happened and was to happen; the look that denied him existence because in time, Indian time, he was without existence. He'd paid off; it wasn't his fault if it backfired. If she turned into a Rosie by next Fiesta. He'd warned her. The rest was up to her.

And if someone had warned him to stick to the straight and narrow when he was fourteen? Someone had. Mac had. Sailor shook away thought. Maybe she'd be better off if she did leave the dump where she lived and the old man beating her and came to the bright lights of town. There was nothing wrong with trying to better yourself. It had worked for him. But then he hadn't been an innocent kid. Ignorant but not innocent. He wasn't either one now. The Sen had taken care of that.

The clouds were a blazing white in the bright blue sky. The Plaza was bedraggled as the flowered skirts trailing in the dust. On the bandstand an orchestra of Spanish kids was squeaking out of tune. The curbs were solid with women and babies and old men getting off their feet. You'd think they didn't have a home to go to. He strolled over to Tio Vivo, knocked the kids out of the way to reach the palings. He felt good for no reason; he'd feel better to get out of the hot dirty square into a place where you could know the feel of a cold bottle of beer. Only he didn't want to be alone. Or with Mac.

He yelled over the fence, "Hey, Pancho."

Pancho heard him. He gave the crank a couple of more turns and left it to unwind. He wiped his face with a blue bandanna as he came over to the fence.

"How about a beer?"

"Un tragito," Pancho sighed and swallowed his spittle. "I would like a beer, yes. Muy bueno."

"Come on. I'm buying."

Pancho shook his head. "But now I cannot go." He gestured to the horde of waiting children. "Come back in a little while, Sailorman. Six o'clock when it is supper time and not so many are here. Ignacio will do well enough when there are not so many."

"Okay." He had to say okay. Pancho was already shuffling back to his labor.

Well, he could get himself a bottle. Nothing wrong with that. He could go sit in the Placita behind the protecting wall. Under a tree. Only he'd run into Mac and it was better not to see Mac. He could go to Keen's. It was a tossup between Mac and the ape; a tossup between luxury and a smoky, smelly bar. He moved on to La Fonda. He could handle Mac. And the Sen might be recovered, might be cooling his fever with beer in the Placita.

The lobby was still like a convention; the Cantina like the El at rush hour. He pushed through them just the same. The Placita wasn't much better but it was quieter. And it didn't smell. In front of the open fireplace, there was a guitarist and a singer that were in tune. There wasn't a table, not just then. There were a half a dozen fancy costumes waiting for a table. He didn't wait. He cut across to where a party was about to leave and when they left he sat down. The crowd at the entrance didn't like it but he didn't mind. The pert blonde was waiting tables again in this corner. When she flipped her starched skirt past him he said, "How's for a big bottle of beer?"

She nodded. She had too many tables to serve and she'd be a long time coming back with the beer. He didn't care. He was comfortable. The Sen wasn't around nor any of his party. The people out here were having fun without thinking they had to make a lot of racket like the hicks in the bar. Sailor shoved back his hat. He could sit here till five o'clock if he wanted to. The blonde finally brought the beer. She poured half of it into a glass. Pouring it right, slowly, handling the head.

He said, "On your next trip in from Gary how about another?" He thought she was eying the empty chairs and he said, "I'm expecting friends."

She said, "I'll be glad when Fiesta is over. This place is a madhouse."

"Yeah." She wasn't as pert as yesterday; there were tired smudges under her eyes. "Why don't you have one with me?"

Her eyes flirted. "I wish I could. But I won't be through till nine."

She wanted him to make a date. She wasn't bold but she was invitational. He pretended regret. "I'm leaving before then."

"You're not staying for the Baile?" She was stalling for a little rest. Resting her feet and her nerves.

"What's that?"

"The big dance. And there'll be street dancing on the Plaza."

He shook his head. "Can't do it. Got to get my business wound up and be on my way."

She laughed. "If you're here on business, you're the only one here on business." She flipped her starched skirt. "I'll bring you the beer when I can."

"Make it two."

He hadn't seen Mac. The copper was sitting there at the table; the waitress had blocked him from sight until she moved away.

"Don't mind if I join you, Sailor?"

"No," he said heartily. As if he didn't mind. "They're pretty busy. You'll probably have to wait for the beer."

"I can wait," Mac said. That was McIntyre. He could wait. For a beer or a man or a story he was after. "How did you rate a table, Sailor?"

"Hijacked it." He lifted a glass. "You don't mind?"

"Go ahead." Mac lit a cigarette, laid the pack on the table. "Sailor?"

"Have my own, thanks." He set down the glass. Good beer. He lit up, left his pack on the table. Mac wasn't the Sen; he wouldn't snitch them. "You see the Sen?"

"No."

"Find out where he is?"

"Yes."

"Where?"

"You can't get to him, Sailor. Doctor's orders. He's to see no one. That's why his room is changed."

If Mac would tell him where, he'd see him. No doctor would keep him out. "What's wrong with him?"

"Nervous exhaustion."

Sailor's laugh was a vulgar noise. "That's a new name for it."

Mac smiled, a faint smile. Then he didn't smile. "You were at the senator's the night Mrs. Douglass was killed."

"Uh-uh." He poured some more beer in the glass. Steady and smooth, watching the amber bubbles lift into foam white as snow-white clouds.

"Fingerprints don't lie."

He drank comfortably. "I was there a lot. But not that night."

"You weren't there a lot," Mac denied quietly.

The blonde brought two more bottles and his change. "Thanks, doll," Sailor said. He left a quarter, put another bill on the tray for the bottles.

Mac was pouring from his bottle. "The senator didn't take his business associates to his home."

"I was his confidential secretary," Sailor pointed out.

"You hadn't been there that week. The panes were washed on Tuesday. Your prints are on the French doors."

He'd worn gloves. Mac wanted him to say he'd worn gloves. He didn't let McIntyre have any idea he'd like to slug him, pulling something like this on him. He brazened, "So you got a witness who'll perjure himself."

Mac said, "When the time comes, I have some good witnesses."

"What have you been waiting for?" Sailor demanded. "If you got all these swell witnesses, if you think you can break my alibi, what have you been waiting for?" He'd let his anger come up and he shouldn't have. He took a quick drink to cool him.

Mac was calm as a mill pond. "Sure, I could have picked you up. In Chicago weeks ago. I didn't want to, Sailor. I wanted to get the man who killed her." Sailor relaxed. "You know who killed her. So do I."

Sailor didn't say a word.

"But until you tell me, I can't get him." Mac spoke mildly, "A confidential secretary knows a lot about what goes on."

"He doesn't spill."

Mac said, "After he's quit?"

"You think I've quit?"

"The senator says that you killed her."

He saw red again, at the dirty, lying Sen. But he clamped his mouth.

"What do you say?"

"I say I didn't. I didn't. You can take me in but you'll never prove I did it. I didn't." Mac said, "How about another beer?"

Sailor's hand touched the second bottle. "I'm all right. You have another." He looked around for the blonde but he didn't see her. He saw another one. She was over in the corner and her shining head was bent to a good-looking blond guy and his head was bent to hers. It wasn't the Prague mucker. Their shoulders were touching. Under the table maybe their knees were touching. More than their knees. Because in their look was longing. They weren't smiling at each other; they weren't happy.

He could give McIntyre the story right now. Then he could walk over and say to Iris Towers and the young fellow, "It's okay now. The Sen's out of it." He didn't. He said to Mac, "I've got to see the Sen. Give me ten minutes alone with the Sen and I'll talk."

Mac should have perked up. But he didn't. He didn't look any happier than Iris Towers.

"It's a deal," Sailor insisted.

Mac said, "I'd rather you didn't see him."

"Why not?" He'd offered Mac a good proposition; Mac ought to accept it, not start making trouble. Mac needed him; he should play ball.

"I don't think it's safe." Mac looked straight at Sailor. The Spanish hat wasn't funny right now; it was a policeman's hat.

"I'm not worried," Sailor boasted. "I can take care of myself."

"I'm not worried about that," Mac stated. "You can take care of yourself against someone else. You know how. Can you take care of yourself against yourself?"

He got it. He wasn't dumb. Mac didn't trust him not to use the gun.

Mac said, "I don't want anything to happen to Senator Douglass. I told you that before. Moreover I don't want anything to happen to you." He took a long drink of beer. "Why I should care about that, I don't know, Sailor," he said in that quiet way of his. As if he were wondering about it for the first time. "All these years, every time I've tried to give you a hand, to steer you right, I might as well have hollered down a well. I don't know why I've thought you were worth saving. Why I still think so."

The sun had gone down, there was already a faint evening chill in the Placita. Beyond the wall, echoing from the Plaza, was singing, wild gay singing, ". . . alia en el Rancho Grande, alia donde vivía . . ." The voices whooped. The Placita was filling with lavender light. Iris Towers and the young man were nearer each other. The tinkle and strum of Tio Vivo was a faint shimmering sound. And somewhere there was monotone of a muffled drum.

"Perhaps because I could have been you. If the wrong person had got hold of me when I was a kid. If the Devil had tempted me, I might not have been any stronger than you were."

Mac was going preachy again.

"You're free of him now, Sailor. You're still young; that part's over. You mustn't make a mistake now."

"I'm not going to hurt him," Sailor smiled.

"You don't know," Mac said. "It could happen. You don't want to take a chance."

He wasn't going to kill the Sen. All he was going to do was get the dough that was due him. He didn't have to kill the Sen; Mac and the State of Illinois would take care of that for him. He laughed. "You got me wrong, Mac. I wouldn't cheat you out of the Sen. I'm not gunning for him." He shoved his hand in his right-hand pocket. All of a sudden he wanted to explain to Mac. If Mac could have been him, he could have been Mac. They'd always been mixed up together, one on one side, one on the other, like one man split in half. Maybe it was explaining to himself.

"Listen Mac," he said. "You don't have to worry about me. I never used a gun in my life except when I had to, to protect myself." Except once. And that hadn't come off. It didn't count. "Against guys you'd have shot it out with yourself. I never killed anyone. It's the mugs that handle that line." He was too good for mug stuff. He was uptown, a confidential secretary. Mac ought to know that.

Mac still didn't trust him. "How do you know what you'll do with a gun in your pocket? Sometimes the wrong person gets in the way. A gun's a bad thing to have handy, Sailor. I don't like guns. I haven't packed one since I quit pounding pavements."

That was all right for Mac. Guns didn't worry Sailor. He spoke with confidence. "This is for protection, that's all."

Mac said, "I can give you better protection. If you'll tell me about that night, I'll see you're protected."

But Mac couldn't give him five grand, even one grand. Mac didn't have it. Mac was a good enough guy for a cop but he wasn't smart about money. He was an honest copper. He'd never be swanking it in Mexico City dressed up in a white Palm Beach suit, ordering champagne cocktails for a girl like Iris Towers. He wasn't that smart. And Mac wasn't going to fix it up for Sailor to see the Sen. He was on his own about that. The lavender light was deepening. "I got a date," he recalled suddenly. Mac was tensed, ready to stick with him.

He laughed. "Not with the Sen. With a friend of mine. For beer." Mac relaxed.

"Think it over, Sailor. I'll be right here."

"Okay."

He'd already got it thought over. He was seeing the Sen if he had to go to Iris Towers to work it. McIntyre, no one, could stop him.

Four

The twilight was hung with early stars and the flowered lights. Sailor cut across to the whirl of Tio Vivo. He was late. He peered over the fence palings. Ignacio was turning the crank. Old Onofre fiddled. Neither one had the heart of Pancho; Tio Vivo was spiritless and the music was tin. Sailor shouted over the hubbub of Fiesta, "Where's Pancho? Hey, where's Pancho?"

Ignacio heard him. He shrugged, "Quien sabe?"

Well, he could catch up with Pancho later. He walked away but before he reached the curb he bumped square into the big fellow. There was a smear of chile on the dirty chin, the smell of garlic would knock you down.

Pancho beamed, "Ah there, Sailor? Where you been?" His hands patted Sailor's shoulders tenderly.

"I got held up. Business," Sailor said. "Listen, we'll have that tragito a little later." He stepped out of the embrace and his hand pulled a bill from his pocket. It was a ten. It didn't matter; he'd be fixed up in a little while now. "Tequila, how about it?"

Pancho's brown eyes took a happy squint at the bill. "Hokay," he said.

A farewell party with his good angel, Pancho. Some angel. A dirty old spic who cranked a merry-go-round. "Hokay," Sailor echoed.

He felt good swinging out of the Plaza, stepping over the curb, into the street. Not paying any attention to the villagers. They weren't so bad; they didn't have much fun. No wonder this tinsel Fiesta looked good to them. Nobody could have much fun living in this one-horse town. He'd be out tomorrow. It wouldn't be Chicago but Mexico City would be even better. Sure it would; no more dirt and cold and sweat; no more jumping when the Sen lifted his little finger. Like Mac said, he'd be starting a new life. He could have it any way he wanted it. He was going to have it good with the Sen's stake.

He returned to the hotel. He tried the Sen's room first. No luck there. The old bitch with the yellow-gray hair was at the desk. He asked her polite, "Will you give me the number of Senator Douglass' room?" She gave it to him like it hurt her.

"He isn't in that room now," Sailor explained. "I just called."

She was snippy, "Well, I don't know where he is."

Somebody ought to push her nose into her face. She ought to learn some manners from the spics. From the Indians. She probably came from some small town in Kansas, so small she thought this was a metropolis. Thought this hotel was the Palmer House.

"Give me Iris Towers' room," he demanded.

She gave it to him with another dirty look. He'd come back here someday and have the biggest suite in the place and he'd get her fired. He rang the room.

A man's voice answered. "Hello."

It wasn't the Sen. It was a young voice. A little drunk.

Sailor said, "I'm trying to reach Senator Douglass. Could you tell me where I could find him?" He talked like he was a rich playboy himself. Casual and a little bored.

"I'm sorry," the fellow said. "I don't know where he is."

Sailor caught him before he hung up. "May I speak to Miss Towers, please?"

The fellow was reluctant. He said, "Well—" And then she was on the phone. Her voice was husky and far away. Sort of breathless. Like she'd been interrupted.

Sailor said, "Do you know where I could reach Senator Douglass?"

"No, I'm sorry. Who is calling?"

He gave a phoney name. The Sen was hiding out in her room. He knew that as he turned away from the phone. She wouldn't have taken a drunk to her room if it was her room. She wasn't that kind. She and the Sen had traded rooms. But he was stalled again. He couldn't have his talk with the Sen with Iris Towers present.

She wouldn't stay there all evening nursing the Sen. She wasn't in love with the Sen. He'd hypnotized her some way, like he'd hypnotized others. But you didn't stay that way. You caught on after a while. You found out the Sen was cold as steel, you found out he was using you. Even a lug like Sailor caught on after a while. She'd be going to dress pretty soon. To dress for dinner and the big Baile. Going with a young fellow. Because the Sen was sick. All Sailor had to do was wait. Wait till she and the young fellow came downstairs. Then he'd go upstairs. Easy as that.

He strolled out of the crowd, to the back portal. There wasn't a place to sit down. The Mexican orchestra in their satins and velvets were playing the dressed-up crowd into the New Mexican room. A crimson velvet rope held off the crowd, like it was the Pump Room. If it was the Pump Room Sailor could go up to the rope and there'd be a reservation. He was one of the Sen's fellows.

The patio outside was ruled too. The fountain splashed and the swings creaked lazily. The bar boys' white coats were luminous under the blue floodlight, the geraniums were dark and scented. Laughter spilled over the fountain, the laughter of those who were young and protected by the best families and beautiful homes with green lawns, who were born right. Who didn't have business here, nothing to do but dance out the Fiesta.

He stood there leaning against the door between the patio and the portal. He wasn't surprised that Mac joined him.

Mac said, "How about dinner?"

"Too early."

"I have a table in the dining room," Mac said. He went on along. But he left hunger behind him.

Sailor didn't have to stand here and wait. He could take an hour off to eat. Kill time, eat and sleep. Get off his feet. No other way to get off them during Fiesta. It would take her that long to get dressed. The New Mexican room had a better smell than a greasy joint. He could get away from Mac easy enough later.

He didn't think about it any more. He followed the way Mac had gone. It wasn't the New Mexican room; it was the main dining room. Another rope, another crowd, but he edged through it. "Mr. McIntyre's table."

He hoped Mac had done something about letting the tall girl on the door know a friend might be along. Mac had. He looked up amused when she brought Sailor to the table.

"Not too early now?"

Sailor took it. "Time sure passes quick during Fiesta." Just as if time hadn't been dragging her heels these days.

Mac held the menu. "Have a cocktail? Forgot, you don't drink." He caught the eye of a nice looking Spanish-American fellow in a dark business suit. "Could I get a martini?"

"I think so." The fellow smiled. He didn't have any accent. "And you, sir?"

Sailor nodded. "I'll celebrate with you, Mac. Make it two." The fellow made him feel at home. Two city-looking fellows in a roomful of gaudy costumes. Even the waitresses in costume. The fellow was polite too, not like the old hag at the desk. She could use a dose of Spanish blood.

"Going to the Baile?" Sailor asked Mac.

"I don't think so. Are you?"

Mac would keep close guard on the Sen tonight. Sailor smiled inside. It wouldn't be close enough. Mac didn't know what room the Sen was in.

"I might," Sailor told him. Just as if he had a girl somewhere that he was going to take care of. A lovely silver girl, not an Indian kid, or a skinny little slut with frizzy hair, or a slattern with sultry eyes and a dirty neck.

The nice looking Spanish-American in the business suit was directing a dumb kid in shapeless whites to their table. The kid had an Indian face. He handled the martini tray as if he were certain he was going to spill it. But he made it, set the cocktails down. Just slopping them a little.

Mac lifted his glass. "Viva las Fiestas!"

"Viva las Fiestas," Sailor echoed.

The martini was cold and dry and right. When he got to Mexico City he'd start having a cocktail before dinner. It gave you a feeling of luxury to be sipping a cocktail in a gay dining room. He'd laid off liquor long enough for the Sen's business.

He could do as he damn pleased from now on. He'd be his own boss tomorrow. Mañana. He said, "They got you doing it, too."

"Doing what?" Mac was writing the order.

"Talking Spanish. Viva las Fiestas. Mañana. Mi amigo. Who'd have thought we'd ever be talking Spanish together?"

Mac handed the order blank to the small dark girl. Her skirts rustled away. "Funny world," Mac said.

Sailor kept on talking. He didn't want Mac to get back to the case. And he didn't want Mac to start preaching. He wanted to enjoy this hour.

"Yeah, it's funny. When I got in here I thought they were all just a bunch of dirty spics. I didn't have any use for any of them. But you take Pancho now."

"Who's Pancho?"

"The guy that runs Tio Vivo." He thought Mac knew about Pancho. Then he saw that Mac did, only he didn't know him by that name. "I call him Pancho. Pancho Villa. He's got a long Spanish name. Don José de something or other. Says he's a descendant of a conquistador way back when Fiesta got started. He looks more like Pancho Villa to me."

Mac smiled, "He does."

"Well, you take Pancho. He's dirty all right. I bet he doesn't take a bath once a year. Probably never owned a tooth brush in his life. But he's muy macho. He'd do anything for you if you're his amigo—" He broke off. "There I go again thinking Spanish." He took another sip. "Not because he wants something out of you but because he wants to do something for you. That's the kind of guy Pancho is."

Mac nodded.

"Maybe they're not all kind of simple that way. But they don't shove you around. They give you a smile. Even if you don't talk their language they don't shove you around. The way we shove them around when they come up to our town."

"I know," Mac said. "I've thought sort of along that line myself. We're the strangers and they don't treat us as strangers. They're tolerant. Only they're more than tolerant. Like you say, they're friendly. They give you a smile not scorn."

Sailor was thinking of Pancho. And he was talking too much, it could be the martini. "They're poor. It isn't good to be poor," Sailor quoted Pancho. "But if you have to be, it's better to be out in this country, I guess. Where nothing matters much."

He was somewhat startled at hearing the words come out of his mouth. If he had to stay here, this alien land would get him, just like it got everyone. He'd be a mañana man himself; he wouldn't have any more ambition than Pancho. He'd start believing like Pancho, ambition and pride got you nothing, only to be conquered by two-bit-fifty-cent gringos. Better to forget grandeur and glory, to sing and dance and work a little, un tragito on Saturday nights, go to Mass on Sunday mornings. Better to be happy in your little life than to be important. You could hold on to your pride because it was all you had left; you wouldn't know it was only a word you'd learned long ago.

This was what the Indians had done to the intruder, this was how they would diminish him to non-existence. The Indians and the land were one, strong, changeless, unconquerable.

The frozen terror he had known as a kid before a piece of sculpture was a chill in him now. For that inanimate hunk of woman had known then that his world, squalid and miserable as it was, was not the rock he thought it was. She had known the rock would disintegrate, that in time there'd be the Sen, and the Sen would run out on him and he'd be driven into this alien land. She hadn't warned, she hadn't pitied or gloated; she'd known. He out of all the kids in the Art Museum that day would be trapped in a land where she knew he did not exist.

He was getting screwy. Why did he keep thinking trap? Why had he thought trap ever since he came here? A piece of land couldn't trap a man. Even if it spread on and on like eternity all over the earth until the mountains stopped it. He wasn't trapped. He was getting out.

He didn't know what McIntyre had been talking about. He heard only what the copper was saying now.

"It's good, for us to see how other people live. We get awfully narrow in our own little lives. We get thinking we're so all-fired important that nobody else counts. We forget that everyone counts, that everybody on this earth counts just as much as we do."

Sailor said, "Yeah. You're right, Mac." He grinned. "Just the same, good as these people are, I'm thankful I don't have to live here. Give me Chicago, USA." He began to eat.

Mac said, "This is the USA."

"This wouldn't be the USA in a million years. No matter what flag they fly." Mac didn't know the secret. "It's a foreign land. We don't belong here." Mac didn't have to worry about the secret. He was going back to Chicago. He hadn't been exiled by the evil of a nasty old man. Sailor wasn't going to be exiled either. He'd get out of here and set up business in Mexico but once he was a big shot with plenty of dough to oil the wheels, he would go back to Chicago. His hands were plenty clean. He'd keep them clean. He wasn't going to use the gun on the Sen. He could collect without that.

This was the way a man ought to eat. Service. No hurry. Clean people around you. This was the way he was going to live from now on. Free. Not just on sufferance as a gentleman with the Sen paying the bills. Nobody was going to look down a nose at him any more.

They both lit up. Comfortable. Waiting for their ice cream. Lulled. "How long has the senator known Iris Towers?"

Mac knew when you were lulled. He was never off his single track even when he pretended to be. He was trying to add up two and two; trying to make the murder the getting rid of an old wife to make room for a young one. As if there were need for any more motive than a fifty-grand insurance policy. Mac didn't need to add it up to five; four was good enough.

Sailor said, "I didn't know he knew her. Until he took this trip."

"She's a pretty girl."

She was lovely as a dream; she was the only lovely thing in this strange dream. "The Sen tell you he was going to marry the Towers girl?"

Sailor snapped it short. "He didn't tell me a thing. He never mentioned her to me." He didn't want to talk about this. Maybe Mac was trying to needle him. Maybe Mac knew how he felt about this girl being mixed up with the Sen. "It's always been strictly business between me and the Sen." He didn't know how to get off the subject. "Ever since he hired me that day down at the pool hall. Remember the old pool hall, Mac? I was pretty good at pool till I moved up with the Sen." He was moving away nicely. He grinned. "Then I learned bridge and gin."

Mac wasn't moving so fast. "You took care of the business records."

"That was Zigler's job." Mac was probably going to impound the records. If he hadn't already.

They wouldn't be pretty. Real estate covered too much in the Sen's books. "You could probably explain them pretty well. A confidential secretary." The ice cream arrived. And the coffee.

Sailor tried the coffee first. "What you after, Mac? A political stink?"

"I'm after the murderer of Senator Douglass' wife," Mac said calmly.

"But you don't mind if you break the organization wide open." It was his turn to heckle. "The Sen shouldn't have opposed you in the elections."

"The Sen offered me his support. Through an emissary. I turned it down." Mac lifted an eyebrow. "You knew that?"

He hadn't known. The Sen didn't talk about his failures. All he'd known, all the gang had known, was that the organization was out to beat Mac's bunch. And they hadn't. Because the Sen's mind even then was on Iris Towers?

"I don't like men who corrupt and destroy. I don't like crooks who get rich off the poor. I just don't like them. The senator offered me a job when I was a young cop, Sailor. I turned it down." His mouth was set. "Ask me why, Sailor? I'll tell you without asking. I'd just fished one of his confidential secretaries out of the lake. After that he picked fellows like you. Those who already had a record. Those who could stomach it."

"Why did he act like he didn't know you today?"

"Maybe he's forgotten. Maybe he prefers not to know me. I've stayed out of his way. But I knew that long ago that he wouldn't let anything stand in his way. What were you doing at his house that night?"

Sailor said stubbornly, "Let me see him and I'll tell you."

Mac picked up the check. Sailor reached out his hand. "It's on me."

"Not tonight. I invited you."

It would help; he was low enough after his handouts. He'd

buy Mac a better dinner in Mexico City. He said, "I won't argue. My turn next." He could excuse himself now but he'd be polite, wait with Mac for the change.

Mac put a bill on the tray. His face was solemn. "You're still determined to take the chance?"

"There's no chance, Mac," Sailor insisted. "Only I got to see him before I talk. I owe him that much."

"You don't owe him a damn thing, Sailor."

He didn't. Nothing good. But he owed the Sen plenty for these three days of bunking on the ground. Plenty for that slit under his shoulder. Plenty for making him wait for his just pay.

He urged, "Let me see him." As if Mac could. As if Mac had the Sen shut up incommunicado.

No Zigler to bust him loose with a habeas corpus. Mac said flatly, "He doesn't want to see you."

"He tell you that?"

Mac smiled, "Let's stop the dodging, Sailor. Give me a name, the name of a murderer, and I'll get you to Senator Douglass quick. If you can't see it any other way, take it your usual way. The way that'll pay you off."

But not in greenbacks. They left the dining room, wading through the crowd still hungering against the velvet rope. Sailor knew how to get away. "Let me think it over. You'll be around?"

"I'll be around."

Five

HE WENT out of the hotel, into the cold night warmed by the
excitement of Fiesta. He turned his back on it, walked away up
the brief street. The dark bulk of the cathedral loomed there, im-
placable as Judgment Day. It didn't bother him any. A long time
till Judgment Day. He turned past it and circled the block. There
could be a back door to the hotel.

If there was he didn't see it. Walls and then the balconies of
La Fonda tiering up to the high flat roof. He could climb up to
a balcony but it wasn't a good idea. Not if someone were inside
the room he tackled, someone who'd start yelling for a cop. He
went on up the street passing under the canopy of the side door,
and again he was smack against Fiesta.

You couldn't escape it tonight. He walked right into it,
through it, drenched with it to the opposite street, to the museum. The Indians were no longer under the portal; their absence
was somehow more frightening than the black, silent, watching
eyes had been. The Indians knew these days must end. They had
never believed in the dream. They had never been of it.

He boosted himself up to the ledge as soon as there was space
and he sat there, marking time until nine o'clock. Just sitting and
watching Fiesta dance by, listening to the musicians overplaying
each other from the bandstand and the platform down below

where the Mariachi sang and the scrape of Tio Viva and the strolling guitarists. It would be too bad if a fellow's life wasn't any more than a merry-go-round, somebody cranking you up to whirl around in style, then letting you peter out into where you started from. That might have been the way it would be for him if he hadn't got what he did on the Sen. Because the Sen was ending the organization; the Sen wasn't carrying it with him into the world of Iris Towers and her wealth and influence. If Sailor hadn't waited around that night, he'd be whistling for his supper. The way Humpty and Lew would be if they ever went back to Chi. Luck had been on his side and he was keeping it there. He'd be just as careful of the Sen as Mac would be. He wanted to deliver the Sen in a neat package to Mac as bad as Mac wanted him delivered. To pay the Sen not only for what he'd done but for what he would have done if he could have married Iris Towers.

He waited until nine and then he started back to the hotel. By now she'd be gone for sure, she and the rest of the Sen's party. Off to dinner and the Baile. The only thing was to avoid Mac. He'd figured it out earlier. At the side door. He didn't even have to enter the lobby.

Through the side door, pass the entrance to the Indian shop on the left; on the right, pass the steps leading down to the barber shop. Then the small flight of steps leading up to a corridor, Women's Rest Room, Beauty Shop, hotel rooms. The corridor ran parallel to the right-hand portal, you came out of it down another small flight of steps and you were by the elevator. You never went into the crowd in the lobby. It was that easy.

The elevator was deserted as usual. "Four," Sailor said. The fourth-floor corridor was as deserted, a ghost walk. No sounds from any of the closed doors. Past the Sen's closed door, past three more closed doors and this was the number of Iris Towers' room. The room she'd originally had.

There wasn't a sound inside. Empty of sound as the corridor where Sailor stood. He knocked, knocked again, kept knocking. The silence within deepened, the echoes of his left-hand knuckles on the door wavered in the emptiness. He couldn't shout in to the Sen; he mustn't attract attention. It could be someone was in a neighboring room. The overhead transom was dark, the Sen could be asleep. He could be lying there in the dark, scarcely breathing, knowing who was outside.

There was only one thing to do now. Go inside. The key was on his ring, the key that opened locked doors. A little present from the Sen, when the Sen needed him to open some stubborn doors. There was no risk in using it. If Iris Towers or any of the others were in there, they'd have answered his knocking.

The door opened noiselessly. He moved with its opening to stand in protective darkness against the wall. His foot kicked the door shut. The gun was in his hand. Its dull metallic gleam would show up even in the lightless room. That much light came from the night outside the windows.

He said, "All right, Sen. It's me." His words dropped into emptiness. Not even a rustle answered him, not the beat of a pulse.

His eyes were beginning to see in the dark. They saw the beds, smooth covers pulled over them. They saw the empty chairs, the empty corners of the room.

He walked swiftly to the bathroom, kicked open the door as he snapped the light. There was no one there. The door of the clothes closet was shut. Before he walked over, pulled it open, he knew what he would find. A closet full of woman's clothes.

He began to curse the Sen under his breath. He didn't bother to turn out the bath light. He left the room. He didn't even re-member the gun open in his hand until he'd used the key on the Sen's own door. He didn't put it out of sight; he slid in, cursing the Sen, cursing the Sen in the room that had once been the Sen's, that was empty now, not even a cigarette butt remained of the Sen.

The Sen had skipped. Mac had kept Sailor entertained with dinner and fine talk while the Sen got away. Sailor shoved the gun in his pocket before leaving the room. He kept his hand on it. Mac had let the Sen go. Knowing he could pick him up, maybe a guy already waiting, to meet the Chief at the La Salle street station. Playing it smart; keeping the Sen safe, keeping him out of Sailor's way. Figuring Sailor would talk any time now. Sailor would think the Sen had run out on him and he'd be mad enough to talk. Mac didn't know about the five grand. Mac thought he was waiting for a payoff; he didn't know how big the stakes were.

He'd go down and see Mac. He'd tell off Mac. But he wouldn't talk. Not until he went back to Chicago and faced the Sen. Even that could be what Mac was after, get both of them back to Chi. Back to where Mac was boss. You never knew when you were playing Mac's game. And how was Sailor going to get back to Chi? He hadn't twenty bucks left. He'd have to let Mac buy the tickets. Travel with Mac, not under arrest, no. Just with a copper bodyguard.

He wasn't alone in the elevator. But he didn't see the faces with whom he rode downstairs. They were paper dolls someone had cut out and pasted there. They smelled like booze and they made a lot of noise. He left the elevator first and he started with angry determination towards the lobby. He had to stop a minute at the opening to the portal. Another bunch of noisy drunks were blocking the way. He wanted to flail through them and their silly faces but he waited. Waited and got the break.

The group of the elevator had moved in behind him. And a girl whined. "Why don't we get Senator Douglass before we go? I want Willie to go with us."

A man said, "I told you he's already gone to the Baile. He and Iris left an hour ago."

"Iris!" the girl cackled.

Sailor didn't turn around. He had no idea who they were. He said, "Thanks," under his breath. He got out of the crowd and strode on to the lobby. It was a whirlpool of color and smell and sound. But he didn't see the black hat with the bobbles. He took the time to look. He didn't want to be followed now. He turned to leave the hotel by the side door when he realized he didn't know where to go. There wouldn't be a chance to pick up a cab quick, not on the last night of Fiesta. He stopped at the newsstand. "Where's this Baile?"

The girl behind the counter didn't smile but she looked him over as if she might if she wanted to. "It's at the Armory."

"Where's that?"

"Out College. The street that runs into the back of the hotel."

"Is it far?"

"No," she said.

He bought a pack of cigarettes from her and left the hotel. Out the side entrance, down the street away from Fiesta into the darkness of College Street. A convent on one side, a filling station on the other. His hands dug into his pockets, right hand closed over ugly steel, left hand cramped in his left-hand pocket. He didn't know what his left hand was shredding until he looked. Pink paper.

The handbill the fancy clerk had given him. To tell him about

Fiesta. If he'd read it, he'd have known the Sen wouldn't miss the Baile. The Baile that was the golden crown of Fiesta.

On up the street, up the hill. Little stores; dark houses, nobody staying home on the last night of Fiesta; another brick school with the cross over it. He walked on. An occasional car roared by. At the intersection a street lamp cast a little puddle of light. On. Nights were cold here, the stars were sharp and cold above the trees.

The narrow street twisted, the street lamps were small and spaced too far apart. Had he known how far the Armory was, he'd have waited for a cab. A rattletrap that passed for a cab in this dump. He walked on. He was alone on the long street, alone on the long, dark, strange street. The houses he passed were dark, soundless. He was alone as before in his bad dream. But he wasn't lost. He knew where he was going. To meet the Sen. To the final meeting with the Sen.

The long street ended on top of a hill. It became a road there, a two-branched road. He didn't know which was the way he should take. Under the white moon both led to empty space, to cold endless wastes of desert, blocked by the finality of mountains against the white-starred sky. He stood there and a car passed, behind it a few paces, another car. They veered to the right and he chose.

It was the right choice. A little further on and he could hear music and the jangle of laughter. The Armory didn't look like an armory. It was another fancy Spanish 'dobe building, pale in the moonlight. There were figures clumped outside, passing the bottle, twining together in the night. Figures gathered at the lighted doorway, peering into the ballroom. Slack-mouthed, gangly boys with their dark Mex faces. No costumes on them, no dough to go inside to the Spanish Baile. They could look but they couldn't touch. It was too long ago they'd been the conquerors; they were the conquered now. The Indians were better off; they didn't want to look.

He went up to the door. The stale hot breath of the big room pushed into his face. It was so crowded you couldn't see anyone inside, only the kaleidoscope of moving color under the muted lights. He'd never spot the Sen in this mob. That was why the Sen thought it was safe to sneak out to the Baile. He didn't think Sailor could find him.

Sailor stepped inside. He wasn't going to shell out dough to talk to the Sen. He didn't have to argue it. There wasn't anyone on the door. Too late for that. Midnight already. He began a slow circle around the outside of the floor. Looking for a little man with a big snout and thin hair, a little man in black velvet pants and a black velvet jacket to cover his black soul. Looking for the white skirts and silvery-gold hair of an ivory girl who shouldn't be let come within miles of the rotten Sen.

Moving his feet snail-like, his eyes not moving, his hand not stirring, sure in his pocket.

Watching the dancers swaying to the rattle of maracas, the scratch of gourds, the sultry frenzy of Latin music; watching the shape of bodies melting to oneness, breaking apart only to melt again. Listening for a voice in the muted thunder of too many voices.

When he saw her, he went rigid. As if he weren't ready for the meeting. Or as if he'd come to act, not talk. She turned in the dance and she was with the Sen. Sailor was all right then. The muscles in his stomach weren't clutching; they were tight. As if he and they were alone in the vast packed room, he cut across the floor, by instinct alone avoiding the dancers who flowed like tide about him. He would have lost them, one couple among so many, but his eyes never left her once they had found her. He would have lost them but the coldness of his anger was a lead wire stretching between him and them. When he came to them he knew what had solidified his anger so that it was no longer anger, but the ice of rage. She wasn't white and beautiful; tonight she was what she was, her skirts dyed scarlet, her eyes blurred by her half-closed lids. He should have known before, the way she'd been with the rich muckers, the way she'd even looked at him once. He hadn't known until he saw her tonight; she was the slattern, Jesusita, with a million dollars. It was the slattern's slow eyes smiling into his now. It was her harlot's mouth that saw him and thought him good. She hadn't been clean for a long time. She was the rottenest part of this dream. The Sen turning, saw him too.

Sailor said, "Do you want to come outside or do you want it here?"

The Sen's tongue flickered over his pale lips. His eyes drooped to Sailor's rigid right-hand pocket, scuttled quickly up to Sailor's face. To Sailor's stone face.

"I'll come outside."

The Sen was a shell, about to break apart. He thought Sailor had come to rub him out. It was a good idea. Let him think so. The scarlet girl swayed against his arm. "Willis, where are you going?" But her eyes were on Sailor. And her mouth.

The Sen said, "I'll be back in a minute." He didn't believe that. He was a yellow-bellied coward, his voice was dust and ashes.

"But, Willis—"

"I won't be a minute, Iris. I'm sorry." He couldn't explain. He had no words to explain to her.

Sailor said harshly, "I don't have all night."

The Sen's eyes flicked the right-hand pocket again. "Find Kemper. I'll be back right away." He left her standing there, alone in the crowd. Annoyed at his leaving her, or annoyed at Sailor because he was leaving her, but she wouldn't be alone or annoyed long. Her scarlet body would be cleaving to another man while the music languored and thudded, while the Sen paid off in the cold night. Paid what he owed.

Sailor said, "Just walk on out that door." His hand in his pocket touched the Sen's side. Guided him to the side door opposite. Past the couples screaming there, swaying hot bodies there. Guided him across the dark stubble, around to the rear of the building. Where it was quiet. Where they were alone.

The Sen quivered his nose towards the ballroom.

Sailor's mouth twisted. "Don't worry about her. All she wants is a man. Any man." The Sen didn't say anything.

Sailor went on harshly, "I don't know what she wants with you. Maybe she thinks she's going to sit in the governor's mansion. Maybe that's what she's looking for. Or is she out for a cheap thrill?" Hate poisoned his words. "The wife of the condemned man looked so beautiful in black—"

The Sen's voice jumped hysterically. "Shut up."

Sailor smiled. He didn't feel like smiling. It hurt him in the pit of his stomach. "What's the matter? You getting cold feet?" He ought to shoot the Sen down, the dirty, sniveling, yellow-bellied Sen. Shooting was too good for him. Shooting was easy. Let Mac put him in the chair where he'd suffer. Let Mac send him to hell. The smile on Sailor's mouth was cold as the cold moon, fixed as the cold, white, faraway stars.

The Sen's voice was a thin whine. He tried to make it rich and full but it didn't come out that way. "Let's talk it over, Sailor.

After all you've been to me. Like my own son. After all I've done for you . . ." He was like one of those shoddy yellow canaries quivering on a cheap stick. It was funny. Sailor began to laugh. He stuck out his chin and he laughed and laughed at the funny little canary that once he'd thought was the most important guy in the world.

When he finished laughing he said again, "What's the matter, Sen?" He could kill the canary easy; there wasn't anyone around out here. They were as alone as if they'd invented this alien wasteland for their final meeting, invented it that they might be utterly alone for their goodbye. He didn't want to kill; he just wanted his money. His honest pay. He said it. "I'm not going to rub you out. I just want my dough. That's all."

He watched the Sen stop shaking, watched the blood fill up the wizened face, watched the shame in the coward turn to vengeful rage. His own hand tightened on the gun in his pocket. Because he knew the Sen's anger. Too well to trust him.

But the Sen didn't start at him. The Sen stood quietly and his eyelids dropped. The bush covered the shape of his mouth. He said flatly, "You've sung. You're waiting for Mac."

Sailor's lips set hard. "I've never sung yet," he said. "You know it. What Mac knows isn't from me. He's guessing." He spat the lie. Only at the moment it wasn't a lie. "Give me what's coming to me and you can handle Mac your own way. I'm getting out tonight. Have you got it?"

The narrow eyes shifted to look into Sailor's. "I've got it," the Sen said in his sweet voice. "Yes, I've got it." He smiled, smiled at him as if Sailor were his white-haired boy again, as if it were the way it was when he'd first moved Sailor uptown.

He reached into his inner coat pocket, where his flat wallet would have been if he'd been wearing a coat, not a velvet monkey jacket. Reached in and Sailor stood there like a dolt waiting for it, waiting for the hand to come out holding a gun, shooting a gun.

Only the Sen wasn't good at it. He'd never been his own gunman. Sailor was good. He could shoot before the Sen did, could watch the Sen's gun explode towards the stars, too far away to know or care; watch the Sen crumple down on the dark stubble of the earth. "God damn you." Sailor sobbed it through his clenched teeth. "God damn you." He was standing over the Sen and he could have emptied his gun into the shadow on the cold earth. He was ready to shoot and shoot again. But he heard the crazy scream in the lighted doorway, heard the babble and he ran.

Ducking around the back of the building, running low to the ground in and out of the lanes of parked cars. His belly sobbing, the breath sucking from his teeth. *God damn him, God damn him, God . . .* He stumbled on; he didn't know where he was going. Only he was getting away. Before they got him. For killing the Sen.

He hadn't meant to kill him. It was self defense. Anybody would know it was self defense. Only nobody would believe it, because the Sen was the Sen, had been the Sen, and Sailor was a mug from down behind the car barns who did the Sen's dirty work. Until the Sen sold him out.

There wasn't anyone behind him. *Hurry, hurry, hurry . . .* He was alone cutting through back yards, around silent sleeping houses. There was no sound of a siren screaming through the night silence. Maybe it hadn't been a scream in the doorway; maybe it was just some bitchy dame with a whisky breath, laughing. Maybe the guns hadn't sounded loud inside where the music was thumping. He swerved away from the houses to the empty street. Not the main highway street; instinctively he'd avoided that one.

Somebody would stumble across the Sen before the dance was done. Mac would be around somewhere; Mac would know whose gun had killed him. If he could hop a late bus, get to Albuquerque quick, get on board a plane to Mexico, he'd be safe. If he could do it quick enough. Before somebody found out what that thing was on the dirty ground by the Armory.

He hadn't enough money for a plane ticket. He hadn't twenty-five dollars left in his pocket. Sickness was a dirty lump in his stomach. He'd been so sure he'd collect. Been so sure the Sen would fork over to save his neck. If he could get to Pancho, borrow back the ten, borrow a little extra, enough to get to Mexico. Ziggy would have something lined up by now. He'd send Pancho back double the loan; he'd send it back right away. *Hurry, hurry, hurry* . . . He had to see Pancho and get away quick. That was no siren; the Sen was still playing his big scene all alone.

He didn't know where he was but he was headed right, the reflection of colored lights lit the sky over the buildings ahead, the quickness of music strummed the night. Under the music he heard the thud of the Indian drum, relentless as heartbeat, as the following footsteps of a smart cop.

He saw the Kansas City steak house, and he crossed, slanted up the hill, turned to the Plaza. As he turned the night was shattered with noise; this was the climax, this was the final glittering twirl of the Fiesta merry-go-round.

Six

THE SQUARE of streets was dense with dancers, with song, with confusion of color and costume and the earth smells that would be forever in his nostrils. With the warmth of life. On the hill the outsiders played at Fiesta with their fancy Baile but Fiesta was here. In the brown faces and the white faces, the young and the old; capering together, forgetting defeat and despair, and the weariness of the long, heavy days which were to come before the feast time would come again. This was Fiesta. The last moments of the beautiful and the gay and the good; when evil, the destroyer, had been himself destroyed by flame. This was the richness of life for those who could destroy evil; who could for three days create a world without hatred and greed and prejudice, without malice and cruelty and rain to spoil the fun. It was not three days in which to remember that evil would after three days rise again; for the days of Fiesta there was no evil in this Fiesta world.

And so they danced and sang in the streets under the colored garlands of light, under the wreathed white smoke of the thatched booths. And the Mariachi shouted their fierce nostalgic songs of the homeland from one corner of the Plaza, and the lugubrious band of the Conquistadores blared their brassy dissonance from another. And the strolling musicians sang with the singers under the dark glittering trees and the children who should have been in bed ran laughing up and down the paths. And the white-haired old nodded their heads to the laughter and the song. And all clutched tightly in their hands the last moments of the Fiesta, as tightly as if they didn't have to let it go, as if tomorrow would never find its way into the dream.

There was cover in this swirling crowd. Sailor fled into it, safe for the moment, making his way to where Tio Vivo spun and tinkled in the far corner. To where Pancho would be, his friend, his amigo, Pancho.

Tio Vivo was motionless and dark. In the whole shimmering Plaza, Tio Vivo alone was still. Not even a small wind stirred the pink and brown and purple horses. Not a big, sweaty, bare-toed brigand rocked the gondola. Pancho wasn't there. No one was there.

In sudden panic, Sailor darted from the dark loneliness out again into the street, into the street crowd. It didn't matter who he was, it didn't matter that he was alien, or what he had done. He could not do wrong in Fiesta because there was no wrong existent. His hands were caught, he was swept into the dance, the girl beside him might have been Rosie, might have been the slut, might have been the abuelita. Or Juana or the woman with his mother's heavy shoulders. Whoever it was, she was honest, not a harlot masquerading in angel white, smirching the ancient and holy Feast. Sailor danced and he sang with the crowd, "Hola, hola!"; spinning around like a merry-go-round horse, "Ai, yai yai yai." He danced and his eye watched for Pancho and his eye watched for Mac. His ears listened for the scream of the siren—and he heard the thud of the drum.

He hadn't imagined the drum. It was right there in the Plaza. A big Indian was thumping it. The dancers were falling in beside him, arms linked, following his slow side shuffling step around the square. All the dancers were joining in the circle. Without knowing, Sailor knew this was the end. Without raising his eyes to see the bandsmen putting away their instruments, without seeing the Mariachi becoming silent shadows in the night. He knew the finality. And panic was gray dust in his throat.

Pancho? Where was Pancho? His friend. His guardian angel. His feet shuffled in the endless linked circle edging to drum thud around the Plaza. Watching the couples fade out of the circle, and he couldn't stop them, neither he nor they could hold back the end of Fiesta; watching the bonfire on the corner flicker lower. He could run but where? Pila was gone. Pancho was gone. Everyone gone. Everyone but Mac.

The circle was thinning, when it reached the corner again, it was small. It broke in front of the museum. Fiesta didn't end in fireworks, it faded away. His hands clenched to keep from reaching out to someone, anyone for help. Before all were gone and the Plaza empty, empty but for him alone there.

Desperately he looked towards Tio Vivo, as if by will he could force it to swing and tinkle.

He breathed again. Pancho was there.

He ran across the street into the park, running until he was stopped short by the palings. It wasn't Pancho. It was a fat man but it wasn't Pancho. Not one of the four men was Pancho. Dark faces, battered hats, worn jeans but not Pancho. Not even Onofre or Ignacio. The four men were taking down the merry-go-round. They knew how; they knew where to lay the pink horse, the brown, where the fence should be stacked.

Sailor said, "Where's Pancho?"

They didn't pay any attention to him. He might not have been there.

"Where's Pancho?" He wanted to yell it into their deaf ears, into their blank faces. "Where's Pancho?" But he mustn't raise his voice. The Plaza was too silent. Fiesta was over, the only sound was the sound of men working, and faintly, far away up on the hill, the plaint, "Adios, mi amigo . . ."

He grabbed the skinny fellow who passed with an armload of red palings. "Where's Pancho?" he demanded. Blank eyes looked into his.

Sailor said in angry desperation, "Don't any of you know what I'm talking about? The guy who owns the merry-go-round? Pancho, Don José? The big fellow. My friend. Mi amigo. Where is he?"

They didn't know. They jabbered Spanish at each other. They gestured, they were vehement.

Then they turned empty faces to Sailor. They shrugged. "Yo no se."

The horses looked like dead things lying on the ground. Pancho would return any minute now, return to put his big brown paw on the neck of the pink horse, to reassure the little horse that tomorrow he would gallop again.

Sailor's head darted at a shadow coming across the La Fonda corner. His breathing was noiseless but heavy. His hand gripped his pocket. It wasn't Mac. *Hurry, hurry* . . . He ought to be running, not standing here. The Sen should have been found by now. But maybe the swells on the hill hadn't stopped dancing to look for the Sen. Pancho would come. Pancho must come.

The four men were leaving. He stood in their path. "Where are you going? Where's Pancho? Where's Pancho?"

They shook their heads. They babbled, "Yo no se," but they didn't stop moving. They were shadows disappearing into the deeper shadow of the Plaza. Going away, gone, leaving him here alone. Alone.

He started to plunge after them. The voice halted him. The quiet voice from behind him, in the black soundless shadows behind him.

"Going somewhere, Sailor?"

He didn't move. He stood like a tree while Mac came up beside him. "I wouldn't," Mac said.

He might have meant Sailor's finger pressing the trigger of the gun in his pocket. He might have meant not to run. Whatever he meant, Sailor's hand came out of his pocket limply.

"You couldn't get away," Mac said.

Mac was always so sure and so right. Mac could be wrong but he was right. There had been no escape from this, from the very beginning no escape. From the day in the pool hall. Sailor couldn't get away.

Sailor said slowly, "I didn't mean to kill him. He was going to kill me. It was self defense."

Mac offered a cigarette to Sailor. Sailor took it; he struck the match for both. Mac sat down on a stack of red palings. Mac, so sure of himself, so sure Sailor wouldn't shoot or bolt. He said, "I know."

Sailor didn't believe him. But Mac's face was plain as truth was plain. He had been there, unseen, silent as a shadow. He had watched it happen.

There was a bitterness on Mac's tongue. "I didn't want you to kill him. I tried to tell you." The bitterness was iron. "I wanted him to stand trial. I wanted him to pay." He looked up at Sailor. "It's too late for our talk now."

Sailor sat down beside Mac. He began to curse the Sen, out of the rage and self pity eating him.

Mac said, sort of wondering, "And you stuck with him despite that. Knowing what he was like."

"No," Sailor said. "I was through. I was getting out. You know I was getting out, Mac."

"Why didn't you get out? What were you waiting for?" And then Mac remembered without being told. "The payoff."

"He owed it to me," Sailor said stubbornly. He'd never collect a dime. He'd be working for Ziggy. Doing the dirty work for Ziggy just like he'd worked for the Sen. Or working for a mug in Chicago, not a gentleman like the Sen. If a smart mouthpiece got him out of this. It wouldn't be Ziggy. Ziggy had got away; he wouldn't come back. Some mug would get him a mouthpiece then he'd be sold down the river to the mug. He wanted to cry.

A guy up from the Chicago streets didn't cry. He'd get out of this. "It was self defense," he said. "You know it was, Mac." Mac was his only witness. Mac would have to testify for him.

"Yes, it was self defense," Mac agreed. "It won't always be self defense, Sailor. There'll be a time when it won't be self defense."

"If I get out of this," Sailor vowed.

"You won't change." He shook his head. The bobbles danced on his black Spanish hat. His voice didn't dance.

"I can go straight," Sailor insisted. "I was going straight."

"You don't want to go straight. You turned your back on the right way a long time ago. You chose the wrong way, the easy way. You can't do wrong and not pay for it." He was matter of fact. "Sure, you could turn around and go back, but it's a long way back and the going would be tough. Twice as tough as it would have been if you'd taken the right turn a long time ago. Too tough for you. You couldn't take it."

Sailor set his chin. "I've taken plenty. I'm not soft. I could take it."

The silence was heavy. "You don't know how tough it would be. You don't know how tough it is to be good." Mac put his cigarette on the ground. Carefully he stepped on the color of fire. "I could be wrong," he said. "I could be wrong all around. Maybe you didn't go bad because that's the way you are inside. Maybe you want to be good. Maybe you just never knew how. I've always wanted to help you, Sailor. I've tried. Because but for the grace of God, there go I." He stood up. "I'll try it again. If that's the way you want it. If you don't, God help you. If you don't, you can't get away from what's coming to you." His eyes were sad on Sailor's face. "You can't get away."

That was the end of Mac's sermon. He was the cop again. "You can have one of my beds tonight. Tomorrow we'll start back. I've fixed it with the locals. I had a warrant for Senator Douglass' arrest. They think you were helping me out."

Sailor got to his feet, slowly, listening to words, words that were like dream words, like in a bad dream.

"It won't go hard on you. He pulled the gun first. If it weren't for your record . . ." His voice was kind. "When you get out, I'll be there. If you want my help, I'll be there."

If the organization were working he'd get off quick. But there wasn't an organization any more. There wasn't a Sen. He was alone.

He'd get off easy. Maybe four or five years. And after he came out of the rotten pen, Mac would find him a job, maybe paying twenty-five bucks a week. He'd brush his teeth and go to church on Sundays and report to Mac once a week and say thank you Mac for helping me be a sucker.

He could do it if he wanted to. He wasn't soft; he could do it. He didn't want to. It wasn't good enough for him.

Beyond the mountains was freedom. So near, just beyond the horizon line. He could hitch a ride, heist a car if he had to, be over the border by morning. With the gun it would be easy. He could make it. Once over the border they'd have a hard time getting him back. He could call Ziggy from Juarez to write him dough. Ziggy needed him as bad as he needed Ziggy. They would make a sweet thing out of a partnership in Mexico; Ziggy, the brain; Sailor, the trigger man. If he had to, he'd be a trigger man. They'd be big shots in no time, white Palm Beach suits and the best hotel suites and the dames hanging around their necks. That was better than stir or grubbing in a factory all your life. Mac was nuts.

The wind blew cold across the dark Plaza.

"Come on," Mac said. He yawned. "Bed's going to feel good tonight."

Sailor said, "No."

Mac's eyes jumped to his face. Cop eyes that quick, colorless, hard as flint. Sailor's hand tightened on his gun.

"Listen, Sailor—" He started to move in.

Sailor said, "No."

He shot McIntyre.

And he ran. Fled down the street, away from the sound that had shattered the dark of the night, the silence of the deserted Plaza. There were no echoing shots; Mac didn't carry a gun. He hadn't wanted to do it. Mac was a good man. But Mac was a copper.

Sailor was weeping as he ran, weeping for Mac. No sound stirred behind him, there was no sound in the night but his running steps, his tears. Somewhere in the silence Pancho prayed for him, not knowing he prayed for the damned. Or Pancho slept with tequila sweet on his lips. Pancho who would have helped him. Who could not help him now. It was too late.

He ran on, into open country this quickly; plunging into the wastes of endless land and sky, stretching forever, for eternity, to the far-off barrier of the mountains. The night was cold, colder than before. All he had to do was keep moving, keep moving on and on until he reached the mountains. On the other side was freedom. Escape from this dread dream.

You can't get away. It couldn't be Mac he heard pitying, Mac was dead. *You can't get away.*

Blindly he stumbled on.

THE END

DISCUSSION QUESTIONS

- Discuss Dorothy B. Hughes' portrayal of New Mexico. How does she depict its culture and its people?

- Was Sailor a sympathetic character in any way?

- In what ways did Sailor's upbringing shape his character in the narrative?

- Did any aspects of the plot date the story? If so, which ones?

- Would the story be different if it were set in the present day? If so, how?

- Did the social context of the time play a role in the narrative? If so, how?

- If you were one of the main characters, would you have acted differently at any point in the story?

- Did you identify with any of the characters? If so, which?

- If you've read other Dorothy B. Hughes novels, how does this one compare to those?

AMERICAN
MYSTERY *from*
CLASSICS

PENZLER PUBLISHERS

*Available now
in hardcover and paperback:*

Charlotte Armstrong . . . . *The Chocolate Cobweb*

Charlotte Armstrong . . . . *The Unsuspected*

Anthony Boucher. . . . . *Rocket to the Morgue*

Anthony Boucher. . . . . *The Case of the Baker Street Irregulars*

John Dickson Carr . . . . *The Crooked Hinge*

John Dickson Carr . . . . *The Mad Hatter Mystery*

Mignon G. Eberhart. . . . . *Murder by an Aristocrat*

Erle Stanley Gardner . . . . *The Case of the Careless Kitten*

Erle Stanley Gardner . . . . *The Case of the Baited Hook*

Frances Noyes Hart . . . . *The Bellamy Trial*

H.F. Heard. . . . . *A Taste for Honey*

Dorothy B. Hughes . . . . *Dread Journey*

Dorothy B. Hughes . . . . *The So Blue Marble*

W. Bolingbroke Johnson . . . . *The Widening Stain*

Frances & Richard Lockridge. . . . . *Death on the Aisle*

AMERICAN MYSTERY CLASSICS

from

PENZLER PUBLISHERS

*Available now
in hardcover and paperback:*

And More! Visit our website for a complete list of titles

Visit penzlerpublishers.com, email info@penzlerpublishers.com for
more information, or find us on social media at @penzlerpub